The Blue Roses of Orroroo

Margaret Visciglio

The Blue Roses
of Orroroo

To my grandmother, Alma Eliza Burge,
who told me of the blue roses of Orroroo

'If you think you're going to die, clean the stove.'
– Mrs A.E. Burge

The Blue Roses of Orroroo
ISBN 978 1 74027 673 3
Copyright © text Margaret Visciglio 2011

First published 2011
Reprinted 2013, 2014, 2015

GINNINDERRA PRESS
PO Box 3461 Port Adelaide 5015
www.ginninderrapress.com.au

1

One of the two horses that had pulled the dray up to our gate began to drop manure on to the road just as the men were unloading the coffin. It was good manure, the round glistening lumps nicely filled with straw. The sharp scent of fresh horse dung filled my nostrils.

I grabbed my nearest son and said, 'Quick, get a shovel. Your father will want that for his roses.'

Charlie shook his head. 'That's Dad's coffin, Mum. He's past caring about the roses.' Then, as I looked at him angrily, he patted my arm and added, 'I'll get the horse shit later when the neighbours aren't watching. None of them will have the nerve to pick it up right now.'

Mr Andrews, representing the Timber-Workers' Union, who were paying for the funeral, joined the two undertaker's men as they lifted the casket. He grimaced when he realised how heavy it was. He beckoned to my eldest sons, Harry and Brian, to help, then recruited a couple of the neighbours who had stopped to watch us welcome Michael's body home. I'll say that much for people in Norwood: they always lend a hand when they're needed, even if it's hard work.

Amy, her eyes full of tears, held the gate open as the coffin bearers stumbled under their grisly burden, down the path and up the veranda steps to our front door. I began to follow them inside, but I paused to remember how proudly Michael had carried me over that threshold as a bride – was it really twenty-eight years ago? 1900 we were married, when I was twenty and he was twenty-four. Now I was forty-eight years old. So it must be twenty-eight years ago. I could not, would not, believe that now Mick was being borne over that same threshold in a wooden box. And where had the years gone?

One of the women took my arm and stopped me in my tracks. 'I've phoned Father Flaherty over at St Ignatius, Mrs Walsh. I thought it was only right, seeing as you're a Roman, like. He said he'll be along shortly. It'll be a comfort to you. Least I could do, love.'

Just like Mrs Williams, interfering old cow. If I had wanted Father Flaherty, I would have sent one of the kids for him. Always has to rub in the fact that she's got a phone and I haven't. Up herself. Mick would have put the telephone on if I had wanted it, but I said I didn't want to be bothered with newfangled things like that. We've got the electricity; that's enough.

And as for calling the priest, Mick and I hadn't been to Mass or taken the sacraments for ages – not since that business with Mary. That wasn't something you would go confessing to any priest, and especially not to Terence Flaherty, sanctimonious old windbag that he is.

I followed the men into our front room and watched them place the coffin onto the trestles they had put there when they had first arrived. Amy carried a vase of Mick's yellow roses in from the kitchen. I saw that she had put them in my best cut-glass vase, and I hoped she wouldn't trip over her feet as she often did. She's a sweet kiddie, my Amy, but a bit clumsy. She walked as reverently as if she was in a religious procession, however, and she placed the vase carefully on the polished wood. I knew she had chosen the yellow roses because they were Mick's favourites.

'No, sweetie, you can't do that,' said Mr Andrews, wiping a drop of water off the wood with his handkerchief. 'We don't want to spoil the veneer, do we? That's rosewood, a very nice bit of timber.' He gave the surface a polish with the hanky, and stood back to admire the gloss.

'Not going to make any difference to the veneer when a load of earth gets dumped on it, then?' I asked sarcastically. 'Amy got up at the crack of dawn to pick those roses before the heat got at them and made them wilt. She wants to put flowers on her dad's coffin and she's going to do it. But right now you can open it up so I can wash him and put his best suit on him.'

'I can't open the coffin!' said Mr Andrews, aghast. 'That's a lead-lined coffin, that's why it's so heavy. It's been sealed by the coroner down in Mount Gambier. Michael's been dead for six days, Mrs Walsh. It's been bloody hot. You don't want to look at him. It's impossible.'

'So how do I know it's really Michael?' I demanded. 'How do I know this isn't all some sort of trick to make me think he's dead when really he's run off with some other woman down in Mount Gambier? You could be in cahoots with him for all I know. The whole bloody union might be conspiring against me.'

'Mrs Walsh, you're overwrought, you're overcome by grief. Michael is dead. He died on the train to Mount Gambier. No one knows exactly when he died. His body was only discovered when he didn't get off the train. He was identified by people well known to him at Mount Gambier.'

Mr Andrews paused to wipe the sweat from his brow with the hanky that he had used to mop the water from the coffin, and then continued berating me. 'As I explained to you three days ago, my dear lady, the railway cleaner found the body when he was emptying the ashtrays and picking up rubbish. The doctor certified Michael dead of natural causes, the local undertaker washed him and dressed him and notified us at the union. We sent you a telegram about it all, and now we have brought him back to you. And,' he said, shifting his glare from me to my sons, 'we are paying for the funeral.'

'You don't expect us to be grateful to you, do you?' demanded Charlie. 'Dad died on union business. You owe us a funeral at the very least.'

'But I don't believe he's dead,' I shouted. 'Who identified Michael? They might have put the wrong body in that coffin! Michael could be alive and walking around with amnesia, not remembering that he's got a wife and children to come home to. We could be burying someone else's husband. What are you going to do about that, you and your union?'

Mr Andrews sighed. 'I assure you, Mrs Walsh, we have got the right body in that box. The people who identified Michael knew him well. Unfortunately, I am not at liberty to say who those people were. They have requested it be kept as confidential information. Now, why don't you just sit down and have a nice cup of tea and a good cry and get over it?'

'So some floozy that Mick was having an affair with down at the Mount identified him, did she?' I demanded. 'How can anything be kept confidential from me, when I'm his widow? That is, if I am his widow and not his wife.'

'That's not for me to say, Mrs Walsh,' said Mr Andrews wearily. He pushed me into the nearest chair and ordered Amy to make tea. 'And I'll have a cup too while you're at it, young lady.'

Mr Andrews sat down in Michael's chair and stared at me as if I was a rebellious child and he was a schoolmaster armed with a cane. Defeated for the moment, I sank down into my chair.

Mr Andrews took a deep breath. 'Now, about the funeral, Mrs Walsh. The body will stay here overnight, of course, and I can arrange for some of the union men to join you in vigil if you like. Although I expect you and your family might prefer to be private with Michael in this last time you will have together. We will pick up the coffin tomorrow at ten a.m., and it will be a really slap-up do – nothing like that dray, that was all I could get today, but for tomorrow I've got black horses with plumes and a glass-sided hearse, and the union members will walk in procession behind it. It will be an old-fashioned traditional funeral, a funeral to remember.'

He paused to sip the tea that Amy had timidly presented to him. I noticed she had used the best cups and saucers. I would have given him a tin pannikin.

'Father Flaherty will do the service, of course. I've teed it all up with him. We had a long chat yesterday. Full Requiem Mass. Father Flaherty insists on that. He said that Michael deserved it, pillar of the community that he was, even though he hadn't been seen in the church for quite a while.'

'You keep out of that,' I yelled, jumping up from my chair. 'If we wanted to go to church, we would have gone. Father Flaherty should keep his mouth shut. Priests aren't supposed to gossip.'

'Sit down, Mrs Walsh, and don't interrupt me,' said Mr Andrews sternly. He leaned over and patted my hand.

I snatched my hand away and sank back into my seat, too disgusted to speak.

'Father Flaherty said he will overlook past omissions, under the circumstances. He said he's sure that Michael died in a state of grace, him being the great family man that he was. Father Flaherty described Michael as a great example to the community. And, the good priest suggested, you and the family might take the opportunity, after this, to be a little less lapsed yourselves.' Mr Andrews gave me a sympathetic smile and sipped his tea again. 'Not quite enough sugar,' he said, reaching for the sugar bowl.

The cup jiggled a little in its saucer and I thought he was going to spill it on my carpet. I'd saved for a long time to buy that Axminster carpet square. I snarled at him.

He didn't notice and he continued his little speech enthusiastically. 'It's all organised. Choir singers, organ player, candles and flowers, the lot. Michael will have the whole kit and caboodle, no expense spared. The union is picking up the tab, since he died on union business.'

Mr Andrews paused to glare at Charlie. 'Or on his way to it, at least. And then we will proceed to the cemetery for the burial.' He paused and frowned at Charlie again. 'In hired cars, paid for by the union.'

He added a further generous amount of sugar to his tea and stirred it vigorously. He banged the spoon against the side of the cup. I winced. I bet the bugger has chipped that cup, I thought.

'Afterwards,' Mr Andrews continued, 'we will come back here for the wake – so I hope you will have some of that excellent fruit cake I well remember Michael boasting about. I will give the eulogy in the church, so there will be no need for your sons to upset themselves by speaking in public.'

'And what if they want say something about their father?' I demanded. 'It seems to me that you and the union have taken the whole matter of Michael out of our hands entirely. It seems to me that this family hasn't had any part at all in Michael's death or in his funeral.'

I never had liked Andrews. Always taking Mick off to union meetings that were really excuses to drink. Did they have loose women at those meetings? Michael had an eye for the ladies. I wouldn't trust him, or indeed any man, further than I could throw them. Not that I had ever caught Mick out, but I had seen the way he looked women over. Even in church, back in the days when we used to go to Mass, he would be sitting there, summing the females up, a gleam in his eye. And after a glass or two and out of my sight, who knew what might happen?

On the subject of drink, I would make sure I hid Mick's whiskey before the funeral. Andrews wasn't getting that. I might need it for medicinal purposes. There would be no shenanigans at my husband's wake.

I sniffed hard. Tears were welling up in my eyes and I wasn't going to let them out. I wouldn't give Mr Andrews the satisfaction of seeing me weep. Was it really possible that Michael was lying, stiff and dead, in that coffin beside the piano in my front room? It couldn't be true.

'That's if my husband is dead,' I said, raising my eyebrows to indicate my doubt. 'I still don't believe that he's inside that box, I might as well tell you that here and now. Michael didn't believe in leaving a job half-done. He never left a party until it was over. He wouldn't go and die when his life was only half-lived.'

I looked up at Michael's sepia-coloured photograph that hung over the mantelpiece. Michael, resolute and brave in his stiff new woollen uniform and slouch hat, head held high and eyes full of hope, every inch the Anzac soldier, posed against a painted background that presaged nothing of the mud of France for which he was bound. He had intestinal fortitude, my Michael, I had to admit that. He had plenty of other faults. No wife could live that long with a husband without noticing her man's faults, but cowardice wasn't amongst them.

'Michael was never a quitter,' I said.

'He was fifty-two years old, Mrs Walsh. His life was much more than half over. You get the pension at sixty-five. Not many people live to that age. The government has it all worked out so they don't have to pay the pension out too often. Not a small man, either. It's not only the lead lining that makes that coffin weighty. He was fond of his food and his beer and his whiskey. And didn't he once tell me his father died of a heart attack?' Andrews sighed, and offered his cup for a refill.

Amy rushed over with the teapot and poured the tea. Her hands shook. I watched, hoping and praying she would pour hot tea into Mr Andrew's lap. She didn't.

He smiled at her indulgently and added more sugar and milk to the cup. 'The science of hereditary is in the news now. That government laboratory that Prime Minister Bruce has been pushing – the CISR – said something about it in the *Advertiser* just yesterday. You are likely to die of what your parents died of. I thought of Michael when I read that article. I believe Michael's time had come. His number was up.'

I frowned at him. Long-winded bastard. Likes the sound of his own voice. I knew he would relish giving Michael's eulogy.

I heard Joseph's voice as he greeted someone at the door, and then there were muttered commiserations as the visitor spoke the same platitudes that we had been hearing for days. These platitudes were more pious than usual, though. There seemed to be a lot of repetition of at peace now and we must accept. Then I recognised the familiar booming voice that Michael and I had tried to avoid hearing in recent years.

Since that problem with Mary, we only attended Mass at Christmas and Easter and when we did go, we always sneaked into the church after the service had begun, and we always stood near the door throughout Mass, ready to run as soon as we heard the words '*Ite, missa est*'.

'Indeed, we all have to accept that when our time has come, it has come. When the good Lord calls us, we cannot deny the call.'

Bloody hell, I thought, Father Flaherty's here.

'I'll be having one of those cups of tea, Amy dear,' said the priest. 'And isn't it a grand comfort to you, Mrs Walsh, to have all the family around you like this? All except Mary, of course. Will Mary be coming back for her father's funeral?'

'No, she will not,' I said.

2

Harry and Brian went home. I said it was best that way. It was getting late. Harry's wife was newly pregnant and shouldn't be left alone at night. They lived two streets away, so Harry didn't have far to go, but Brian lived on the other side of town and he had to catch two trams.

It had been a long, exhausting day and we all needed rest before the ordeal that tomorrow would bring. I sent Charlie and Joseph out to their beds in the sleep-out. I said I would keep the vigil with the dead. I wanted to be alone for a bit. It was so hot in the house that the boys were glad to escape to the relative cool of the enclosed veranda.

I knew my sons were upset about their father's death, but they were men enough to put a brave face on it. It was best that they should talk it over, a couple of lads together, and get their sorrow off their chests. I knew enough about boys of sixteen and seventeen, half-boys, half-men, to let them do that. In their eyes, if not mine, they were men now. If their dad had been here, he would have taken them off to the pub and given them a beer each, even though they were under age. A rite of passage, Mick would have called it. But of course their dad wasn't here. Or was he?

Amy was asleep in my bed. She had burst into tears when her bedtime came, crying that her daddy would never kiss her goodnight again. I didn't have the heart to push her into her room and shut the door on her. If I really was a widow, it was *my* bed now, not Mick's and mine. I could share it with Amy if I wanted to. I could share it with anyone I wanted to, in fact. Not that I would ever want to share my bed with another man. One man in my life was enough.

I had put Mick's best suit back in his cupboard. It had been a waste of time brushing it and ironing his good shirt and polishing the shoes that I was going to put on him. Those clothes might fit one of the boys in a couple of years' time. Harry was filling out now. Waste not, want not.

I sat beside the coffin, knitting. The wood gleamed in the candlelight. Father Flaherty had set candles around it when he was prancing about with the incense and the holy water, wearing his black stole so he would look the part for the service of the dead.

The priest had a new censer for the incense, which he showed to the boys while he was lighting it. It had bigger holes in it than the one he had previously used. Joe tried to look interested, but Charlie shrugged and said the incense would fall out and burn the floor if the holes were too big. Mindful of my carpet, I watched carefully while the priest was waving smoke about.

Amy was impressed. I wasn't sure about the boys, but personally I thought Flaherty looked like a red Indian doing a war dance. You see that sort of thing in those cowboy and Indian films that Joe is so fond of. Personally, I like a bit of romance. I really enjoy those films starring Rudolf Valentino.

I had left the candles in place. They had burned down now, but they still gave some light, and it saved using the electricity. A bit of religion didn't do any harm, I reasoned, though I wasn't sure that it would be much use, either. What was God's attitude towards Michael and me, I wondered. Was Mick in heaven now if he was dead? How did God feel about Mary?

The candles flickered. The cloying smell of burned wax, combined with the incense, hung heavily in the hot room. This house held the heat dreadfully when the weather had been warm for a few days. The temperature had been over ninety degrees Fahrenheit for almost a week now. The fact that I had put the oven on to do some baking for the wake wasn't helping either.

This didn't feel like my front room. My home had been invaded by death and by the church. I didn't like that, or the idea of tomorrow's funeral. Mick would have been furious. He said it would be over his dead body before he set foot in a church again.

He was right, too. He wouldn't be setting his feet in the church. He was going to be carried in. Would it be head or feet first? I wasn't sure about that. If, in fact, he really was in that coffin.

I looked up at Michael's photograph on the wall. On each side of Michael's portrait hung similar ones of my two brothers, Patrick and Daniel, who had also gone off on what they had called the great adventure. But unlike Michael, they had never returned.

So much hope, so much promise, so many dreams of glory, and it was all for nothing. And now had Michael also embarked on that journey from which he would never come back? When the children were grown and gone, would I be alone as my mother had been when my father had died? She had told me once that only the love of her children helped when she lost her husband, but even that could never replace the lack of a man in her life. And then, soon afterwards, she had lost my brothers too.

My poor mother had prayed every night for her boys from the day they had been reported missing in action, and lived every day in hope that her prayers would be answered. She expected them to walk in the door at any moment, laughing and saying it had all been a joke, a trick they had played on the British army.

I knew Paddy and Daniel were dead, long before the door bell rang. I had had a feeling of dreadful loss a week before the telegram boy handed the envelope to Mum, before I read the words on the yellow paper. Because of the emptiness in my heart, I had accepted the deaths of my brothers.

But I could not believe that Mick had gone. How could Michael die on a train, in broad daylight, in peacetime? It was beyond acceptance, beyond belief.

The cat had jumped up onto my lap. I stroked its head for a moment, and then decided I was too hot to bear its body heat as well as my own. I pushed it onto the floor. The cat turned, arched its back and spat at me. I threw a knitting needle at it. I missed. The cat stalked out of the room. I put down my knitting and went to lean against the coffin.

'Are you really in there, Michael?' I asked the wood.

There was no answer. It was so quiet in the night, in the ringing silence of the stifling hot, dark house. It would be even hotter and darker inside that box, I thought. I knocked on the coffin. Nothing. It sounded hollow, like the ripe watermelons that Mick, grinning with pride, used to carry in from his garden. And never would again, if I could believe what I had been told.

Would I truly never see his face again? Never again to hear his voice, never to lie beside him in the cosy companionship of our bed, with our feet together on a cold night? It was just not possible that all that warmth, all that life, all that energy could be gone, evaporated like the steam from a train's funnel, somewhere between Adelaide and Mount Gambier.

I had to know the truth. Either he was in the coffin or, as I suspected, he had run off, and the coffin was full of sand or bricks or wood from the pine forests of Mount Gambier.

If Mr Andrews was telling the truth and Michael was in the box, after six days he would not be a pleasant sight. Even so, I had to be sure. The truth must come out.

I took a torch and went out to the shed and found a screwdriver. I checked the fruit cake in the oven as I went through the kitchen. It was almost done. It smelled rich and spicy. I would make scones in the morning. I hoped we would get a cool change tonight, though. It was nearly unbearable in the house. How could we hold a funeral in this heat? Funerals ought to be held on gloomy, wet days, not in the middle of summer.

I longed to sit outside in the relative coolness of the garden with a cold drink of water from the icebox. I felt breathless and light-headed. I had to do my best, though. If Michael really was dead, I must give him a good send-off. Otherwise people would talk. If Michael really was dead and in the coffin, he would expect his widow to put on a good show. I owed him that much. But I must know the truth.

As quietly as I could, I went back into the front room and gently lifted Amy's roses, which were drooping sadly now, off the lid of the coffin. I wondered if she had remembered to put some sugar and a Bayer's Aspro in the water. That always kept flowers fresher longer. I moved one of the candles closer so that I could see what I was doing. Mr Andrews was right: there was a white watermark on the wood.

I put the screwdriver into one of the holes and tried to undo the screw. It wouldn't turn. I shone the torch into the hole and realised that a piece of lead had been melted over the head of each screw to prevent the lid being removed. 'Bastards,' I said.

I went back through the kitchen again and out the back door. The axe that we used to chop wood, and sometimes to kill chooks, was leaning against the chopping stump, beside the wood heap next to the tank stand.

I picked up the axe and carried it into the house. I leaned it against the dresser while I checked the cake again. It was done. I took it out of the oven and put it on the table. If any of the kids touched that cake, I would kill them. I carried the axe into the front room.

'Thud!' The noise reverberated through the sleeping house.

I lifted the candle and peered at the small hole I had made in the side of the coffin. I hadn't hit it hard enough. I could see the dull grey of the lead lining through the wood, but I couldn't see into the coffin. I lifted the axe again to take another swing.

Charlie burst into the room, and paused for a moment, then shrieked, 'Mum!'

He told me later that it looked like some sort of horror show – like something he had seen in the movies down at the Odeon. He said he had nightmares about it for a long time afterwards. Apparently the shadows cast by Father Flaherty's candles were magnified on the walls. But then it isn't every night a lad comes into a room and sees his mum attacking his father's coffin with an axe.

His screams woke his brother, and the two of them shouted and wept and I shouted and wept and it was enough to wake the dead. I think the boys got their feelings about their father's death out in the open then, more than they had the whole time since we had had the awful telegrammed news from Mount Gambier.

The yelling and screaming probably did them the world of good. But Michael didn't wake up, and neither did Amy. Poor little thing, she must have been worn out by the events of the day.

'I should have sent Amy off to Harry's place to sleep,' I sniffled, when we had all calmed down a bit and Charlie had taken the axe out to lean against the stump again. 'I didn't think. It would have been better for her if she had stayed with Harry and Mavis. You shouldn't keep a kiddie in a house of death.'

'There wouldn't be room over at Harry's, Mum. Mary and her husband Fred and their little boy, young Patrick, are there,' said Joe, handing me a cup of tea.

'Joe, we weren't going to tell Mum that Mary was back until tomorrow morning when she came around. We all agreed on that. It was going to be a surprise to cheer Mum up. Now you've gone and let the cat out of the bag, you dope.' Charlie glared at his brother and then turned to me. 'She named her baby after your brother, Mum. She said she hoped you would like that. She's really keen to see you.'

I was furious. The cup rattled in its saucer and tea spilled into the saucer and then over the edges. I thought I was going to drop it, so I rested it on the coffin lid. 'How dare she? Your father and I told her we never wanted to see her again. After what she did! She couldn't have the cheek to show up here again. And at her father's funeral too.'

The tears started again. I was beginning to be ashamed of myself, bursting into tears like this. I am not one of those women who go around weeping and wailing. I pride myself on bottling things up. I had bottled everything up for eight years since I had last seen Mary, and suddenly it was all coming out.

'I don't want Mary to see Amy. We have to keep her away from Amy. She might corrupt her. Everything your dad and I did over the past eight years will all be for nothing. We both swore that we would never see Mary again. Never even think about her.'

But I had thought about Mary. I had never told Michael, but I found that Mary, little sneak that she was, crept into my thoughts constantly. Eight birthdays, eight Easters, and eight Christmases had passed without me hearing her voice. It was eight years since I had last seen her, since I had hugged her, braided her long auburn hair, ironed her frocks, scolded her for untidiness or for not doing her homework.

Every May I still remembered how proud I had been when the nuns had chosen Mary to lead the procession at the church when the young girls had worn white dresses and veils and sung 'Salve Regina Coelis' as they crowned the statue of the Blessed Virgin with flowers. That last May, before it all happened, it had been Mary who had lifted the crown of flowers and placed it on the smiling statue's head. I was the proudest mother in the church.

And then disaster had struck. But life was full of disappointments. There was always sorrow amongst the laughter and the little joys. You had to expect that.

And we had paid for what we had done. I had paid in guilt-ridden sleepless nights. I was torn between my anger at what Mary had done and my concern about her safety, but Michael insisted that we must cut all contact with our daughter for honour's sake and for the moral welfare of the other children.

He said that although his heart was broken, he knew that Mary would be all right with his friends at Mount Gambier. He said that thought consoled him in his grief. He must have been convinced of that, because I often heard him snoring as I lay awake beside him.

Had Mary paid for her sins, I wondered. Of course she must have done. It can't have been easy for her, the suffering and the pain, being separated from her baby, and the exile from family and home. And she was just a slip of a girl, after all. She was still just a child herself. But after eight years, did she still regret her sin? Was she ashamed of her past? How could she come back to face me and her father's coffin?

'Your father never forgave her. He wouldn't want her at his funeral,' I said.

'Dad forgave her years ago,' said Charlie, pouring more tea into my cup. The liquid ran out of the saucer and pooled on the coffin. He picked up a newspaper to blot it. 'He'd be happy to have her at his funeral. And what did Dad used to say? "If I'm happy…"' Charlie broke off and looked at Joe.

Joe grinned and joined in with '…everyone's happy.'

'Your father never said that,' I gasped. 'That's a horrible thing to say.'

'Yes, he did, Mum,' said Joe. 'He said it all the time. All of us kids hated it, but that was his favourite expression. "If I'm happy, everyone's happy." We all used to chant it behind his back. We never repeated to his face, though. He would have belted hell out of us. You didn't hear it because you didn't want to hear it.'

Charlie nodded his agreement. 'You just shut off when something doesn't fit the way you think things ought to be, Mum. You've ignored a lot of stuff that's happened in this family because you didn't like it. Well, we won't be hearing that expression again.'

'Mary lives at Mount Gambier, Mum,' said Joe. 'Dad went to see her every time he went down there. He paid friends of his to look after her for years until she got a job in the local drapery shop. He even paid for her wedding. Harry found out somehow, and then we all knew, but Dad made us swear not to tell you.'

'You know what Dad was like, he could persuade the rain to fall out of the sky if he wanted it to,' said Charlie. 'Dad told us to keep quiet about Mary, so of course we didn't tell you. Mary's really nice, Mum. She forgave Dad and she's forgiven you too.' Charlie nodded again. 'It wasn't easy, keeping the secret, but Dad said you mustn't know. He said it would upset you. She's a real saint, our Mary, she ought to be canonised. Only you have to be dead for that, don't you? She really has forgiven you, Mum.'

'She's forgiven me? What has she got to forgive me for?' I shouted. 'The hussy! I took her baby in, saved her from being shamed in front of everyone. Pregnant at fourteen and didn't even have the grace to say who the father was! Your father and I brought up Amy up as our own, registered her as our own daughter, took away the stigma of being born out of wedlock, we gave Mary the chance to have a respectable life in another town, and now she thinks she can forgive me? I have never heard such rubbish in all my life.'

A dreadful thought occurred to me. What if Mary took Amy back to Mount Gambier with her? 'Amy mustn't ever find out.'

'We told Mary that. And she agrees. She's going to tell Amy she is her long-lost sister. She's going to be sensible about it, Mum. She promised,' Joe said.

My son was pleading that I accept Mary's return to our lives. And the boys had said that Michael had been seeing Mary every time he went to Mount Gambier. And Michael had paid for her wedding and he didn't even tell me she was married. My only daughter. I didn't even get to see my own daughter's wedding. I didn't even know what my daughter's married name was. I couldn't write her a letter if I wanted to. Not that I would want to write to her. But the rest of them all knew about it. I sniffed back my tears. Was it anger or grief that made me want to weep?

They all knew except me. I had been kept in the dark. I had been tricked, betrayed by my whole family, but it was different to the betrayal I had suspected. Perhaps this was worse. I had had the wool completely pulled over my eyes by my own family whom I had trusted. They had all known and they had all hoodwinked me completely. I had been a complete and utter fool.

'What about this husband of hers? What does he think about her having a child before he married her? Is he a Catholic?'

'He knows all about it. He's a great bloke, Mum, and a really nice fellow. Modern, forward-thinking. You've got to move with the times, Mum. It's 1928 now, not the 1800s. And Fred's a Methodist, but Mary loves him,' Joe said. 'Protestants are probably more progressive-thinking than we are. Look at King Henry VIII, for example. He was a Methodist, wasn't he? And he had lots of wives. No one complained about that.'

'Henry VIII was an Anglican, Joe, and his wives had plenty to complain about. Most of them got their heads chopped off like chooks,' Charlie said scornfully. 'Haven't they made a film about him yet? It would be a real pity if you read a book once in a while instead of going to watch films all the time. You're cooking your brain with all those movies.'

Charlie turned to me. 'But Mum, Joe's right about Fred. Fred Mudge is his name. So Mary is Mary Mudge now. It's not Irish, but that doesn't matter. Fred is a good man. And there's nothing wrong with a mixed marriage these days. It happens all the time. Brian is keen on an Anglican girl whose father is the captain of his cricket team. You'd better get used to the idea of mixed marriages in the family.'

I began to choke. Joe banged me on the back and Charlie ran to the kitchen and got me a glass of water. He thrust it into my hands and I took a deep drink.

When I could talk again, I glared at them both. 'That idea depends on the company you're in,' I said.

'Well, yes, I wouldn't mention it to Father Flaherty,' Charlie said. 'No need to go asking for trouble.'

'Fred's hardworking,' Joe broke in. 'He's got his own butcher's shop down at the Mount. And you can see he loves Mary and the little kid, it's written all over him. Just wait until you see young Patrick, Mum. He's the nicest little kid. About two years old. He's your first grandson. You'll love little Paddy.'

'Why would I care what she called her brat when I'm never going to see her or him anyway? She's mad to give a name like Patrick to a half-Protestant kid. He's going to have problems all his life, poor little tyke. He won't know if he's Arthur or Martha.'

I wasn't too sure that I could love any child that Mary had brought up, anyway. It was bound to be a sneaky, defiant little troublemaker, just like its mother. Amy was all right because I had brought her up. And I had had my fair share of children anyway. I didn't have any ambition to take on any more at my age.

'Just keep Mary and her kid away from me. I don't want to have any dealings with any of them.'

'You have to see Mary and her family, Mum. She is definitely coming to Dad's funeral. The rest of us want her there. You can't make a scene at the funeral. What would people think?' Joe pleaded.

'I'm not going to make a scene. I can't stop her from coming but I'm not having anything to do with her. She can sit on the other side of the church from me. And you just make sure she doesn't go anywhere near Amy. Amy's upset already and I'm not letting her get any more upset. She's delicate. She needs protecting. She's at a difficult age. She's just lost her daddy too. And don't you let that kid of Mary's run riot in the church either. I don't want Father Flaherty having a go at me because of some kid who's got nothing to do with me.'

'He's your grandson, Mum,' said Charlie in disgust. 'And you shouldn't keep saying Amy's at a difficult age. You're always making excuses for Amy, trying to baby her. It's time you let her grow up a bit.'

I don't baby Amy, I thought to myself. It's just that she's my youngest and she does need more looking after than the rest of them. And if anyone thinks I'm going to go chasing after Mary's son, they've got another think coming. Grandson, indeed! I might have a grandson if Harry's wife, Mavis, has a baby boy. I think I'd prefer a girl, though. I've had plenty of boys in my time. Plenty of children, actually, and I've reared them all safely, which is not something everyone can say. I've had five kids, six if you count Amy, and I do count Amy. All right, I didn't actually give birth to her, but I've looked after her since birth. But the gloss wears off babies, after a while. You can only take so much wiping snotty noses and dirty bottoms before you begin to think there has to be more to life than that.

I've never had the chance to get out and do anything for myself. I gave up my whole life for Michael and this family. I never went anywhere, never did anything exciting. I was always tied to my home. I could have been a nurse or a teacher or a nun. I could have worked on the Missions or even travelled and gone as far as Melbourne or Sydney. Instead I married Michael and that was that.

And of course, as far as grandchildren goes, Mary's little boy wasn't actually my first grandchild. Amy was, although she didn't know it. And never would know it, either. Mary was not going to take her away from me. Amy was mine. I had earned her.

3

It was another blazing hot day after a smouldering hot night. The cool change I had hoped for had not arrived. I had not slept a wink. The thought of confronting Mary was enough to keep me awake even if I hadn't had thoughts of Michael running through my mind all night. At least being awake all night kept the dreams of Molly away.

My bed was huge and empty, despite Amy's presence, and I couldn't find the right way to place my limbs. They kept assuming the position I knew Michael was in, legs straight, arms crossed over the chest. Why did it have to be Michael who was dead, and not me? Every breath I took seemed an insult to my poor dead husband. What was the point of living, anyway?

I should have insisted on sitting beside the coffin. It was my duty, a widow's duty, to keep the death vigil. But after the incident of the axe, the boys had said they would keep the watch throughout the night beside their father, and they had sent me off to bed.

Perhaps the whole thing was a dream. Perhaps there was no coffin in the parlour. I pushed my feet into my slippers and looked into the front room. The piano was still pushed against the wall. The candles had burned down to puddles of wax. The morning light filtered through the edges of the brown holland blinds and the red velvet curtains and lit the room dimly. It was not decent to raise the blinds with death in the house.

The coffin still stood on the trestles. Charlie had found some wood filler and some varnish in the shed and had tried to repair the damage I had done. It still showed.

The cat was curled up on top of the coffin. It woke and stretched luxuriously as I walked into the room. I pushed it off. Michael wouldn't have been happy if he knew Mulligatawny was sitting on his face. Mick had always hated cats. Years ago, when Mrs Williams gave that cat to Mary, Mick had said he would make soup of it. That was why we named it Mulligatawny. Mully was always kept outside except when Michael was away on one of his trips. Now the cat could be inside as much as he liked, I reflected.

'I hope Mully didn't scratch the veneer,' I said sarcastically. 'Mr Andrews wouldn't like that.'

'What are we going to tell Mr Andrews?' Charlie asked from the depths of the armchair. 'That coffin is a real mess.'

'We'll say the damage must have happened on the train or when they were getting it off the dray,' suggested Joe from the other chair.

'The varnish is still a bit sticky. I was hoping it would dry before they came to take it away. Blimey, now it's got cat fur stuck on it, too,' said Charlie, trying to pull the grey hairs off, and removing a strip of the veneer with them. 'It's a good thing Dad doesn't know about this. He'd have kicked Mulligatawny all the way down the road. And can you imagine what he would have said if he knew what was happening last night? We'd never have heard the end of it. No one would have been happy.'

'Plumbers shouldn't do carpentry. I told you that varnish wouldn't be dry in time, but you said with this heat it would be all right. What's for breakfast, Mum?' asked Joe. 'A chap gets pretty hungry sitting up all night. Is the kettle on?'

Grief didn't seem to have dampened the lads' appetites. The boys need a bit of sustenance to get them through the day, I reasoned, as I fried eggs and bacon for them. Amy and I weren't very hungry, so we just had toast and tea. Perhaps females react to death differently to males, I told myself.

I made scones and sandwiches (some egg and curry and some fritz and tomato) and I put the sandwiches in the icebox. Just as well that the ice man had called yesterday. The boys had put the last of Mick's beer in to cool for the union men and for Mick's army mates. They would all be expecting a drink at Mick's wake. I hid the whiskey bottle in the wardrobe in one of Mick's shoes.

Mrs Williams brought some of her anaemic-looking scones around, along with a jar of her runny fig jam. I thanked her. I said I would tell everyone that they were her scones.

There was a commotion outside and Harry, Mavis and a lady wearing a cloche hat and a very slim, short, modern dress burst in. She was holding a small red-haired boy by the hand. A young man stood behind her. He looked ready to defend her from wild animals if the need arose.

The lady looked so much like Amy grown up. And so very much like Mary, my own lost Mary. The old grey cat must have had the same thought, because it made a bee line for the lady's legs and began to rub itself against her.

The cat hadn't made a fuss like that about anyone in the family since Mary had gone. Mully had been Mary's pet. He had tolerated the rest of us, but he never really liked anyone except Mary. I looked at the cat and I looked at the lady, and I nearly dropped the tray of sausage rolls I had just taken out of the oven.

'Mum!' cried the lady in the cloche hat. She burst into tears.

The sausage rolls slid off the tray onto the floor.

'Mum!' yelled Amy. 'Look what you've done. There'll be cat hair all over them.' She bent to pick up the sausage rolls. 'They're hot, Mum! I'm burning my fingers. Mum, help me.'

'Mary!' I cried. 'Surely you haven't had your hair cut – not in a bob?'

Amy pulled at my sleeve. 'Mum, what am I going to do with these sausage rolls?'

'Feed them to Mr Andrews,' I sobbed.

Then Mary was in my arms and I was in Mary's arms and the tears were flowing and we were hugging and kissing each other, and her cloche hat fell to the floor and got sausage roll crumbs on it, and Amy was picking the hat up and handing it to Mary and trying to get between us, and the cat was trodden on and hissed and flew out of the room, I was stroking Mary's bobbed hair and she was gazing into my eyes, and we were both talking at once, and it was as if we had never been apart.

I really don't approve of carrying on like that, but there are times when it can't be helped, and this was one of them. I don't know what came over me. It just shows you can't tell what's around the corner.

I looked up, and there was Amy watching. I've never seen her eyes so wide.

Mary, bless her, saved the day. 'Hello, Amy. You don't remember me,' she said, between sobs. 'I'm your big sister, Mary.'

Amy shook her head. 'I don't have any sisters, only brothers.'

'You were very little when I went away. I remember you, but you don't remember me. I've thought about you every day since I left. Will you give me a kiss?'

Mary smiled wistfully at me over Amy's head. I saw the longing in her eyes.

4

The damage to the coffin looked even worse in the sunlight than it had in my parlour. The pall-bearers, Charlie, Joe, Brian and Harry and a couple of the undertaker's men, carried the casket up the steps of St Ignatius's church.

Father Flaherty was waiting at the door, wreathed in smoke from his brass censer of incense. He raised his eyebrows when he saw the state of the coffin. He looked at me. I looked away. I wasn't about to make apologies or explanations.

Then the priest saw Mary beside me and smiled a welcome which was at odds with his sombre robes. 'It's little Mary come back!' he said joyfully. 'And little Mary is all grown-up.'

'Little Mary's a respectable married woman, Father,' I said. 'With a husband and a child and a house and a butcher shop in Mount Gambier.'

Mary smiled wanly at the priest. I was afraid she was about to say something to him, so I pushed her forward into the church. With horror, I saw a chunk of sausage roll pastry dangling from her hat. I brushed it off, and it fell into the openwork censer.

'Mum, the coffin has to go first,' Mary protested, pulling me back from the doorway.

I stepped aside so that the bearers could carry the coffin through the door. The priest, turning to smile at Mary, followed the cortege, swinging his censer. The rich aroma of cooking pastry blended with that of the frankincense.

The coffin was settled in place at the front of the church, and Mr Andrews draped an Australian flag over it, in accordance with Michael's status as a returned soldier. It was obvious that Andrews was angry at the way the woodwork had suffered overnight. I doubted that he believed the feeble explanation the boys had given him, but he had shaken his head and said nothing. At least the flag hid the damage.

I sat in the pew at the front of the church with Amy on one side of me and Charlie on the other. Joe and Brian sat together and Michael's sister Bridget took up the rest of the pew. Bridget's husband Frank sat in the pew behind her because we were a bit cramped. Some of Bridget's bulk disappeared behind the fragrant smoke which filled the hot air in the church.

Bridget leaned forward and whispered to me. 'Are they cooking pies and pasties out in the church hall for afterwards?'

'No,' I said. 'The wake is at my house after the funeral. You and Frank must come.'

In my mind, I ran through the amount of food I had prepared, hoping that there would be enough. Bridget's appetite was legendary. I wondered how many of the nuns sitting in the pew opposite looking like a row of crows on a telegraph wire would come to the wake. Nuns are a hungry bunch. Poor things; I didn't know how they could wear those heavy black veils and long robes in this heat.

Amy turned round to look at Mary, who was sitting in the row behind us. I pinched her arm and she jumped.

'Sister Mary Leon is looking at you,' I whispered. 'Behave yourself or you'll be in trouble when you go back to school.'

I listened to the choir caterwauling. Most of them were members of the Ladies' Auxiliary. The singing had gone down hill since I left the choir. The Latin pronunciation wasn't too good either. I really ought to rejoin that choir and sort them out, I thought. I knew I could do that now that I had my Mary back. With her by my side, nothing was impossible. And Michael wouldn't be around to object to my going to church.

I gazed at Michael's coffin standing in the centre aisle. It looked lonely there, and I wondered how Michael must be feeling at this moment. Was his soul hovering up there near the high pointed ceiling of St Ignatius's church? Was Michael looking down at us as we all knelt together in the wooden pews? Was my dead husband happy that Mary had come all the way from Mount Gambier for his funeral? Was he pleased to see the family reunited?

The undertaker had placed a wreath of roses on the coffin. They were florist's flowers, red roses that were so perfect that they could have been made from crepe paper. I looked down at the bunch of roses I was carrying. My roses had a few spots and blemishes on them, and maybe an earwig or two, but they were alive and perfumed. The flowers in the wreath looked as lifeless as the corpse below them.

When I looked at the roses I held, I remembered that Mick had once told me that different coloured roses meant different things. Golden roses are a symbol of spiritual power and teaching, he had said. Michael liked yellow roses because he believed it was his duty to teach his union men how to overcome their troubles and also he had to instruct his children how to live good moral lives. Also, he said, yellow roses stood for resurrection and immortality. I couldn't help smiling when I remembered how Michael always liked to explain the reasons behind things.

He once said that red roses stood for love and lust, so I knew they were not really an appropriate choice for his funeral wreath, even though red also meant blood and sacrifice. Michael had gone to the Great War, but he hadn't shed much blood. We all said he had the luck of the Irish.

White roses were for purity. Blue roses, Michael once said, were a symbol of the impossible, because blue roses could never exist.

I was sure Mr Andrews had selected the flowers. Of course Andrews was a Protestant. He wouldn't have had Michael's education. Say what you might about the brothers who taught Michael, their pupils learned a lot. I had brought yellow roses and white roses to throw into the grave. Yellow roses for resurrection, and white ones for virtue, in the hope that Michael's soul would be purified by the ceremonies of his funeral and that he could look forward to resurrection on the Last Day when the angels sounded their trumpets.

'I am the resurrection and the life,' intoned Father Flaherty.

'Bloody hell,' I thought. 'Now that bugger is reading my mind.'

I decided to block the priest out by thinking about Michael. You wouldn't have thought Michael was a deep thinker, but now, at his funeral, I was remembering things from the past. That's what widowhood does to you: makes you remember things. Good things and bad things.

But of course you should only remember good things about the dead. Mick had a book of Shakespeare's plays that he liked to read aloud in the evenings before we got the radio. I always thought it was mainly because he liked the sound of his own voice, but he did make those words sound impressive. I thought about how at Julius Caesar's funeral, Antony spoke about good and evil. There was something about good being buried with a body, but evil living on long after a person was buried.

Well, there wouldn't be anything nasty living on in our family. That was the only good part of Michael dying, the fact that Mary was back with our family, and that she had forgiven Michael and forgiven me for sending her away. She even seemed to have accepted losing Amy. As the boys said, Mary was a living saint. Everything would be all right from now on. Any evil from the past that Mary and Michael and I had done was laid to rest. It was probably evil of me to feel so full of joy at my husband's funeral, but when I looked at my daughter I didn't care. I hoped that the smile I felt inside wasn't showing on the outside.

I realised that Mr Andrews had begun his eulogy. I must have missed the first part of it while I was thinking about Michael and Mary, but Andrews had so much to say that it probably didn't matter a great deal.

'Bowled a maiden over,' Brian whispered to Joe.

Scandalised, I turned and glared at him. 'How dare you talk about girls when you're at your father's funeral?' I whispered furiously.

'It's not girls, Mum, it's cricket,' Brian whispered back.

'I don't believe you,' I whispered. 'Lust is a mortal sin. Pay attention to the ceremony! Have a little respect for the dead.'

The eulogy went on and on, but Mr Andrews did say some nice things about Mick. He mentioned Michael's devotion to the union cause, and how he and Michael were still striving for a shorter working week. The living wage was secure, and three out of five men were now members of trades unions. Michael's philosophy, Mr Andrews told us, was that of a fair day's work for a fair day's pay.

Mr Andrews spoke of Mick's above-and-beyond-the-call-of-duty attitude, how Michael had fought in the war to end all wars, and that, thanks Michael and his Anzac mates and to the wonderful League of

Nations, the world would never again suffer the horrors of a world war. Now, with the Treaty of Versailles in place, we were living in a new era of international cooperation. War was abolished for ever.

I looked around the church at my four sons and my little grandson, and I was greatly comforted by the thought that because we lived in 1928, they were safe. Michael, Daniel, Patrick, and their mates had not suffered in vain.

Mr Andrews spoke of Michael's upholding of true Australian mateship and of his strength of character and how Mick exemplified moral values for the whole Australian community. At the very last he mentioned Michael's care for, and devotion to, his family.

I shed a couple of tears when I thought that Michael was embarking on his last journey, and that he would never come home from this trip to the cemetery. I suddenly realised what a heart of gold Michael had had, and what a fortunate woman I was to have been married to him. I wished that I had realised all this while Mick was alive.

Father Flaherty invited us to bow our heads and reflect. I thought about my behaviour last night. I must have been mad to act like that. How could I have doubted that Michael was dead? As Mr Andrews said, the coroner at Mount Gambier had examined him, and someone must have identified him. Who had done that? Was it Mary or her husband, or was it the people from the hotel he always stayed at, or perhaps one of the union men down there? I hoped that my poor Mary had not had to look at her father's dead face.

It must have been grief that made me act so badly last night. Grief, and unfounded suspicion. After all, Michael had never given me real grounds to suspect him of anything untoward. He had been a good husband and a wonderful father. I had often wondered about his morals, but there was never any proof. Perhaps I should examine my own conscience, question my own character. I said an act of contrition to atone for my doubts about Michael. 'Mea culpa, mea culpa, mea maxima culpa,' I whispered to God and to Michael.

Mick had doted on Mary in particular. I will admit I always thought it was going a bit overboard when I saw her sitting on his knee long after the age when you expect a kiddie to be doing that. Usually that stops at about the age of six. But you could see how much he loved her.

Mary was ten years or older and Michael was still reading her bedtime stories. I often told him she was old enough to read for herself, but he wouldn't listen.

He liked to take Mary for long walks, just the two of them. They would hold hands as they set off on those walks. Mary adored her daddy. She was the apple of her father's eye. He said it was because she was the only girl.

Of course, that was why it hit him so hard when she fell pregnant. He probably didn't think his little girl would ever look twice at a man other than her daddy. Some men are like that. Naïve. You have to accept that children grow up. But I hadn't expected her to grow up that fast, either.

Mary sat in the row behind us with her husband and son and Harry and Mavis, and Bridget's husband Frank, with a couple of Michael's cousins jammed in. Poor Mary. She seemed very upset about her father's death. She kept dabbing at her eyes with a little lace hanky and leaning against her husband for support. Fred seemed to be a very nice man. And the little boy was so well behaved. Nothing like Charlie, who had once stolen the collection plate and run out of the church clutching a handful of pennies. Little Patrick just sat there quietly and gazed around with his big blue eyes.

The union men, led by Mr Andrews, were behind the nuns on the other side of the aisle. Behind them were Michael's army mates and the rest of the church was filled by our cousins, our friends and our neighbours. You don't realise how many people you know until there's a funeral or a wedding, and then they all come out of the woodwork.

I was worried whether I had provided sufficient food for all these people if they were all coming back to the house. It was a loaves and fishes situation.

Would there be enough chairs? We could bring in the bench from the back garden and maybe we could borrow a few chairs from Mrs Williams. We would need a good solid chair for Bridget. Mick's sister took after her mother; she was a fat cow too. Thank God that Mick's mother, Sheila, was dead and buried. She always criticised everything I did. I wouldn't have been in the mood for her brand of nastiness today.

Mrs Williams had come to the funeral but you could see she was uncomfortable in a Roman Catholic church. She didn't know when to sit and when to kneel and when to stand. I will admit our ceremonies are confusing for an outsider, and the Requiem Mass did go on for a long time. I kept turning round to see what she would do next and it was hard not to smile. You had to admire her for coming, though.

Like Mary, Mrs Williams clung to her husband's arm all through the ceremony. I wondered if she was expecting fire and brimstone to rain down on her head. She told me later that it was the Latin that had bamboozled her. She hadn't realised we spoke another language.

Father Flaherty turned to bless the congregation. He looked up from his book and caught me turning round to look at Mrs Williams. He glared at me as he raised his hand in blessing. I had the feeling he thought I was a lost soul and probably beyond redemption. I bowed my head and tried to look devout.

Harry, as eldest son, insisted on saying a few words, and he stood up there and did his father proud. He talked about Michael taking the boys fishing in the River Torrens and how they never caught anything, but it didn't matter.

I was glad that Harry didn't mention that Michael had taught the boys to swim by throwing them into the river near the weir. I was horrified when I found out about that. Those kids could have drowned.

I was also relieved that Harry didn't say anything about the constant arguments that occurred whenever the family sat around the table for a meal. Michael could be quite overbearing at times with his sons. He was an opinionated man. That was probably why Harry and Brian had left home as soon as they could, and why Charlie and Joe weren't as devastated by the loss of their dad as they should have been. Mary and Amy were the most affected by Mick's death. I hoped that people would not judge me harshly because I displayed less grief than they did.

The Mass dragged on and I think we were all glad when it finally ended and Father Flaherty dismissed us all, saying his final words, '*Ite, Missa est.*'

The pall-bearers lifted the coffin to carry it out to the hearse but Father Flaherty stood in the aisle and gave the coffin a thorough dousing with holy water before it left the church. I gave Mr Andrews a good hard look when the water hit the wood. So much for damage to the veneer now, I thought.

They loaded Michael's coffin into the hearse, and we all got into the waiting hired cars and went off to the cemetery. The union was paying for it, so we might as well enjoy it. But when you think about it, trams or bicycles are a better way to get around, really. Noisy, rattly things, cars are. All that smelly stuff that comes out of the exhaust pipe, too.

We dropped Michael's white and yellow roses on top of the coffin after it had been lowered into the grave. They would muffle the sound of the hard dry earth pounding down on it. Brian, of course, had to make a show of it and bowl his rose into the grave like the cricket fanatic he was. When I remonstrated with him later, he said that his father would have expected that of him.

It occurred to me how awful a feeling it would be if you were lying in a coffin and you suddenly woke up and heard the earth raining down from above. You'd be absolutely helpless. There would be no escape. There would not be a thing you could do about it. I felt a wave of panic go over me when I thought about that. My throat tightened up and I began to choke. For a moment I thought I might die too and join Michael in his grave. But then I thought that if Michael hadn't woken up when I was hitting the coffin with the axe, he wasn't going to wake up now. So perhaps my frenzy had not been in vain.

I whispered a couple of lines I remembered from an old Irish blessing: 'May the earth rest easy over you when, at the last, you lie out under it.'

While Charlie played *The Last Post* on his trumpet and the RSL and union men stood stiffly to attention, I clutched the hand of my daughter Mary with one hand and with the other I held the trembling hand of my beloved Amy.

Softly I whispered, 'Goodbye Michael', and I shed a couple of tears, because now I really did believe that we were burying my husband.

5

Mary and her family stayed for two weeks after the funeral. I got to know her better in those two weeks than I had done all through her childhood. The times when she had been a difficult, wilful child seemed amusing now. I saw what a good mother she was to young Paddy. Paddy was the sweetest, best behaved little fellow you could meet. He called me Grandma from the beginning, and was quite happy to have me feed him his semolina. He reminded me so much of Charlie at the same age.

I even became quite fond of Mary's husband, Fred. As my boys said, he was a good-hearted bloke, for a Methodist. And you couldn't hold religion against him, could you? It wasn't his fault. You can't choose your parents, after all. All the same, some secrets are best kept within the family, so I told the kids not to tell anyone that we had a Protestant in our midst.

Amy worshipped Mary. It was all 'My sister, this' and 'My sister, that'. She followed Mary about like a lost dog.

I found it difficult to watch them together. It was like eating grapefruit marmalade to see them together. Bitter and sweet at the same time. I envied Mary the easy manner in which she persuaded Amy to do things. If only I had had those skills when Mary was growing up, I thought to myself. Not that I would admit it to anyone, but Mary was a good little mother. Perhaps almost as good a mother as I am.

Once I came into the sitting room and found them sitting together looking at our old photo album. Two red-gold heads bent over the heavy book, serious when they looked at the picture of my poor little sister Molly, who had died in childhood, and at the photos of my two brothers.

Patrick and Danny had died in the mud of Flanders. Bishop

Mannix was right to oppose conscription, I reflected. But in the end there had been no conscription in the Great War. There was no need for it. The men rushed to join up. Like all the Anzacs, Pat and Danny and Michael had joined up voluntarily even though volunteering for the British Army wasn't a thing that all our community agreed with.

We of Irish descent remembered how the Poms had treated the Fenians back home in Ireland, with the hangings and the persecution, and even though we were second-generation Australians, we didn't feel a part of the British Empire the way the rest of Australia did. And look what they did to Ned Kelly! We never felt comfortable singing *Rule Britannia* or *God Save the King*. Our fellow Australians knew that and were suspicious of us.

But for Patrick and Daniel and Michael, their loyalty to Australia came first. They believed Australia was in peril and they went off to protect their country without a second thought.

In the end, it was those pictures in the newspapers of that young girl, Alma Cowie, shot by those two Turks at Broken Hill on New Year's Day 1915, that made our men decide to go. They said Australia had to be defended against people like that. And of course they knew that their youth made them immortal.

I began to lose my faith back then, when Pat and Danny died. It took our troubles with Mary to finish the job. It's hard to believe in a God who lets bad things happen.

Michael had gone to the Great War too, even though I protested that he was too old at thirty-eight to fight. He left me with twelve-year-old Harry, eleven-year-old Brian and eight-year-old Mary to care for. I was terrified that the war would not end before Harry and Brian could join up. If the Armistice hadn't happened in 1918, I don't think I could have stopped those boys from going.

They were damned fools, my brothers and my husband and their mates, carried along by a wave of hysteria. Prime Minister Billy Hughes had a lot to answer for. So did all those politicians who said that the war would be over by Christmas. It was a miracle that Michael had survived. Mick never spoke of the war, apart from mentioning the mud, the cold, the lice and, when he had had a few drinks, the noise of the shelling and his dead mates. I learned from other men's wives of the real horror of the trenches. Of the bodies and parts of bodies that stuck out of the walls of the trenches in which our men lived, bodies rotting and eaten by rats in the mud. Some of them spoke of it, and some of them screamed of it in their sleep.

I knew little about his life in Europe. Had he known French women over there, dark-haired French women who spoke soft seductive foreign words and who wore berets pulled low over one eye and elegant black lacy underclothing? Had Michael committed adultery in France? Did some French family have photographs of Michael in their photo album, standing arm in arm with their daughter against a background of the Eiffel Tower? Had Michael left a few red-haired French sons or daughters back there in a foreign field? Of course I haven't got a jealous bone in my body, but a woman always wonders.

I heard my girls laughing. They were looking at our wedding photos. I knew that after the wedding photos would come the one of Molly. I couldn't bear to see that photo of Molly's smiling little face. My sister died a long time ago, but it still hurts to see her photo. I didn't want to see the pictures of Mary and Amy either. Mary and Amy in childhood were as alike as peas in a pod. I would have to go out to the shed before they got to those pictures.

'I don't see what's funny about my wedding photos,' I said, pretending to be cross, although I could see why the girls laughed. We were all so stiff and prim and proper in those photos and my dress – well, it was fashionable then, but my wedding was a long time ago. With a sudden pang I realised that I had not seen Mary dressed as a bride. She would have been a lovely bride, my daughter. Did she have photos that she would show me one day, photos that we could weep over together?

'We're not laughing at you, Mum,' said Amy. 'It's just that you look so young and happy and so different. It's hard to believe that people change so much. And your Uncle Sean looks awful. I just found out that you told the same stories about him to Mary that you told me. And look, there's Grandma Moira with all her wrinkles!'

Yes, I thought, I did look young and happy then. Well, there is a time to be young and happy and then there's a time that comes after that. And now, seeing my two girls together, I felt as if I was recapturing a tiny bit of that happiness. A little of what might have been if Michael and I had not been so harsh. I felt guilty about our treatment of Mary, and I felt guilty too that I was so happy now, what with Michael's death and all.

I had to excuse myself and go out to the shed. Even before Michael's death, when Michael was away on one of his trips and I had had to cope with the kids on my own, if I was worried or confused or upset, I always escaped to the shed just to think things over. Now, since Michael's death and funeral, I was going out to the shed quite a bit.

Years ago, when he came back from the war, Michael had hung his old woollen army greatcoat on a nail behind the door. He used to wear that coat in the winter when he was fetching in the mallee stumps for the fire or when he was mucking out the chook run when it was cold. I used to warn him that the coat would get muddy and he would laugh and say Australian mud wasn't as dirty or as sticky as the Somme mud. Not as much body in it, he used to say.

Now, whenever I felt guilty about my new found joy with Mary or when something suddenly reminded me of Mick – silly things like seeing someone else sitting in his chair at the table, or when a man was needed to carve the meat and one of the boys did it for me – things that brought back thoughts of my dead husband, I would run out to the shed, hide behind the door and bury my face in the rough wool of his coat. Then I felt close to Mick again. That old coat, stinking of chook droppings and of Mick's sweat and cigarettes, comforted me. Hiding in the depths of that smelly old coat, I could almost believe Michael's arms were around me again.

6

Mrs Williams was thrilled to see Mary back, especially since Mary had a husband and child in tow. Of course, Mrs Williams hadn't had any children of her own, so children were a novelty to her. No wonder that her house was always so spotless. She should have been the president of the Housewives' Association, although she was busy enough with the Women's Christian Temperance League. I had trouble keeping the old busybody out of my kitchen. I didn't want to be rude to her, but I badly needed some time alone with my daughter after all this time.

Mrs Williams wasn't the only one who kept popping in for a cup of tea and a gossip. In the first few days after Michael's funeral, all the neighbours visited. The ladies from the church came as well. I hadn't seen most of them for years except when I was taking Amy to the school or picking her up, and I didn't particularly want to see them now. Nasty stuck up lot they were. I am sure they only go to church to show off their hats. Unless you were a member of their Ladies' Fellowship they would have nothing to do with you. I was sure they were only coming around now because Father Flaherty had told them to come. And Father Flaherty himself hung around like a bad smell. Hardly a day passed without someone knocking on the door.

So when Mary said she wanted to take the tram into town to buy some boots for little Patrick, I jumped at the chance to get out of the house. Amy wanted to come with us, but I reminded her that her school friend Dymphna Murphy and her mother had asked if Amy could go with them to the zoo and that I had agreed. Mrs Murphy thought it would cheer Amy up. It was kind of Mrs Murphy, of course, but since Mary's arrival, I doubted that Amy had given her father's absence a lot of thought. Kids are easily distracted, I suppose, and a long-lost sister was distraction enough for any girl.

When I reminded her about the zoo visit, Amy threw one of her tantrums. Mary's jaw dropped at the sight of Amy in action. I think she had thought Amy was perfection embodied until she saw the child stamp her feet, pull at her own hair and scream blue murder.

'You used to carry on just like that, Mary,' I reminded her. 'Just ignore her and she'll get over it.'

I turned my back on Amy and made a pot of tea. When she had reached the sniffling stage, I looked at her again.

'You told Dymphna yesterday that you wanted to go to the zoo with her and so you will have to go. As I recall it, you said you wanted a ride in the elephant's cart. And you wanted to feed peanuts to the monkeys. You can't chop and change and let people down because it doesn't suit you. Who do you think you are, Lady Muck?'

'But I want to go to town with Mary,' whined Amy. 'She'll be going home soon and I'll never see her again. It's not fair. I didn't know you were going to town or I wouldn't have said I'd go to the zoo. Dymphna's really silly, anyway. Sister Mary Leon says she's the silliest girl in the class. Sister says it's because she's named after the patron saint of madmen.'

'Dymphna can't help her name,' I snapped. 'I don't know what possessed her mother to give her a name like that. It's a filthy story, that tale about Saint Dymphna. I remember reading it in the *Lives of the Irish Saints*, but I still don't believe it. It couldn't possibly have happened. I burned my copy of the *Lives* when I read about it,' I glared at Amy. 'But silly or not, you are going to go to the zoo with Dymphna and Mrs Murphy, and I won't hear any more about it. Mary's not going home just yet and anyway you'll see her again next time she comes back to Adelaide.'

I glanced at Mary and saw that she had gone pale. She opened her mouth and seemed about to say something, but then she closed her mouth again and turned around to pick up Paddy, who had been watching Amy's performance with great interest.

'I hope Paddy hasn't been learning how to throw a tantrum from you, Amy,' I said. 'A nice example you'e setting for a little boy.'

Mary sat down at the kitchen table and grabbed the edge of it as she did to steady herself. She did look a bit shaky. 'Saint Dymphna,' she muttered, stroking Paddy's hair.

I hoped Mary had never read the story about Saint Dymphna. It was enough to turn anyone's stomach. The nuns at my school used to caution us about impure thoughts, and then they handed out a book with rubbish like that in it, about a girl raped and murdered by her own father, and him an Irish chieftain who should have known better. Dymphna was the saint for madmen and for incest victims.

I was sure I had tossed that book out before any of the children could read. You wouldn't believe that the church could sanction filth like that. I remember looking to see if the book had the word 'Imprimatur' at the front of it, and being disgusted when I saw it did.

Mary might just be feeling a little unhappy about going back to Mount Gambier, I told myself. It would do her good to have a day in town with me, away from the rest of the family. It would do me good, too. I always say there's no need to go into the city, you can get everything you want on Norwood Parade. But still, it is fun to have a good look around the shops in town once in a while.

'But Mum, you change your mind when you want to. Why can't I change mine?' Amy asked.

'Because you are a child and children don't make decisions. I will decide what you are going to do. And you will behave yourself nicely and smile and say thank you to Mrs Murphy for taking you to the zoo, or I'll box your ears.'

Mary drew Amy to her and hugged her. 'I'll come back here as soon as I can, Amy,' she said. 'Whenever Fred can get someone to look after the shop, we'll come. But it is expensive to pay another butcher, so we can't do it very often. Maybe you could come and stay with me at Mount Gambier next school holidays.'

I wasn't sure that I liked the sound of that. Amy needed a firm hand at times, and I doubted that Mary would be able to control her. She was good at wheedling Amy to behave, but a child needs a bit of discipline too. Amy was better off with me. I had had a lot more experience with children than Mary had.

I didn't say anything, though. I wasn't going to upset Mary or Amy if I could help it. But I was glad Amy would be out of the way at the zoo the next day. I wanted some time alone with Mary very badly. I intended to find out who Amy's father was, if I could, and this would be the perfect time to do it.

7

We found the boots for young Patrick in the first shop we went to. Miller Andersons were having a sale and we got a bargain. But we didn't go home straight away. There was plenty to look at in Adelaide and it's always nice to have a good browse through the city even if you aren't spending a lot of money. We were both enjoying ourselves. We hadn't had a day out in town since Mary was fourteen.

We visited all the big shops, Miller Anderson, Cox Foys, Harris Scarfe, the Myer Emporium, and lastly John Martins. Balfour's Café is at number 74 Rundle Street, not far from John Martins, so we left Johnny's for last. We had planned on lunch at Balfour's Tea Room. There's nothing like a nice cup of tea and a pasty in Balfour's after a morning shopping in town.

Little Paddy was very good. I thought the tram ride in to town would frighten him, but he seemed to like the noise and the being shaken about and he looked through the windows, interested in everything he saw. I enjoyed it when Mary and I took turns to propel his stroller around the streets. It was like having a little kiddie of my own again. At last we were hungry and headed for Balfour's for lunch.

I usually go upstairs because you feel as if you're a real lady up there. The waitresses upstairs seem nicer too, and you can look out of the window at all the people and the traffic in Rundle Street. There are quite a few motor cars in Adelaide these days, not just horses and carts. I don't mind looking at motor cars from a distance. But we had Paddy in his stroller to consider, so we sat downstairs.

When we had our tea and food in front of us, I decided it was time to have a mother-and-daughter chat. If I didn't do it now, it might be a very long time before I had the opportunity again. As Amy had said, Mary would be leaving soon.

'Mary, how much does Fred know about what happened eight years ago?' I asked, hesitantly.

I saw the tears well up in Mary's eyes and I immediately regretted my question. Sometimes you wish that you could take back words that you've spoken, but of course you can never do that. Mary bit her lower lip. I knew I should have bitten my own lips before I had interrogated her. But I had to know. I held my breath and waited.

'Fred knows everything. He lived in the house next door to Mrs Conyers. That's the lady I boarded with at Mount Gambier. Fred and I became good friends. He helped me a lot in the beginning when I was really lonely and unhappy. We used to sit on the front porch together and then we started going for walks in the pine forest, and he never asked questions, he just waited until I wanted to talk. He was so patient and kind. That's when I fell in love with him. I needed a shoulder to lean on and he gave me that shoulder.'

Mary looked me straight in the eye, but her voice trembled and I knew she was having difficulty talking about the past.

'Fred knows as much about me as you do, Mum. In fact, he probably knows more than you do.'

'How could he know more than I do?' I began, but then I thought about all the years we had been apart, and all the pain that Mary had been through during her exile in Mount Gambier. I could never know how she had suffered. I had seen events from my own perspective, but I realised now that there was another way to see what had happened. There was Mary's point of view too. I had never thought about that before. Thank God for Fred, I thought.

I suddenly knew just how selfish I had been. If I had not been so anxious to protect the family's name, if I had had the courage to stand up to Michael when he had insisted we send Mary away, we would all have been better off. I had been weak to give in to Michael. But I had always given in to Michael. It was the only way to keep the peace at home. And I was so ashamed that my daughter was pregnant. It reflected on the way I had brought her up. I could not admit my shame to the whole world.

All those wasted years, I thought. All those years when I could have been hearing her voice, seeing her face, sharing her life. All gone for a stupid principle, a stupid out-dated, outmoded set of values.

Surely we could have covered it up somehow, without going to the lengths that we did.

I still couldn't imagine how the problem could have been fixed, but there must have been another way. Perhaps we should simply have admitted the truth and taken the blame ourselves. It was only a baby, after all. It wasn't the first time a baby had been born without an official father. Look at the Blessed Virgin. She must have had a bit of explaining to do to her family, when you think about it.

'We didn't come back for the funeral because of Dad, you know,' Mary suddenly burst out.

She was groping in her bag for a hanky, and I found one in mine and handed it to her. I reached over the table to grasp her hand.

Paddy, who was sitting in his pusher, realised his mother was upset and began to wail. I picked up a frog cake from the plate on the table with my other hand and thrust it at him. Balfour's Café is famous for those cakes.

From the corner of my eye I saw him look at the green cake. He turned it so that he could see the little frog face drawn in icing on top. He squeezed the cake. The cream oozed out of the frog's mouth. He licked the cream and grinned and apparently forgot about his mother's distress. Just like a boy, I thought. Girls are far more sensitive to people's feelings than boys are.

'We came back because of you, Mum,' Mary said. 'I had wanted to see you for so long. I was angry with you too, because I thought you should have defended me from Dad, but I missed you so much that I just wanted to hear about you even if I couldn't see you.' She hunched over the table and hid her face. Then she looked up at me and went on speaking, but so softly that I had to strain to hear.

'Dad insisted on seeing me when he came to Mount Gambier. At first I was afraid and I refused to see him because of all that had happened, but I had to know if my baby was all right and I needed news of you and the boys, so I started talking to him. It wasn't easy, though. I always made Mrs Conyers sit with me when he came. I never wanted to be with him on my own.' Her body shook with sobs and she looked across at me through eyelashes thick with tears. She blew her nose loudly.

I got up from my chair and put my arms around her and she leant her head against my chest. She drew a deep breath and her voice became more confident.

'I've wanted to come back for such ages. Fred always said I ought to come. He said I needed to get everything out in the open. He said I would feel better if I did it, but he knew that it would be hard for me to come back to Adelaide and face you, especially if Dad was around.'

I sat there feeling as if the world had collapsed about me. I knew Michael was a difficult man in many ways, and that the boys resented the way Mick treated them. Brian had moved out because of the constant arguments, and I knew Harry had been unhappy at home before he married Mavis.

And of course, the older boys had worked out what was going on when Mary was pregnant. Michael told them he would thrash merry hell out of them if they breathed a word of it outside the house. Charlie and Joe had surely been too young to understand at the time, but they had learned about it later, of course.

But to hear Mary speak about her father like this astounded me. I thought she had worshipped her dad. Of course he had been horrible to her about the pregnancy, but Charlie said Michael and Mary had been reconciled in Mount Gambier. Either Charlie was wrong, or Mary had pretended forgiveness. Perhaps she was not the saint she was made out to be. I remembered how she used to tell lies a lot to avoid trouble when she was little.

'Dad was always so much in control of everything. He even tried to take charge of Fred and me down in Mount Gambier. We did let him help us out a bit financially.' Mary sniffed hard and looked at me.

I thought she looked a bit furtive, somehow.

'Fred said Dad owed me something for the harm he had done me in the past. Fred stood up to Dad and he told Dad how he felt about things, and Dad agreed. That was the only time I ever saw Dad back down on anything. Fred said it wasn't blackmail, it was just payment owed me. We knew Dad had plenty of money or he wouldn't gamble on the horses so much, so we knew we weren't taking it from you.'

She smiled tentatively at me through her tears. 'But I never felt comfortable being with Dad. He always made me feel guilty about things, even though I know now it wasn't really my fault. I blamed you for not standing up to him, for not protecting me, especially when he sent me away, but I know you couldn't. He was such a hard man. So when we heard that Dad had died, it seemed the perfect opportunity to come back. For the funeral. To see you. And to see Amy. We've lost so many years that we should have had together, Mum.'

'Have a sip of your tea, Mary, it will make you feel better,' I urged.

I was confused and almost as upset as my daughter, although I had no intention of letting her know that. Why wasn't it really her fault? It couldn't have been an immaculate conception. There hadn't been one of them since that first Mary. But perhaps my Mary had not sinned willingly. Had someone raped her? Who? Why didn't she tell us who had hurt her? How much money had Michael given Mary and Fred, and why? I couldn't ask her any of these things, not when she was so emotional. I should never have said anything. We had been having such a lovely day together until now. And now I had spoiled the day, ruined everything with my curiosity.

'You don't have to talk about this if you don't want to, Mary.' I said, reassuringly.

'But I want to talk to you, Mum. It's just that I've been trying to forget it all and I honestly thought I had done, but now it's all coming back. I've shoved stuff into the back of my mind and I've hoped it would stay there, but it always comes to the surface. Mum, I wasn't crying in the church because Dad was dead. I wasn't sorry that he was dead. I think I was probably relieved, even glad, he was gone, although I know I shouldn't say that. You shouldn't think ill of the dead, after all. No matter what they have done.'

She blew her nose again and made a loud honking noise that would have made me smile if I hadn't been so concerned about her. The words poured out of her almost as quickly as the tears flowed.

'He thought I had forgiven him, but I hadn't, not really. I couldn't. There are some things that can't ever be forgiven. No, I wasn't crying because Dad was dead. I was crying because of all those wasted years that I'd been away from you. And these last few days since the funeral have been so wonderful. I haven't been as happy as this for years. And seeing Amy and knowing she's safe and well have made me feel so much better about it all. You have no idea what I've gone through, missing you and missing Amy and missing home, Mum.'

She was sobbing quite loudly now. It was all very embarrassing. I looked around and saw that the lady at the next table was staring at us quite shamelessly. I felt like telling the woman to keep her nose out of our affairs, but I didn't want to make a scene. Well, more of a scene. A woman like that, in an expensive silk dress that had obviously come from David Jones' shop, had no business sitting downstairs any way. She should be upstairs with all the other stuck-up old biddies. Old ladies who didn't know what it was like to have children.

I patted Mary's hand and glared at the woman. 'There, there, Mary, it's all right now. You're back and we're all together and we will never lose contact again. We're a family again now.'

I realised that this was not the time or the place to ask who Amy's father was. I couldn't bear to upset Mary any more. It was strange, though, that Mary had said she had come back for my sake, not for her Dad's. And that she was more upset about the years we had been separated than by Michael's death. I sighed. I would have to wait a bit longer. If a secret could wait ten years before it was solved, it could wait a few more months. One of the local boys must have fathered Amy, but which one? She didn't look like any of them. With that red hair, she was pure Murphy.

There was a shriek from the next table. Paddy had tired of the frog cake and had hurled it at the nosy lady at the next table. He would make a great bowler for the Sheffield Shield or even for the Australian test team in years to come, I thought. A great little cricketer. Brian would be proud of him. Paddy'll bowl the Poms out every time.

The frog cake had landed fair in the middle of the woman's elegant frock. Perhaps it was time to take a run, though.

'You need to add a few drops of glycerine to the water when you wash that dress, love. Rinse it out with a bar of Velvet soap. That takes cream out of silk like a charm,' I told the woman as I pushed back my chair.

She stood up. Her chair fell over. She glared at me and picked up the little silver tea pot from her table.

'Quick, Mary, she's going to throw that tea pot at us!' I said.

I grabbed the handle of the pusher and ran towards the door. Paddy screamed and held on to the side of the pusher with both hands. Mary gasped an apology at the lady, scooped up our bags and followed, her tears turning to giggles.

'That's the sort of thing I've missed about you, Mum,' she gasped when we were out in the street. 'It's so good to be back and to see you haven't changed. You're corrupting Paddy, though.'

'Young Paddy's going to be another W.C. Grace,' I chuckled. 'Did you see how he threw that cake? Better than Brian's bowling, that was! Paddy'll be a credit to the Australian cricket team one day.'

'Dr Grace was an Englishman, a Pom, Mum, and he was a batsman, not a bowler. Ask Brian, he knows all about it. Dr Grace was the one who put the bail thing back on the wicket after he was bowled out and then said what a windy day it was. He was really arrogant.'

I looked back at Balfour's Cafe. Through the window I could see the waitresses clustered around the angry customer. They were looking in our direction as they sponged the cream from her frock. She looked as if she was about to break free from them at any moment.

'Let's dash back inside John Martins, Mary,' I suggested. 'The summer sales are on and there are a lot of people in there. We can mingle in the crowd. Just in case that woman comes after us.'

8

One night, towards the end of Mary's visit, when dear little Paddy was asleep, I carried a tray of tea into the front room from the kitchen and found my family gathered around the piano. I still shuddered when I looked at that side of the room and remembered how Michael's coffin had lain there.

'*The Rose of Tralee*,' said Mary as she picked up a sheet of music. 'This was Dad's favourite song. He said I was named after the girl in that song. He used to sing it to me when I was little. I'd forgotten about that.'

'He used to sing it to me too,' I said. 'Yes, we did name you after the girl called Mary in the song. He always said that song was about his two loves, his Rose and his Mary.'

'We did have something special once, Dad and me,' said Mary. 'Even after everything that happened, I can't forget that. Even all the horrible stuff can't erase all the good times. When the rotten things come back to me, I try to make myself think about the happy times.'

I noticed that Fred was sitting in Michael's armchair and was looking at Mick's photo over the mantelpiece with what looked like disgust on his face. I wondered why he felt like that. After all, Mick had paid for their wedding. Mary said Michael had tried to run their lives but they had not allowed him to, so perhaps there was a bit of animosity involved. And there was that money they had from Mick to set up the shop. I wondered how much money that was. I didn't begrudge them the money, but I was a bit curious about the amount. Did Fred resent having to thank Mick for the money?

Perhaps I was mistaken. Maybe Fred just had indigestion after the roast hogget and the pudding and the fruit cake I had fed him. Or maybe he was bored at being made to spend time with a noisy family of Irish descent. It might offend his more restrained Protestant upbringing. I knew things were a bit more sedate in Mrs Williams's house than they were here. Fred probably preferred a bit more decorum. He might be longing to have his wife and his son to himself again. He could be missing the peace of Mount Gambier and his butcher shop.

No, I decided, the expression on Fred's face went far beyond indigestion or boredom. I had the feeling that Fred detested his father-in-law. I remembered that Fred had declined to act as a pall-bearer at the funeral. At the time I had thought Fred was being a bit stand-offish, but perhaps there was more to it than that.

Michael had probably rubbed him the wrong way just as he had his own children. Mick and Fred had probably had heated discussions over religion, or philosophy, or trade unionism. Michael could be pig-headed about all those subjects and had clashed with all of us at one time or another.

I wondered just how much any of my boys missed their father. They seemed to have got over their loss very quickly, because I could see that they all were itching to have a good sing around the piano. Joe was actually polishing the top of the instrument with a tea towel, and Brian had lifted the piano seat and was looking through the sheet music in the little tray under the cushion.

'Would it upset you if we had a bit of music, Mum?' asked Joe, giving me a hesitant smile. 'I know it hasn't been long since we buried Dad, so we will understand if you say it wouldn't be decent, but we've always had music in this house. I really miss our musical nights. I don't think Dad would be upset if we had a sing-song, do you?'

'I suppose playing the piano would be all right, but I don't think I'm ready for Charlie's trumpet yet. Not that jazz stuff, anyway. It sounds like tomcats fighting.'

Mary played. The nuns had taught her the piano just as they were teaching Amy now. Amy sat on the stool beside her and turned the pages of the sheet music and the electric light gleamed on the dark wood of the piano and on their two auburn heads. I felt at perfect peace with life and with my family.

We began with the *Rose of Tralee*, and we sang of the pale moon declining into the blue sea and of the lovers who strolled beside the pure crystal fountain that stands in the beautiful Vale of Tralee. When we reached the bit where it goes 'Twas the truth in her eyes, ever dawning, that made me love Mary, the Rose of Tralee', I looked at my daughter Mary, and wondered what indeed was the truth? Who had fathered Amy?

I felt that I could not ask Mary yet, but perhaps when I had really gained her confidence, some time in the distant future, then I would ask her. It was still too soon for that. One day we might talk about it, but not now.

I looked up at the portrait of Michael over the mantelpiece. Did I detect a smile of approval at the corner of his mouth as he looked down at his family gathered around the piano as we had so often done when he was still with us and he was leading the singing? I longed to hear his voice again, but I knew that I never would.

I almost made a dash for the shed and the sanctuary of the old woollen greatcoat again, but then Charlie started to sing *Danny Boy* and I had to stay and listen. He's got a lovely voice, my Charlie.

9

The time passed too quickly and Mary had to go home. The tears on my cheeks mingled with the tears on hers as she and I swore that we would never lose contact again. We were mother and daughter and what was past was past. It was the future that mattered now.

The whole family went to the Adelaide railway station to put her, Fred and little Paddy on the train back to Mount Gambier. Amy had picked every rose in the garden and had wrapped damp newspaper around them. She presented the flowers to Mary at the station.

Mary wept and hugged us all, but she hugged Amy the tightest. She showered kisses on Amy's head and, with tears in her eyes, made me vow to take good care of her dear little sister. She promised to come back as soon as Fred could take holidays again. Not this year, though; he couldn't take more time away from the butcher shop. Perhaps next year. But we all promised to write.

After they went, I felt lonely and unable to settle to anything. It was an effort to water the garden, though I forced myself to do it for Michael's sake. I couldn't let his tomatoes die. Or his seven-year beans. Or the apple cucumbers. But the ground dried out so quickly. Was it the heat, or had the plants withered as my heart had withered? I felt empty, sucked dry, as I had felt when one of my babies had suckled its fill and my breasts hung flaccid and drained.

This is what life did to a woman, I told myself. It was all demand, demand, demand. Michael had stolen my youth in order to breed his children. The children had taken, and still took, all my energy to feed, clothe and care for them. And when they were ready, they would leave and I would be cast aside like yesterday's potato peelings.

Unconditional love, that was what a mother had to give. And if you failed at it, as I had failed Mary, you could never forgive yourself.

Even if the child forgave you, the dark stain remained on your soul. There was no bleach to remove that mark.

And now Michael had died and had forced widowhood and loneliness on me. I was no longer a married woman. I was the Widow Walsh, even my name diminished. I was a husk, blown about in the hot wind. Soon I would know more dead people than live ones.

But the demands of daily living continued. Demands I could no longer fulfil. Even the cat, winding between my legs and purring for milk, exhausted me. I wanted nothing more than to sit in the morning sun, too tired after another sleepless night to think about anyone's needs, the kids or my own, even too drained for tears. It was an effort to breathe.

I used to sit out there on the bench under the apricot tree, just looking at the vegies Michael had planted when he could still talk about his expected harvest. It takes hope to plant a garden, and now hope was gone.

I knew I was waiting for something, but what that was, I had no idea. Time was suspended. Perhaps Michael's soul was in limbo, and mine was there with it. My soul felt like one of those endless, lonely jazz notes that Charlie sometimes played on his trumpet when he wanted to sound artistic, the sound hanging in the air and going nowhere.

Some mornings I didn't even bother to get dressed. There seemed no point in it. I sat there on the bench in the sun in my nightie and my slippers with a cup of tea that I couldn't bother to drink growing cold in my hands.

Once, I was certain that I saw Mick kneeling in the onion patch in the sunlight, weeding. It was definitely him. Despite the heat, he was wearing his old army greatcoat. I blinked hard to be sure my eyes were not playing tricks. He was still there when I opened my eyes. I stood up. The cup fell to the ground and shattered.

'Mick!' I shouted. I ran towards him, wishing that I had made the effort to dress and to comb my hair this morning. As I ran I screamed, 'It wasn't you in the coffin! You've come back to me!'

I raced down the path around the apricot tree, jumped over the hose coiled beside the peach tree, almost fell over the cat which was sunning itself on the cement path, dodged past a bucket of half-rotten seed potatoes with their green shoots sprouting that Mick had intended to plant when he came back from Mount Gambier and hadn't lived long enough to cover with earth, and which we had all forgotten about until now. But when I arrived at the onion patch, Michael had gone.

I saw that the onion patch was badly in need of weeding. Between the dry rows, the onions wilted. I fell to my knees and pulled out the thistles that had grown since Mick had died. I watered the onions with my tears.

Another day, I forgot to feed the chooks until their frantic clucking reminded me of them at midday when I was forcing myself to hang the washing out. I nearly dropped the sheets on the ground when I realised. Poor bloody chooks, I told myself. It wasn't their fault that I was falling to pieces. I mustn't neglect the fowls or there'll be no eggs for the kids' breakfast.

Amy and the boys had had to sort themselves out at breakfast time lately, because just I didn't have the energy to get out of bed, and sometimes the dishes were still there when Amy came home from school. I spent a lot of time sitting in my chair, staring at the space where Michael's coffin had stood, my mind as empty as the house. I wasn't sure if it was Mick or Mary I was missing the most, but I had a guilty feeling that I was grieving more for Mary.

In a way, I envied Michael. It must be quite luxurious to be dead and not to have to worry about anything any more.

10

'What's for tea, Mum?' Charlie called as he came back from work. He had an apprenticeship at the local plumber's shop and was always starving when his day was over. He was still a growing boy, after all.

I should make a big effort to have the meals ready for the kids, I thought. I had no appetite myself and didn't want to cook or eat. My clothes were getting looser and I knew I should make an effort. I wasn't being fair to the family, but I was so very tired.

'I don't know, I haven't thought about it yet. I'll send Amy down to the butcher's to get some sausages.'

'You did that last night and the night before. We're all sick of sausages. You've got to snap out of it, Mum. I know it's hard for you. We all know you always relied on Dad to do the thinking, but you have to pull your socks up and get on with life.'

Joe was already home from his job with the bricklayer. He was looking through the cupboard for something to eat to tide him over until the meal was on the table. 'There's nothing here. No biscuits, no cake, not a crumb. You haven't done any baking for a while, Mum,' he complained. 'Not since Mary left. I'm hungry. I've got to eat something now. I'm going out with my mates tonight. There's a new Buster Keaton film on at the Odeon. Did you iron that white shirt for me? I asked you this morning to get it ready for me.'

'No, I forgot. Sorry, Joe. I seem to have lost my get up and go lately. I just don't have much energy at the moment. I'll do it after tea. Amy, get some chops from the butcher and then help me peel some spuds.'

'This isn't good enough, Mum. You can't spend your life moping like this. Life goes on. I know you used to rely on Dad for a lot of things, but you've got to realise he isn't coming back. You've got to get over it. You're just going to have to pull your socks up and stand on your own two feet,' said Charlie, looking through the mail that Amy had brought in from the letter box.

'There's a lot of bills here, Mum. There's an electricity bill and the council rates and we owe the grocer quite a bit. And the butcher. You booked up a lot of meat when Mary and her family were here.'

'I had to,' I protested. 'Fred's used to eating meat.'

Charlie interrupted me. 'How much money is left in Dad's account?'

'I don't know, Charlie. I just can't be bothered with any of it. I'll get around to having a look at it later.'

'No, you won't. We'll all sit down now and look at it. Joe, get those other bills from the shelf. Bring paper and a pencil. Let's work out how much we owe and how much we have got. Mum can go and pay the bills tomorrow. Dad'd turn in his grave if he knew we were in debt. I can still hear him saying "Take care of the pennies and the pennies will take care of the pounds." He was always careful about money. Except for his gambling, of course. He was a selfish old bugger, in a lot of ways, when you think about it.'

'Don't speak ill of the dead, Charlie,' I snapped. But privately, I agreed with him.

He shrugged and opened another envelope. 'This bill's for that hat and coat you bought for the funeral, Mum. Six quid. That was a bit extravagant, wasn't it?'

'I wasn't going to look as if I was in the poor house at my own husband's funeral. What would the neighbours have thought?'

'Well, tomorrow you can go and settle the lot. It'll do you good to put your new hat on and go for a walk in the sun down to the Norwood Parade and get these bills out of the way instead of sitting here with the blinds down.'

'If I put the blinds up, that busybody Mrs Williams comes round. I don't feel like listening to her gossip.'

When Charlie had worked out the debts, we looked at Michael's bank book. We all had a shock. There should have been more in it. No one knew where the money had gone, and Michael wasn't there to ask. He might have known which horse he had put it on at least.

The memory of the time when my family had had big financial

troubles came back to me. Things were tough when I was growing up, back in the 1800s. My parents were renting a house. My dad was a bit of a drinker, so we were never in a position to buy our own home, and the landlord put the rent up just after Dad got really sick. It was his liver that was the problem.

I had to leave school and get a job cleaning rich people's houses over in Toorak Gardens. I walked there and back from Norwood every day, summer and winter, although it's not something I have ever told my children.

I was thirteen years old, not much older than Amy now. The money I brought in wasn't much, but it helped. If it hadn't been for Michael, I would have had very little education. That's one thing he did for me: he opened my eyes. He was a great reader and we always had books in the house.

My parents and I weren't the only ones who had problems. Most people did towards the end of the 1800s. Some people said the reason the economy nearly collapsed was due to the big floods that came down from Bourke after that terrible drought of 1888 broke, but other people said it was because of the unions making demands.

1891 was the year that the miners got the eight-hour day award up at Broken Hill. The men worked for eight hours, they had eight hours' recreation and eight hours for sleep. The bosses said this was extravagant, and they blamed the miners for the recession. Management wasn't happy that the miners' pay went up to ten shillings per day, either. I remember Michael talking about it.

Ten shillings a day was a lot of money in 1891. It still is a lot of money in 1928. The other unions envied the miners, and they wanted more money too. But Michael always said Australia's problems weren't caused by the unions. We had problems because the investors and the bosses got greedy and over-extended themselves.

I remember many of the banks failed in the 1890s. People stood outside the banks and tried to get their money and there were riots. I've never trusted banks since then. The memory of those times has taught me to keep a careful track of my money. Money only goes in one direction once, my mother used to say. She was right. She used to talk about the riots of 1870 before I was born, when the government tried to make the unemployed work for one shilling and ten pence per day. I remember how Henry Lawson talked about an uprising in which blood would stain the wattle.

The workers have always been exploited, and unless people are really prudent and keep track of their money, they can get into a lot of trouble. Unfortunately, the memory of bad times in the past didn't stop Michael from being a gambler. While he was bringing in good money, it didn't matter all that much. We were never short of a quid.

'Mum, what are we going to do?' Amy asked, her voice shaking.

'Don't worry,' I said with a confident smile, 'everything will be all right. I'll just see the insurance people. I've been meaning to do that, when I got around to it. Your father had life insurance. There should be a tidy sum in the policy. He's been paying into it for years. He cared about this family. You all heard the eulogy at his funeral. He wouldn't leave us unprovided for.'

Next day I dressed in the new black coat and black hat that I had worn to Michael's funeral and I caught the tram into town to the insurance company.

11

'Your husband cancelled that insurance policy last year, Mrs Walsh,' the man behind the desk said apologetically.

'What? Why?' I asked, flabbergasted.

'He said now that the boys were working there wasn't such a strong need to make provision for the family. He said he wanted the money to pay off your house. He said the interest rates were going higher and it was more important to keep the roof over your heads than to have money tied up.' The man shook his head. 'He did say he had heard that there was some sort of worldwide financial problem looming, but we've all heard those rumours. Australia hasn't had any real economical problems for thirty-seven years. Hardly anyone even remembers back that far. I admit there were problems back then, but it won't happen again.' He shuffled the papers on his desk.

I thought he looked a bit guilty and I wondered if he was telling me the truth. How did I know whether Michael really had closed the account or not? Maybe the insurance company had done a fiddle with the money. Maybe we were being swindled. But how could I prove it? I didn't know anything about banks or insurance companies. Michael always handled that sort of thing. Money was men's business, not women's business.

The insurance man sighed. 'I told him those rumours were all nonsense. I said the American economy is in sound shape. And if America is safe, Australia is safe. I warned him that a family man needs insurance, but he laughed it off. He said he might buy an insurance policy again when his ship came in. Those were his very words, "when his ship came in". He insisted that he wanted the money then and there. He cashed in the lot. So there's nothing left in the account. I'm sorry, Mrs Walsh.'

Back home, I went out to the shed and hid my head in Mick's army greatcoat and I sobbed. I just could not believe it. We really were in trouble. What were we going to do? How would I feed the kids?

I had a sudden thought. There could be some money in the pockets of the coat. Mick liked to squirrel money away. He hadn't been as personally affected by the problems of 1891 as my family had been. His people were better off than my family was. They owned their own house and had money behind them. His mother, Moira Walsh, never let me forget that, old witch that she was. She never had to clean houses for pennies at Toorak Gardens. She just sat on her fat backside and ordered people around. Me, usually.

But still, Michael must have remembered how the land investment companies went bankrupt back then. His Uncle Phil had been one those who lost money. It happened all across Australia. In all the capital cities, big companies and banks went bad. In fact, it happened across the world, London, Paris, Rome, New York. It was nasty. Neither of us wanted to relive those times, so we were always careful with money. Not mean, but careful. Although Michael did like a flutter on the ponies from time to time.

Since his death I had found few pounds in the pocket of the jacket he used to wear to the races and there had been ten pounds under the mattress. Maybe there would be some money in the old coat pockets, just enough to tide us over for a bit. Until our ship came in.

I went through the pockets but all I found was some torn-up betting tickets for the Melbourne Cup from a couple of years ago. Obviously that horse had not won the race. Had Mick cashed in the insurance and used the money for gambling? He was fond of the horses. He had won some money last year, I remembered.

That story the insurance man had told me about paying off the house sounded a bit peculiar to me. I thought that Mick had paid it off years ago. I could remember seeing the papers, in fact. At one stage he had put them in a tin box on top of his wardrobe. I could have sworn I had seen them there. But when I had forced that box open with a screwdriver last week, all that was in it was our wedding papers and the kids' birth certificates, including Amy's, which didn't tell the whole truth. He must have put the mortgage papers somewhere else. I was gradually working my way through all of my husband's hiding places, finding all out all his secrets.

But what had he done with the insurance money?

Could he have spent the money on Mary's wedding? But a wedding wouldn't cost all that much, surely. Not in Mount Gambier. I remembered with a pang of bitterness that I had not been invited to Mary's wedding. My only daughter, and I had not seen her wedding. She would have been a lovely bride. I bet Mick had been there. He had probably gone to Mount Gambier for it. Another secret I had discovered. He probably even gave her away. He could have managed the trip easily enough by telling me he was off on union business. He was always off somewhere on union business.

How many other lies had he told me over the years? What sort of marriage was that? It was a marriage in which I had been continuously deceived. I had lived with the wool pulled over my eyes for most of my life.

Infuriated, I pulled the old coat off the nail and lugged it into the kitchen. I threw it on the table and got the scissors out of the drawer. I opened the seams in the hem. He might have sewn money into it. Even enough to buy food for a week would help. The hem was empty.

Bloody Mick! Went off on one of his union trips and died and left his family to starve! The selfish bastard! Him and his ship coming in. He was always talking about what he would do when his ship came in. When the horses came in was more like it. If he was here right now I would hit him over the head with the cast-iron frying pan! What sort of husband, what sort of father, what sort of man, goes and dies and leaves his helpless wife and family to fend for themselves?

Same attitude that sent him off to the Great War, when you thought about it. Off he went on the great bloody adventure, him and his army mates, went off to save the British Empire wearing this damned woollen coat, all bluff and bravado, and left me for four long years to cope alone with all those little kiddies.

It wasn't as if he had to go. No, he volunteered, didn't he? He said it was the honourable thing to do. What had he quoted at me? 'I could not love thee more loved I not honour more.' Some crap like that. Honour was more important than family.

Not that he was the only one. All the men were infected by that madness in 1914. The whole country went mad. The patriotic insanity spread just like that Spanish flu had spread when the killing finally stopped in 1918. First the war, and then the flu. It was a miracle any of us survived, soldiers or civilians.

It was only a fluke that he actually came back. I could have been a widow years ago if you thought about it. Or he could have come back with his lungs ruined by the gas or with one leg blown off and then what would we have done?

He'd have sat by the fire, like Mr Roberts down the road, weaving baskets that no one wanted to buy. And I would have had to go out and clean other people's toilets again to put a bit of bread on the table. That's what would have happened. Just like a man. Get your legs shot off with never a thought for the consequences of it. Bloody selfish attitude.

I looked down at the coat and realised that I was cutting the stiff wool up into little squares. Instinctive revenge, I suppose. It was a waste, I realised when I thought about it. I could have used the wool from that coat for a door mat and wiped my feet on it when I came in from the garden. No, I decided. I was going to dispose of it and of my memories of Mick now. I wanted revenge.

It wasn't much of a revenge, but it was better than nothing. I hacked further into the material, shredding the coat to pieces. Damned men, all of them. The men had all the fun in life, drinking and smoking and gambling on the horses. Going off to war and to work. Travelling on trains. Women never got to travel on trains.

What did women get out of living? Periods and pregnancy and childbirth and looking after kids. Blood and pain and shit and tears. Look at my poor mother. She did everything that was wanted of her, everything the family and the church and the community expected a woman to do. She spent her entire life at it. Six children born, two of them stillbirths, so she had all the labour pains with no reward for it, then Molly, her youngest daughter, died of the diphtheria at two years old, and then her two sons, full of bravado, ran off to the Great War and got themselves killed, and I was the only one left. One out of six. What were those odds if you were a gambler? No wonder she went to pieces in the end. Well, I wasn't going to go to pieces. Mick's coat could go to pieces instead.

I put the scraps into the slop bucket and carried the bucket out to the incinerator. It took a few trips. It was a big coat. Heavy too. The wool was heavy and so was the history of the coat. I found some kero in the shed and doused the incinerator with it and struck a match. The pieces of coat smouldered and caught fire. I felt a pang or two of guilt and of regret when I saw the smoke rising, but then I thought about how Michael had ruined my life and my children's lives and how we would all have to suffer because of him.

'Dust to dust, ashes to ashes,' I said, and I poured a bit more kero on the fire. It flared up and singed my eyebrows and I yelled.

Mrs Williams put her head over the fence. 'What on earth are you burning, Mrs Walsh? It smells dreadful.'

I had to agree. Nothing stinks like burning wool, especially burning wool soaked in kero.

'Just some old rubbish I found in the shed,' I said. 'My husband was a hoarder. It clears the air to have a clean out once in a while.'

'Well, it's not clearing the air over here,' said Mrs Williams. 'You might wait until the wind is blowing the other way. I'll have to do all my washing again now because of the smell. I've closed my windows, but I'm sure my curtains are going to be ruined.'

I looked over the fence at her clothes line and saw her nightgown and Mr Williams's striped pyjamas hanging companionably together amongst her snow-white sheets. If she was making the point that she had a husband and I didn't, it didn't wash with me. I knew now that all men are rotten if you look at them closely enough.

I went back into the house to get away from her. I walked through to the front room to shut the windows in case the wind changed, so my curtains wouldn't be stinking too.

I saw Michael's portrait hanging over the mantelpiece. 'Bastard!' I said. 'Leave your family destitute, would you?'

I got a chair and climbed up and took down the portrait. It was heavy and I nearly dropped it. I shouldn't have to do things like this, I thought. This is a man's job. Michael should be here doing the heavy work.

But even when he was alive, half the time Michael was away looking after the union men. If the men at Broken Hill won a reduction in working hours, Michael wanted it for the Timber Workers Union. If they got more pay at the Hill, his men had to have a pay raise. He looked after their interests more than he ever looked after his family's welfare.

I was the one who, single-handed, had to keep this place running when he was away. I was the one who had to do all the heavy work until the boys and Mary were big enough to help. Lifting the clothes out of the copper with a stick when I was pregnant. Moving furniture to clean behind it. Killing rats and mice and spiders.

Mrs Williams always screams whenever there's bit of wildlife in her house. Mr Williams always has to come running to save her from any unfortunate creature foolish enough to intrude. That never happened in my house. Even when Mick was home, I had to do my own killing.

And as for the state of that place next door! I don't believe in being dirty, but Mrs Williams takes it too far. Her house is so clean you're scared to breathe in there in case your breath makes a mark on something. It's like something out of *The Ladies' Home Journal*. My house is clean enough to be healthy, and dirty enough to be happy. Well, some of the time we're happy.

This was all Mick's fault, I told myself again. If he hadn't died, if he hadn't left us penniless, I wouldn't be struggling like this to take his picture down. Useless waste of space that he was.

I yanked the picture off its hook. A dark rectangle showed on the wall where the photo had stopped the wallpaper from fading. I would have to put something over it to cover it up. Michael's photo wasn't going back, though. I lugged Michael in his frame out to the shed and leant him against the corrugated iron.

I looked around the shed. There must be something here I could use to cover the dark rectangle of wallpaper in the front room. Leaning against the corrugated iron was a picture of Jesus wearing a mournful expression as he pulled back his scarlet robes to display his sacred heart. This picture had hung over my mother's bed. Mum had gazed at every night as she knelt and prayed, her rosary beads passing through her work-worn fingers.

I think my mother thought she could keep her nightmares about Molly's and the boys' deaths away by praying. I doubt that it helped her because I often heard her sobbing in her sleep. I didn't dream of my brothers, but I still dream of Molly, and prayer has never helped me in that regard.

Jesus' picture had come to me when Mum died. I had inherited all that she had, come to think of it. Which wasn't much. My inheritance consisted of Jesus and memories.

Michael had hated that picture. He said when the Brothers were caning him for smoking in the toilets at school he used to look up at the very same picture of the Sacred Heart hanging in the class room. Michael felt that Jesus approved of the punishment that the brothers were giving him. Michael said the shed was the best place for the sacred heart.

'Just the thing,' I said, brushing off the cobwebs with a bit of rag. 'Come on, Jesus, you've got a new home. I reckon you're just the right size.' I put the two pictures back to back to check the measurement. Exactly the same dimensions. The less faded rectangle of wallpaper wouldn't show at all.

I dragged the religious picture into the living room and had another look at it. 'If I was your mother,' I told Jesus, 'I'd make you get your hair cut. Short back and sides, that's what you need.'

I climbed onto the chair again. Then I had to heft the picture up and lift it up to the hook. It wasn't easy getting the string to catch on the hook. I almost gave up, but I'm not one to give in easily. Eventually I succeeded. Then I had to get up and down from the chair a few times to make the picture hang straight.

At last I stood sweating and triumphant in front of a correctly aligned Sacred Heart. 'At least Father Flaherty won't be able to say this is a Godless house without a religious picture in it next time he calls,' I told Jesus. 'Not that I want him calling and drinking my tea and giving me advice on how to run my life. And now Michael won't be able to smirk at me again knowing that he has won and that I have lost. He can grin all he likes out in the shed. I won't be looking.'

I was dismayed when I realised that if Jesus had had a short back and sides hair cut, he would bear an amazing resemblance to Michael.

The clothes were different, of course, but there was something about the shape of the nose and of the mouth that reminded me of Mick. They both wore that holier-than-thou look in their eyes. It must be a trick of the light, I thought. I've wasted my time changing the pictures over. I might as well have left things as they were.

Jesus' eyes seemed to be following me about the room as if he was accusing me of something. I could almost hear one of Father Flaherty's sermons exhorting wifely obedience and meekness and acceptance of a woman's lot in life. 'A wife should accept her husband's rule, just as the church accepts God's ruling,' I remember Father Flaherty saying.

'It's all codswallop. A complete load of nonsense,' I told the picture.

But when I went out of the room I shut the door. Just in case. I knew I was being superstitious, but I didn't care. God knows what the kids will say when they find out I've put Michael in the shed, I thought. Or what they will say when they find out there is no money?

12

'We're skint. We're completely broke,' I told the boys and Amy. I had used the last of my cash to give them a roast dinner – hogget and baked spuds with gravy, carrots and peas. I thought we ought to have a decent meal in our bellies while we digested the hard facts. Bread and butter pudding to follow, washed down by a good strong cup of tea.

Charlie put his fork down. 'We could sell the house,' he said. 'Sell it and rent something smaller. We could live off the money from the house until Joe and I finish our apprenticeships and we get a decent wage.'

'We're not selling this house,' I said. 'I've lived in a rented house once and I'm not going to do it again. You can't choose your neighbours if you rent, either. You might have to put up with horrible people next door. Your father and I put our heart and soul into this place. He might have left us in the lurch, but I'm not giving our house up.'

Charlie and Joe looked at each other. Amy sighed. I knew I had said things like this before when I was telling the kids how hard we had worked to get the place in order, but I didn't care.

'Those concrete paths around the place, for example. Your Dad and I mixed that cement by hand. Three squares a day. Three shovels full of sand, two of gravel, and one of cement. Then you mix it together and add water until it's sloppy. That's hard work. In the winter rain and in the summer heat we worked on those paths.' I thumped the table with my fist in case they didn't believe I was serious.

'Even when I was looking after Harry and expecting Brian, I worked. We did all the painting ourselves, we sanded and polished these floors by hand. We sweated blood for this house. It's my home now, anyway. My parents rented a place, but now I own one and I'm not giving it up for love or money. I'm not letting some stranger come and rip out the garden and dirty my clean floors.'

'I could leave St Joseph's and go to the public school,' said Amy. 'Then we wouldn't have to pay school fees.'

I looked at her. Ever since she had started kindergarten with the nuns, the kids who went to the public school had teased her. What was the jingle they sang at her – 'Catholic dogs jump like frogs, in and out the Irish bogs'? They all knew Amy, those Protestant kids. They'd seen her wear her Catholic school uniform. They were a rough lot, the public school kids. Amy would never survive at the public school. My other kids had been teased too, but they had had older brothers to stick up for them. Amy, the last of my children, had no one. And Amy was a quiet, gentle little thing. A real lady. Even the nuns said that. Except when she threw screaming tantrums. But that wasn't all that often. And she was still just a baby, after all.

'Kids at the public school get nits in their hair,' I said.

'We get nits at St Joseph's too, Mum,' Amy protested, running her fingers through her hair and looking at her hands. 'Sheila McDeed had nits in her hair last week. Everyone gets them. I feel itchy when I think about it, but I haven't got any yet. The nuns say lice are dirty but not unusual.'

She watched me as I began to scratch my head. There's something about the word lice that makes you uncomfortable, even though you know that your hair is clean. Amy shrugged. I could see she was relishing giving me a lesson for once.

She continued. 'Lice is the correct name for nits, Sister Mary Leon said. She said you just use kerosene, comb it through and then wash your hair with Velvet soap. That gets rid of lice.'

'All of us boys went to St Joseph's, so did Mary, and we all got nits. Or lice if you want to call them that. You've just forgotten about it, Mum,' said Joe. 'You always forget the rotten stuff. You only like to remember nice things. We've all noticed that about you. Sweep the horrible stuff under the mat and look the other way, that's your policy.'

'We've paid the school fees for this year already, anyway,' said Charlie. 'So outgoings aren't the problem. We need to increase our income. They're paying good money at Broken Hill for labourers down the mine. We've been thinking, Joe and me. Even before you said about the insurance money, we thought it would be a good way to help. We could go up there on the train, board somewhere cheap and send money down. I reckon that's a really good idea.'

'I think Charlie's right,' said Joe. 'If we do that, you won't have to feed us and we can help towards keeping this place going as well. You're going to have to face facts, Mum. Dad's gone. His money won't be coming in. Things have to change.'

'Well, I reckon it's a really rotten idea,' I said. 'The reason they're looking for labourers down the mine is that men get killed at Broken Hill all the time. Men and boys. A sixteen-year-old lad has just been killed in a rock fall up there. I was thinking this morning that Saint Barbara is the patron saint of miners, and she's not doing her job properly. That lad's death was in the paper today – I'll find the article.'

I looked for the story in the *Advertiser*. The boys must have been looking at the employment section for mining jobs while I was serving up the meal because those were the pages I found open. I forgot about the mine-death article and began to skim the job advertisements – there might be some sort of work a middle-aged woman could do. I knew it was unlikely, but it wouldn't hurt to look.

'What if we ask Brian to move back in?' Charlie was saying. 'There's plenty of room now. Amy can share Mum's bed and Brian can have Amy's room. After all, there used to be a lot more of us here when we were all little.'

Joe agreed. 'Brian says he hates his landlady. She can't cook to save her soul, and the room he rents is putrid. She doesn't wash his cricket togs properly. He's fussy about his cricket whites. He says Mum used to look after them much better than his landlady does.'

'That's right. He can pay his board here instead of to his landlady,' Charlie went on. 'That will help us and him too.'

I was half listening to Charlie and thinking he had turned out to be a really sensible lad despite his obsession with playing jazz on that trumpet of his, and at the same time reading the ad I had just seen in the paper.

'Wanted, housekeeper lady to care for widowed farmer and two children on mid-north property near Orroroo. Wage and board. Four pounds, four shillings and two pence per week. All found. No followers.'

There was an address to send a letter of application. I had no idea where Orroroo was. The name sounded a bit uncivilised, and I didn't remember Michael ever mentioning it. It couldn't be anywhere near Mount Gambier. But there must be a train that went there. The trains went everywhere these days. It would mean cleaning a stranger's house again, but a farmer, especially a widowed farmer, would be better than working for some snooty lady at Toorak Gardens. I could always come home if I didn't like it.

'That's a really good idea, Charlie,' I said, tearing the advertisement out of the paper and putting it in my apron pocket. I smiled at Charlie. 'Can you get hold of Brian and see if he agrees? I was thinking of taking in a lodger, but Brian would be better than a stranger.'

I wouldn't tell the kids about the job until I had it. I was certain that I would get it. I don't know why. Maybe I was finding some faith in God again, or even finding faith in myself for once in my life. Perhaps I was fooling myself that I could live independently without Michael or my family making all the important decisions for me, but somehow I knew that I could and would do it. I would show them all that I was able to cope without Mick. They'd change their tune when they found out I could stand on my own two feet. This job would be something to tide us over, to pay a few bills until our ship came in. And I might not miss Mary quite so much if I got away from home for a month or two. Above all, if I got a job, the boys wouldn't need to go to work at Broken Hill.

I wrote a letter and posted it the next day. That very night I found a bundle of banknotes rolled up in pair of socks in Michael's sock drawer. Thirty pounds, it was. I don't know how I had missed that money the first time I went through his drawer.

I thanked the God who I was not sure existed, and I paid the grocer and the butcher. The boys' payday was next week, so we could pay something off the council rates or off the electricity. I wasn't sure which was the more pressing. Probably the electricity. My family would find it hard to live without electricity, and so would I, now, although we hadn't had it when I was a girl. I'd forget about the rates for the present. What do you actually get from a council for the money you pay them, anyway?

Brian moved back in and Amy slept beside me in my bed. I was relieved to have her, to tell the truth. I won't admit it, but I hate to sleep on my own. If I haven't got someone beside me, the dreams are worse. I used to bring the cat into my bed when Michael was away. A cat helps a bit, though if you roll on it you can get scratched badly, but I really need a person beside me at night, when the darkness tightens around my throat. Amy didn't have fleas, either.

There were a few disadvantages in having Brian home again. It cost more to feed an extra mouth, but we killed a few chooks and ate lots of home grown vegies and of course there were the preserves I had put down last year. Brian's board money helped, although the situation was still difficult. We had spent too much before we realised there was no money to fall back on. I wished that I hadn't bought that new hat for Mick's funeral.

There was more washing and ironing for me to do with an extra son in the house. As Joe had said, Brian was very fussy about his cricket clothes and I had forgotten how hard it is get grass stains out of white trousers. I had to buy more bleach than I had done lately.

The three boys did argue a bit, so there was more noise than before, but that's only natural. Michael wouldn't have liked it, but Michael wasn't there. Put three blokes together and they're bound to raise a bit of a ruckus occasionally.

At least Brian didn't play the trumpet like Charlie. His cornet was almost as bad, though. I banished my musicians to the shed in the end. Mrs Williams complained a bit but I turned a deaf ear to her whingeing.

And it was good to have my second eldest son home again, even if he had grown a bit independent since he had moved out. He had acquired a few ideas about when and how he liked his meals served and he thought he could come in at any old hour of the night. I soon changed his mind about that sort of thing. You have to have some sort of standards, and tomato sauce on fried eggs and toast at eleven o'clock at night wasn't going to be one of the standards in my house.

Brian admitted he was glad to be back. His dad had been getting on his nerves, he said. That was the real reason why he had moved out. A fellow gets sick of being treated like a kid at the age of twenty-three.

Now that Dad was gone, Brian said, he was happy to come back to his mum's cooking. Also, he complained, his landlady wouldn't let him smoke in the house. I wished I had thought of that rule. I get sick of emptying ashtrays. Michael and the boys have never considered disposing of their own cigarette ash.

Even before I heard that I had got the job, I threw myself into a flurry of spring cleaning, although January is well into the summer and it was a bit hot for cleaning. Curtains were taken down and washed, ironed and re-hung, I cleaned off the Vegemite that Mary's son had spread on the walls. I did regret not seeing the Vegemite, though. Those brown smears had reminded me of young Paddy every time I looked at them.

The floors were waxed and polished, the windows gleamed, and when I could find nothing else to do, I made apricot jam and plum jam by the gallon. It wasn't runny either. I cleaned the stove. I got a ladder and climbed up and put a tablespoon of kerosene on top of the rainwater tank to stop the mosquitoes breeding. At night I mended and darned the family's clothes. If I would not be there, they would want for nothing.

It was Amy who worried me the most. To be separated from my little girl, to leave her in the care of someone else, almost broke my heart. It was like losing Mary all over again, but somehow this was worse, because back then I had had the anger and the shame to sustain me. Now there was only fear. And I was the one who leaving this time. I was abandoning my children. I toyed with the idea of sending Amy to live with Mary at Mount Gambier, but I couldn't bear the idea of doing that. Sending one little girl away was bad enough. To dispatch two of them into the unknown was more than I could bear.

And if the job didn't work out and I had to come home, I would have lost both my girls. I was sure that Mary wouldn't let go of Amy once she had control of her, reconciliation or not. Amy should stay close to home in familiar surroundings. She wouldn't like going to another school in another town, I reasoned. I wasn't too sure about leaving home myself. It would be an adventure, but it would be frightening too.

But if I didn't make the first move, if I didn't bring some money into the household, Joe and Charlie were determined to go to Broken Hill. I remembered the things that Michael had told me about the mines. Men and boys died in their hundreds there. It was a unionist's nightmare. The money was good, but it had to be, or men wouldn't work at Broken Hill.

If the miners weren't crushed by the mine caving in, they were blown up by explosives that went off before the poor devils could leave the blast area, or they were injured or killed by the heavy ore carts hitting them in the darkness. Sometimes people fell off the high slag heap.

And, according to Michael, any miners who were lucky enough to escape all these earlier fates died of lung disease. What had Michael said about the miners, something about 'bodies wrecked and lives destroyed by lead and by poisonous gases'? Mick knew all about the miners' working conditions from his own union work. He had talked to other union leaders and read articles about it.

Michael would turn in his grave if he knew Joe and Charlie were working down the mine at Broken Hill. He might not have provided properly for his family and he might often have been cantankerous, but he would never have wanted his sons to be miners. You had to have some respect for a father's feelings and wishes. No father would want his children harmed.

My husband was dead and buried but I would not allow my boys to be buried alive in the dark depths of a mine. Even if it meant that I had to sacrifice myself and be exiled from all I loved, if I must put my body and my soul in jeopardy by living with a Protestant family, so be it. The farmer's surname was Pascal, and that didn't sound Irish or Catholic to me.

But would the farmer want me? I wasn't sure what sort of qualifications he was looking for. I knew I was well qualified for housekeeping and caring for children, but how did he know that?

All I had said in my letter to him was that I had had six children and reared them all successfully. They had all turned out well and I considered that looking after two children would be as easy as falling off a log.

I had stated that I was a good plain cook and anyone who wanted to, could eat off the floor in my kitchen. Well, they could if they wanted to, I suppose. I've always thought that's a pretty stupid expression. Why would anyone want to eat off a floor? You'd have to be mad. Only Mrs Williams would be fussy enough to have a house like that.

But I might not even get a reply to my letter. I was getting all worked up for nothing. As time went on, I decided that I would never see Orroroo.

<h1 style="text-align:center">13</h1>

A letter came from Orroroo. I had the job on appro. I was to catch the train up on the 12 February, and would have three months on spec to see if I suited the farmer and he suited me. His wife, he wrote, had died of cancer. The household consisted of himself and two children aged ten and six years. The letter was brief and I wondered what I was letting myself in for. But the money would help my family. There had been a final demand letter for the council rates. They would remove goods and chattels unless some payment was not made soon. They would accept small regular payments, though.

When I showed the Orroroo farmer's letter to the family they were dismayed.

'You can't do this, Mum,' Amy sobbed. 'We've just lost Dad and we don't want to lose you too. I need you. Who'll iron my school uniforms? Who'll brush my hair?'

'Mavis will,' I said. 'You'll live with Harry and Mavis and she'll look after you. I've already talked it over with her. You'll have to give her a hand in the house. She'll need a bit of help now she's expecting. They won't charge any board for you, but you will have to do your share of the housework.'

'And who'll look after us?' asked Joe. 'Who'll cook our meals and do our washing? Who'll clean the house?'

'You're just going to have to learn to care for yourselves. It was going to happen sooner or later. What if I dropped dead like your father did? Just don't burn the house down while I'm away. And look after the garden. If you look after the vegies they'll look after you. Don't forget to water the plants, especially the pumpkins.'

The boys groaned, but I was implacable. 'The garden needs a lot of water this time of year, drought or no drought. Use the water in the rainwater tanks. You can do your own washing and ironing, it won't hurt you. It'll do you the world of good to see how much work I do around this place. If you get into trouble, ask Mavis for advice. Just don't ask Mrs Williams next door. I don't want her poking about my house. Especially if I'm not here. She'll run her hand over the furniture to see how much dust there is. As bad as your father's mother, she is.'

'How do you know what sort of people you're going to meet up there, Mum?' asked Joe. 'How do you know they're not white slavers? This Orroroo place, that's way up in the bush. It could be desert up there. You've seen that film *The Sheik* with Rudolph Valentino. This bloke might drag you off to a harem or something.'

The two lads looked at me, then looked at each other. Charlie was trying to hide a grin. Joe didn't even try to hide his expression. I could see they both doubted that I was white slave material. Even I knew I didn't quite fit the role of the slender, blonde English lady Rudolph Valentino kidnapped in the film and carried off into the romantic desert sands to be ravished on cushions in a tent. I remembered how that lady was very delicate and elegant and wore floating silk scarves. She protested mildly as the sheik lifted her onto the back of a large white horse. She said she didn't want to be married because she would lose her independence. If I interpreted the smouldering look in Valentino's eyes correctly, she was about to lose more than her independence.

I've given birth to five children and I'm more solidly built than that lady in the film. My once flaming red hair has turned grey, and although I still have most of my teeth I admit I have lost the odd one or two. I have stretch marks across my belly and my breasts, having fed all those babies, droop. There are wrinkles on my face.

Somehow Michael still found me attractive, or he said he did. But I was aware of Michael's roving eye. I had never actually caught him out with a female, but he was a great flirter at parties. I know, with his powers of persuasion, he would have been able to seduce women if that was what he wanted to do. He had a golden tongue, my husband. He could talk his way around me when he wanted to. Mick had never called me slender, though. And I very much doubt that Rudolph Valentino could have hoisted my weight on to his protesting horse.

I must admit I am partial to Rudolph Valentino. I've often wondered what Michael would have looked like with a tea towel on his head. I shouldn't say this, but I have sometimes pictured Valentino instead of Michael taking me in his arms when we performed the marital act. That's probably the sort of thing a woman ought to confess to a priest and do penance for. I expect it amounts to a sort of mental adultery. But I certainly wouldn't tell Father Flaherty about it even if I did go to confession. It would come into the impure thoughts category.

It was dreadful when Valentino died. I remember the date, 23 August 1926. He was just thirty-one years old, and as handsome as they come. I wasn't the only woman devastated by his passing. I did hear that some women even killed themselves when they heard the news, even though suicide is a mortal sin.

I shouldn't say this, and I certainly wouldn't admit it to my family or confess it to any priest, but I think I was more grief-stricken when I heard that Valentino had died of that burst stomach ulcer than I was when I heard that Michael was dead in Mount Gambier. After all, Rudolph Valentino's death was a worldwide, an earth-shaking tragedy. Because so many women shared my grief, the loss of Valentino seemed more real than Michael's death, and therefore more believable. I suppose every woman takes her husband for granted and thinks he'll always be there. Familiarity breeds, perhaps not contempt, but complacency.

But a good film gives you the chance to escape ordinary life, so it's only natural that you develop certain feelings about those film stars. If they die, it breaks your heart. The tragedy transcends reality, one of the newspapers said at the time of Valentino's death. And Michael, callous as he was, laughed. 'Mass hysteria,' he said.

I decided I'd pack my scarf just in case. It's not silk of course, just paisley-patterned cotton. It certainly wouldn't float in the desert air like the silk scarves worn by the bashful English lady in *The Sheik*. But it would have to do.

'You spend too much time going to the movies, Joe,' said Charlie. 'There's no future in films. You're wasting your time. I've told you that over and over. You want to wake up to yourself. You ought to take up a musical instrument and learn jazz. That's where the opportunities are. You need to come down to earth a bit. You're getting your brain pickled, sitting in theatres, breathing in all that cigarette smoke and eating Jaffas. You'll rot your teeth and your lungs.'

'You know what, Charlie?' said Joe. 'You're starting to sound just like Dad. Don't give advice unless it's asked for. Don't tell me how to spend my spare time. And you can stick your bloody trumpet where the sun doesn't shine. This whole family has gone mad, if you ask me.' He turned to me. 'Mum, you can't go to Orroroo. You've never been on a train in your life.'

'He's right, Mum,' whimpered Amy. 'You could get lost up there in the bush. You could even die on the train like Dad did. Trains are dangerous. It's not fair. You mustn't go away. We don't know how to live without you and you don't know how to live without us.' She flung herself onto my knee and hid her face on my chest. 'I need you, Mum!'

'You'll probably get off at the wrong station and we'll never see you again. You haven't got a clue how to travel on a train,' said Brian.

'I know all about trains,' I said, extricating myself from Amy's embrace. It was just too hot for that sort of thing, and I was feeling smothered by all the emotion the family were displaying. 'I went to Victor Harbor on my honeymoon. All you have to do is show the ticket to the conductor and sit on the train for a bit and you get off when the name of your destination comes up on the board at the station at the other end. I'm not a complete nincompoop, you know. I'm a grown woman and I'm going to make my own decisions for a change. I'm off to Orroroo and you'll all just have to put up with it.'

They all moaned and groaned and predicted that I couldn't cope away from them and from Norwood, but I had made up my mind. It takes me a while to make up my mind, but once it is made up I won't change it. Never back down, that's my motto.

Well, I did use to back down all the time when Michael was alive, because I had to keep the peace, but now Michael was dead and gone. And even if I had been wavering in my resolve to leave home, the very fact that they were all so sure that I couldn't manage to live on my own without them had made me even more determined to go through with my plans.

I filled the bag that Michael used to take to Mount Gambier, and I packed a few tears in with the clothes. I was excited, but apprehensive.

I had agreed to go and work as a housekeeper for four pounds, four shillings and tuppence a week and all found, which meant my food and accommodation would be provided. That might ease the burden on the family a bit and keep the wolf from the door, although I knew it would not bring in any ships. But it would keep the boys from a career in mining.

The whole family came to see me off. Going to the Adelaide railway station brought back memories of those other departures when I had farewelled my loved ones. Of course, Pat and Danny hadn't lived long enough to see this splendid building with its brown marble interior. If they had, they would have said it made Adelaide even more worth saving from the Germans. My brothers were convinced the Germans were going to invade us, march down King William Street and bayonet the citizens. Especially the babies. There was a lot of talk of Germans bayoneting babies in those days.

Back when the boys went away, the old railway station was wood and galvanised iron. The government has nearly gone broke building this new station, or so I read in the *Advertiser*. Some people are scandalised about the cost. It's taken two years to build, but it's nearly finished now. Opulent, Michael called it. He said the new building was a credit to Adelaide. I remember him saying that people from interstate see this place when they first arrive, and first impressions are important. I wondered what the Orroroo station would be like. Probably just a tin shed.

My mother, Michael and I went to see Pat and Danny off to the war on the train. The memory still brought tears to my eyes. The boys looked splendid in their stiff woollen khaki uniforms with their polished belts and boots and their slouch hats with the excitement and anticipation of adventure shining out of their eyes.

Then my mum and I, with little Harry, Brian and Mary, had been there for Michael's departure when he, also wearing khaki and full of confidence, had followed my brothers to the Great War. His mum was dead by then. If she had been alive, she might have stopped him going. She would have used her stomach pains as an excuse to make him stay home. She always complained about her gut. Didn't stop her eating, though.

But worst of all had been that awful day when Michael had forced Mary onto the train to Mount Gambier while I stood on the platform with Amy in my arms. He had pushed Mary through the train door, prised her hands off the door frame and shoved her inside, while I, clutching Mary's screaming baby, watched with my heart torn between shame that my daughter had given birth out of wedlock and terror that I would never see my Mary again.

Of course, Michael travelled on the train for his frequent union trips, although that happened so often that we didn't bother about seeing him off. I might have gone that last time if I'd known he would come back dead, but then I suppose he wouldn't have gone if he'd known what awaited him at Mount Gambier.

And then, just a month or so ago, we'd said goodbye to Mary, Fred and little Paddy. But she would come back, so it was not as heart-wrenching, although it still hurt. Yes, the Adelaide railway station was full of memories for my family.

But this was the first time I had gone away alone. The only time I had ever left Adelaide in my entire life was when we went to Victor Harbor for our honeymoon. Three days, we had had. And it rained the whole time. Not that that had mattered when we were newly married and in love. The rain was just an excuse not to leave our room.

All the rest of my life I had lived in Norwood, with only the occasional trip on the tram into the city to the shops. As I always say, you can get everything you want on the Norwood Parade, so it was an indulgence to go to town.

But now I had committed myself to leaving everything I held dear. I was even leaving Amy, whom I had promised Mary I would always look after. I was breaking promises. I was as bad as Michael. Well, almost as bad. I must be crazy. The kids certainly thought I had lost my senses.

'You'll be back in a week,' said Brian, grinning and patting my arm. 'Don't be afraid to admit defeat, Mum. Australia wasn't too proud to evacuate the soldiers from Gallipoli. There's no shame in knowing when to turn back.'

I shrugged and jammed my hat a bit harder on my head. I wasn't about to let them see that I agreed with them. 'Nothing ventured, nothing gained,' I said. 'Change your sheets every couple of weeks and wash your socks before they walk away from you. Don't just soak the dirty clothes, give them a good wash with Rinso and Velvet soap on the scrubbing board and then boil them up in the copper. Feed the chooks and water the garden. And…' I suddenly remembered the advice my mother had given me, the same advice her mother had given her. 'If you think you're going to die, clean the stove.'

They looked at each other, puzzled. I gave Amy one last hug, threw my case up the high steps on to the train and pulled myself up after it. Amy acted as if I was climbing the scaffold to be hanged. She shrieked and tried to follow me. Either the dirt on the train window or my tears made her figure blur as I watched her running beside the carriage as the train began, slowly at first, to move.

The train gathered speed and so did Amy. She raced alongside my carriage and put out a hand to try to grab the train. She lost her hat. I pressed my hands against the window and held my breath, terrified that she would fall off the platform and be crushed under the wheels. Charlie ran after her and caught her and grabbed her hand and pulled her, sobbing, into his arms.

I sat back in my seat, feeling a bit sick. I wasn't sure if that was because of the way the train shook and rattled or because of the noise it was making or the speed at which it had begun to travel, or if it was just the thought of leaving home and the thought of being separated from Amy.

I was helpless now. My bag was in the baggage-rack above me, and now the train was going faster and faster and the whistle was hooting. It was too late to change my mind.

I would have to put up with the consequences of my decision. When I had earned some money to save the family from financial ruin and stopped the boys from going to their deaths in the Broken Hill mines, I would come straight back. It couldn't be that far to Orroroo.

14

When the engine whistle blew, the long, low lament echoed through my heart. The carriage shook and swayed as we sped away from the city. The grime on the windows muted the landscape to grey, despite the glaring sunlight. The houses and trees and the factories on the outskirts of Adelaide had given way to the drab, dry fields of summer. Thin sheep grazed bare earth. They looked as miserable as I felt.

I dabbed at my eyes and then blew my nose hard. I must get hold of my feelings. 'You can't give way to emotion like this,' I scolded myself. 'Put a brave face on it, Rose. Grow up, woman.'

I settled back on the hard green leather upholstery. I would have a sore backside from thudding against it as the train bumped along if this turned out to be a long trip, and I would probably become deaf from the noise, too. I inspected the high wooden back of the seat that screened me from most people's view. There was only one other person in the carriage, anyway.

It could do with a bit of waxing, that wood, I thought. It was in better condition than Michael's coffin had been, though, the last time I saw it. The soot-streaked carriage windows could have stood some soap and water and a nice hard rubbing with newspaper. A good dose of elbow grease, that's what was needed on this train. Perhaps I could have found a job with the railways, cleaning the carriages, polishing the brass, rubbing blacklead stove cleaner onto the engine, instead of rushing off to Orroroo.

Of course, the coal fire in the engine spewed out grime. Personally, I've never liked the smell of coal. It reminds me of Michael's mother. She used to burn coal. The cleaners would have their work cut out to make the carriages sparkle. Dirty things, trains. Mrs Williams would not have put up with sitting in here. She would have demanded a bit of rag from the conductor and some Brasso to polish up the fittings.

Firemen on trains must suffer like souls in torment. It was hot enough outside without having to stand shovelling coal into a fire. It must be at least ninety degrees in the shade today, I thought, and God knows what the temperature is next to the firebox on the engine. I wondered whether the railway union was a strong one. These men certainly deserved a fair wage for the sort of work they were doing. Michael would have known all about it.

More tears welled up in my eyes when I thought that I couldn't ask Mick about the railway union, or indeed, about anything, ever again. He was feckless, stupid, arrogant and perhaps not as nice a man as everyone said he was in his eulogy, but he had been my husband for a long time and, despite everything I had learned about him recently, I did miss him. And it would have been nice to have had someone with me to point things out to and to chat with on a long trip like this. In many ways it was sad to be a widow woman. I stifled a sob.

The woman in the seat across from me smiled in sympathy. Oh no, I thought. Not another Mrs Bloody Williams. Michael always said it never paid to talk to people on trains. He said you meet a lot of daft people on trains. He always carried a newspaper or a book to hide behind when he travelled.

'Had a death in the family, love?' she asked. 'You've got the black coat and the black hat. Widow, are you?'

'Black is all the rage in London, Paris, and Rome' I said. 'You should read the woman's supplement from *The Daily Telegraph*. Sydney newspaper, that is.'

I had only ever seen the one copy of *The Daily Telegraph*, but this lady wasn't to know that. Mavis's sister in Sydney had sent it to Mavis. Load of old rubbish, I thought. All that talk about fashion, as if you could change your clothes at the drop of a hat.

There was that article on hats, for example. It was so silly I'd remembered it. I decided to repeat it for the nosey lady, and I put on an appropriately posh accent. 'One no longer buys a winter hat for the winter months and a summer hat for the summer months. Instead, one purchases a hat when the need arises.'

With a puzzled expression on her face, she scratched her head under a rather dowdy hat which looked as if it had been sat on by my sister-in-law.

'So where do you get the money for buying hats like that? You don't live in the country, do you, love? Farmers don't have that sort of cash. Last time I looked, hats were eight shillings and eleven pence. And that was at a sale in Adelaide.'

'Well, nor do city folk have that kind of money either,' I admitted, feeling a bit sorry for trying to be stuck up. After all, who did I think I was, anyway? This lady was probably not a bad stick. 'But that's what they put in the paper. There must be more money around in Sydney.' I blew my nose again.

She was about to ask why I was upset. I knew it, but I didn't want to talk about myself just now. If we had to talk, I would change the subject. I would make her talk about herself. People usually like to talk about themselves.

'These summer colds are the very devil. Where do you come from, dear? What were you doing in Adelaide?'

'It's me legs,' she said, lifting her skirt to show her huge swollen limbs. 'I've got the dropsy. I was in Adelaide to see a specialist but he said there wasn't nothing he could do for me. Keep me legs up, he said. Me, a farmer's wife, and I'm told to keep me legs up. Fat chance of that happening. So I'll just have to put up with it. I live on a property out from Black Rock. Fair way out, actually. It takes us a good hour and a half from the railway station by buggy to our door. Where are you headed?'

'Orroroo,' I said. 'I'm going up to visit a friend of the family. I decided I wanted to see the countryside for a change.'

'Not much to see around Orroroo, love,' she said. 'Unless you like sheep. Of course, there's dairy cattle now too, since they got that new dam on the Pekina creek and done all that irrigation business. Made a big difference to Orroroo, that reservoir did. And they've got a real big gum tree over at Orroroo. It's a huge thing. You could get a lot of timber out of it, but the town council won't let anyone cut it down. It's supposed to be very old. Maybe you could go and see that while you're there.'

She turned out to be a decent enough woman. Ada Jenkins, her name was. She gave me her address and said if I was ever up her way, the kettle would be on. I said I'd be happy to give her a cup of tea if she came to Orroroo, although I wasn't sure how long I'd be visiting the friends of the family.

I felt sorry for her, and sorry for the wife of the man I was going to work for, another farmer's wife, who had died in this desolate place. In fact, I felt sorry for any woman who had to endure life out here. I felt sorry for myself too, when I saw the vast distances between the little settlements.

I even felt sorry for the sheep I could see in the paddocks, grazing fields that held only short, parched stubble. I'd never really looked at a sheep before. I'd only ever thought of them as mutton or hogget, hung on a hook in a shop where their blood dripped onto sawdust and the smell of wood and flesh filled your nostrils, or cut up in lumps and wrapped in white butcher's paper. Now I saw what a miserable life the animals led before they ended up in the roasting pan. Dun-coloured sheep in a dun-coloured land.

Not a drop of water in any direction. How often did sheep need to drink? I realised I knew nothing about these creatures. Did sheep need shelter? There weren't even many trees, and the few trees I saw were stunted and bent and gave no shade. It was hard to believe any of those trees could grow big enough to waste time going to look at, as Ada had suggested. This was a terrible place, a landscape bereft of feeling, even for sheep.

The Lord might be my shepherd, but he wasn't doing much for these animals. He leadeth me beside the clear waters, that psalm Father Flaherty had read out at Michael's funeral had said. There was no clear water here. No dirty water either, for that matter. This landscape looked more like the valley of the shadow of death. If you didn't believe in a God, as I was still trying hard to do, this must be what death was like, total oblivion, a complete absence of any compassion.

Every shudder of the train reinforced in me the absolute indifference of this country to humanity. If the train broke down, if it were derailed, if it hit one of the scrawny brown cattle I saw from the window or one of those kangaroos or emus running on the empty flat plains, we would all die. There was no water out there, no food, no shelter. Eagles would pick our bones and eventually the sparse and spindly grass would be fertilised by our flesh. And the land would not even notice our death, just as France had been indifferent to the death of my brothers who lay somewhere over there in no-man's land in unmarked graves.

I remembered how Michael had been a changed man when he came back from the war. A lot of the joy of life seemed to have left him. He seemed to be driven by the need to change the world that had let him and his generation down. That was why, he said, he had joined the union movement. He wanted to make the world a better place. He said anyone who had survived the Great War deserved a good life.

Mick had never been much of a drinker before he went away. But after he came back, whenever he wanted to make excuses for himself for going on one of his occasional binges, he said he was trying to forget the memory of absolute desolation.

I bet this place is more desolate than France, I thought. They've got vineyards and the Eiffel tower and the Louvre in France. And I bet the river that runs through Paris is bigger than the River Torrens that we've got in Adelaide. They call Paris the city of romance. No one says that about Adelaide. Adelaide is the City of Churches. Churches and wowsers, that's Adelaide.

But wowsers not withstanding, Adelaide was home, and now I had left home behind me. I could see how loneliness and desolation would drive you to drink. And not water either. Perhaps the shock of this harshness came because it lay just outside the lush green, safe gardens and parklands surrounding Adelaide. These vast flat lands held a silent menace hidden from and unsuspected by the Adelaideans. Here the hot sun baked the earth and absorbed the heat and magnified it and reflected it back to the train windows. I hoped that the farmer I was going to work for wasn't a drinker. I didn't need another Michael in my life. On the other hand, I could use a glass or two of something myself right now.

It was hot enough in the train, but at least we were moving. What would it be like to be out there, alone in the centre of this empty plain? How would you protect your soul from such emptiness? How did anyone live here? How would I live here, even for a short time?

'It won't be nothin' like Adelaide,' my friend was warning me.

I jumped. I had forgotten she was there. Had she been talking the whole time I was looking out the window? I hoped I had nodded in the right places if she had. Otherwise she might think me rude.

'You won't be able to get to the shops much and the neighbours are a long way away. Once a week, we go into Black Rock. When we need tea and sugar and suchlike. On a Friday afternoon, usually.' She sighed. 'Like I said, it takes an hour and half in the buggy. And the same back. So you spend three hours eating the dust from the track and smelling what comes out of the horse's backside. Horses pass a lot of wind. It's all those oats, I suppose.'

She sighed, perhaps thinking about the buggy ride that awaited her when she got off the train. 'There's no electricity or telephones. On our farm, we use kero lamps, but I don't know what the place you are going to is like.'

She shook her head, and I realised she was feeling sorry for me and that she thought I was mad to want to go to Orroroo. I had the impression that she didn't think I was going to cope with farm life. The trouble was, I knew she was absolutely right.

'I did hear they've had electricity in Orroroo for four or five years now,' Ada continued, 'but I don't reckon they'd have it out on the farms yet. I use a wood stove. Messy things they are, though they work all right when you get the hang of them. The ice man doesn't deliver out here like he does in Adelaide. And when the dust storms blow, all you can do is shut the doors and windows and hold your breath. Windy place, Orroroo.'

'My mother had a wood stove,' I said. 'And kero lamps. So I know what they're like. A bit smelly, but you get used to it. We used to sit around the wood stove in the winter to get warm. Nasty in the summer, though, when you have to do all the cooking on them. Mum used one of those flat irons for the ironing. You put it on the wood stove to get it hot and then you had to be careful not to scorch the clothes.'

She nodded. 'I still use one of those. Look, there's the blue roses.'

I looked out of the window and saw a field full of weeds. I shrugged. Ada must be crazy. I could see that this country would affect you like that.

'There's no such thing as blue roses,' I said. 'My husband, Michael, always said that. He knew all about roses. He said you'll see white roses and red roses and pink and yellow ones but you will never see a blue rose. It's impossible to have a blue rose. They can't be bred. It's in the genetics, like the CSIR says.'

'We call them roses,' she replied. 'The blue roses of Orroroo. So you're nearly there.'

I looked again. There were acres and acres of Scotch thistles in full flower. It did look pretty, after all the scorched earth we had been travelling through, but all the same, thistles were thistles.

'They're Scotch thistles. Artichokes, that's what Michael would have called them,' I said. 'Michael would have taken a hoe to them. He would have made a hole in the middle of the plant and poured kero down the hole. That would kill them. They're a weed. Some homesick Scotch drongo brought them out to remind him of home. They brought out rabbits and foxes too. And sparrows and starlings. The Acclimatisation Society, they called themselves. Michael told me about it. They were trying to make Australia look like England.'

'They're the only roses you'll find out here,' the lady replied. 'You find roses where you look for them, love. You'll learn that in this country.'

She reached up and pulled my bag down from the luggage rack and handed it to me. Despite her legs, she was pretty spry. 'This is your stop, love. Good luck and I hope you get to have a hat for every occasion.'

15

My suitcase beside me, I sat on a bench in the shade of the wide veranda of the Orroroo railway station and watched the train depart. It emitted another long low whistle as it went, as though mourning its own departure. I mourned its departure too. That train was my only link with home. Now I was absolutely alone.

I envied the other passengers who had got off the train at Orroroo. They knew where they were going, but I had no idea what lay ahead of me. Loud, enthusiastic voices had greeted them. There was a lot of hugging and embracing and shaking of hands. Their luggage was quickly handed down from the train and carried to the waiting traps and carts by eager helpers. Those other people were sure of their welcome. I was not.

Soon I was the only one left at the station. I straightened my black hat and looked down the dusty road along which the farmer should come to meet me. Even in the shade it was very hot. I wanted to take off my black coat and my hat and gloves, but it wouldn't do to be half-naked when I was about to meet my future employer. First impressions are important.

I waved away the flies. I had never seen so many flies. They seemed to want to drink the sweat from my face. I couldn't blame them. They were probably as thirsty as I was. At least they were at home, I thought.

There were a few houses in the distance out among the dry grass. Further out there were low brown hills. Nothing like the Adelaide hills. It wasn't a desert, but it wasn't lush farming land either. And there was no sign of a town. What a dead and alive hole Orroroo is, I thought.

'Someone coming for you, missus?' asked the porter, shaking tobacco into a paper and rolling a cigarette, as he paused beside me.

'Yes, a farmer called Pascall. I'm going to be his housekeeper.' I said. 'Where's the town, anyway?'

'About half a mile up the road. So you're going to work for Pask. I heard he was getting a housekeeper. He's the bloke whose wife up and died,' said the porter, striking a match and lighting his cigarette. He sucked on the cigarette. 'Cancer, she had. Yeah. Well, good luck then.' He lit the cigarette and walked away inhaling the pungent smoke deeply.

I wondered what he meant. Was he wishing me good luck with the housekeeping job because there was something peculiar about the farmer, or was he telling me that I would get cancer too if I spent time on the farm, or did he mean that I would need good luck to have the farmer arrive to collect me? How long would I have to wait at the railway station?

I considered my situation. Had I been forgotten? Maybe the farmer wasn't very bright and didn't know what day it was. Farmers weren't renowned for their intelligence. What was that expression Michael used to use? 'A few sheep short in the top paddock.' Yes, that was what he used to say about some of the farmers he met in the south-east.

That was it. The farmer had forgotten I was coming. Or perhaps he had changed his mind and decided he didn't want a housekeeper after all. A more attractive housekeeper, one who looked like some of the actresses in the films, might have turned up on his doorstep, and he had taken her on to look after the family. Did people in Orroroo know about movie films yet?

Or maybe, like his wife before him, he had died in the time between sending the letter to Adelaide engaging my services and the time it had taken me to come up here. Accidents did happen on farms. He might have caught up in a mob of stampeding sheep or set upon by wild dogs. I might not have a job after all. When would there be another train back to Adelaide? How would I face the kids if I arrived back home tomorrow? I'd never it live down.

And what if Joe was right? What if the farmer was a white slaver and I was going to a fate worse than death? Of course, if he looked like Rudolph Valentino, it might not be too bad. It was not as if I was a virgin. I had given birth to five children. I knew what life was all about.

But even so, a woman had to have standards, I reminded myself sternly. And Michael had only been in his grave a month or so. What sort of immoral woman was I anyway? My standards seemed to have dropped terribly since Michael's death. I had accepted a position working for a man I had never met, agreed to go to a place I had never seen, jumped on the first train that came along and here I was, sitting here without a chaperone, miles from any female companion in fact, waiting for goodness only knew what fate.

The whole population of Orroroo might be maniacal axe-murderers for all I knew. That porter didn't really look me in the eye properly. Some of those people who got off the train here looked a bit dishevelled. Although, I had to admit, I probably looked a bit dishevelled myself after a long journey on a dirty train. But what if the farmer didn't look like Rudolph Valentino but still acted like the sheik?

And if he did turn up, what sort of accommodation was I going to? Would I live in a tent out here? Nothing had actually been said about a house, come to think of it.

From memory, in the film the sheik's tent was quite luxurious, filled with carpets and tasselled cushions. You didn't really know what colour the carpets and cushions were. Films, of course, are in black and white, but I had coloured the furnishings as red and purple in my mind.

The tent in the film had big copper vessels to hold food and water and probably wine. But I had a feeling that a tent out here would probably be made of canvas with holes in it that would let in the sand and the rain. Any containers for food and water would probably be old kero tins. I didn't expect wine. That would be too exotic.

Would there even be water? Did it ever rain out here? It didn't look as if it had rained for a very long time.

At last, through the dust and the heat haze, I saw a cart drawn by a brown horse slowly coming my way. This must be the farmer. So he had a brown carthorse, not a white stallion. The colour of the horse matched the colour of dust that clung behind the cart.

That was reassuring, although perhaps just a little disappointing. A bit boring, really. Mundane, that was the word Michael would have used. Nothing romantic about a brown horse and a cart. Our milkman had a brown horse, and so did the bread man and the rabbito. Every one except Rudolph Valentino had brown horses. I shook my head.

Had I expected white horses, adventure and romance at Orroroo? You really are going mad, Rose Walsh, I told myself. This sort of behaviour is not quite normal. It has to stop. I shook my head. I would have poked myself in the chest if I wasn't scared the porter or the stationmaster might be looking at me.

Ever since you attacked Michael's coffin you've been edgy, I thought to myself. And you must admit, my girl, that whole episode was a bit over the top, really. I mean, Mrs Williams wouldn't have done that, would she? She would have been rubbing furniture polish into the coffin because it wasn't shiny enough, not taking an axe to it. You'd better come down to earth and get a grip on yourself, woman.

There was a large figure slumped in the driver's seat of the cart and there were two smaller ones sitting in the back swinging their legs over the edge. It had to be my new employer and the two children, aged ten and six, as described in the letter. At least I hoped it was.

My backside was going numb from sitting on this bench, I badly needed to go to the lavatory but I had been too scared to leave my seat lest the farmer come while I was gone, and I was dying for a nice cup of tea. I willed the man to flick the reins and push the plodding horse to move a bit quicker. There was no change in the slow progression across the flat landscape or in the amount of dust raised by the wheels.

Eventually the cart stopped. I couldn't see the driver's face under the battered hat he wore, but he was tall and thin and stooped. Droopy, I thought. He must have been a soldier, though, because that hat looked as if it had once been a military one, although it also looked as if a cart drawn by several horses had driven over it. Clydesdales, probably.

He pushed the hat to the back of his head and nodded to me. I saw that he wore an eye patch over one eye and his face was heavily scarred. I knew he must have been in the Great War. Had he been on the Somme with Michael, I wondered, or had he been in the middle eastern desert? He was nothing like Rudolph Valentino, though.

I felt vaguely disappointed, but I was a bit relieved too. I should be safe with this man. He wasn't the ravishing type. He was just a middle-aged, rather sad-looking farmer with a pipe stuck between his teeth beneath a sandy moustache with streaks of grey in it.

He took the pipe out of his mouth to greet me. 'G'day, Mrs W,' he said. 'Sorry we're a bit late. It's Friday afternoon and I had to get a few provisions from the general store before I picked you up. It's a real busy time in Orroroo, Friday afternoon. I'll get your bag.'

The two children didn't move from their seats in the back of the cart. They were sandy-haired and silent. A boy of ten, and a girl of six, as the letter had said. The boy looked away as I approached. The girl stared at me but said nothing. Gormless pair of kids, I thought.

'Hello, kiddies,' I said. 'I'm pleased to meet you. I'm your new Auntie Rose, come to look after you.'

There was no response.

'Move over a bit, Bob. I need some room for Mrs W's bag. Did you both say hello to her?'

The two children nodded vigorously. I decided to ignore their lies and rudeness. I wasn't sure how my children would act if they had a new auntie suddenly thrust on them. Amy had been happy about a new sister arriving out of the blue, but that was probably an entirely different kettle of fish.

'I'm Cedric Pascall, by the way,' said my employer. 'But I don't like being called Cedric, I'll tell you that right from the start. Everyone calls me Pask. I hope you will too. So,' he extended a large work hardened hand, 'so I'm Pask.'

'Rose Walsh,' I said. 'Pleased to meet you, Pask.'

'Likewise. And the kids are Bob and Annie. So we might as well get back home, all right? We're a bit outside the town, out on the Pekina road. Not out as far as Pekina, though.'

I had no idea how far Pekina was, so I smiled and said nothing. I sat and listened to the steady clop, clop of the horse's hooves. Conversation had evaporated in the heat. I gazed at the round backside of the horse for a while, wondering how much manure it contained.

After a bit the silence became oppressive, so I tried to think of something to say. 'What's the horse's name?' I asked.

'Dobbin,' said Pask. 'The wife named him. Before she died, that was. Here's Orroroo.'

'Why is the street so wide?' I asked, still trying to make conversation.

'You need the width to turn a bullock team around,' said Pask.

I wondered how often bullock teams went through the town. I couldn't see any bullocks, or anything that looked like bullock droppings, although there was plenty of horse manure in the street. Roses, the sort that Michael grew, not just the blue roses of Orroroo, should do well here. If there was any water for them, of course. Perhaps, I thought, the bullocks didn't come to town on Fridays. But as my new employer didn't seem to want to talk, I decided not to pursue the conversation further.

A few horses and buggies were tied up to the hitching rails outside the general store, the horses shaking their heads occasionally to keep the flies out of their eyes. People were going into the shops beyond the shady verandas with empty shopping baskets and string bags, and others were coming out with full ones. As Pask had said, Friday was a busy time in Orroroo. I wondered what happened on the other days of the week. It wasn't a patch on Rundle Street, though.

A few women stopped and watched us go by, and one woman raised her hand in greeting. I wasn't sure whether to respond or not. Pask nodded to her, just as he had nodded to me. I glanced back at the children to see if they would greet the lady, but they were whispering together.

Anxious to fit in, I decided to nod in the same way that Pask had done. I raised my hand in the way I had once seen Queen Victoria do, in an old photo that Mrs Williams had shown me. The lady stared at me for a moment, then turned away and hurried into the general store. I didn't feel that my arrival in town had aroused much interest among the Orrororians.

After we had gone down the main street for a short distance, Pask flicked the reins and the horse turned off onto a dusty track. The animal seemed to know the way well. Perhaps it could see its way better than the farmer. Unlike its owner, it had two eyes. Pask appeared to do little to guide it.

Away from the town, the vast brown land stretched under a hot blue umbrella of sky. The desolation I had seen from the train continued here. Only the angle was different. You couldn't see quite as much of the land from the cart as you could from the train. The hot air burned my lungs. I thought I knew how that man shovelling coal into the train engine must have felt. And the flies wanted to climb into my mouth every time I opened it. Perhaps that was why the family spoke so little.

At ground level the emptiness of the land had become more intimate. It was a desolation that reached into your body and your soul if you let it. I made up my mind to keep thinking of my home and not to allow room for this barren place in my heart. I was feeling desolate enough already. Orroroo was so far from my family and my home.

And I wouldn't let these miserable kids get on my goat either. Surly little devils, both of them. The boy seemed worse than the girl, but I didn't think I could ever take to either of them. I would do my job, earn some money and get away from here as quickly as I could.

The boy, Bob, had the task of jumping down each time we came to a gate. There were lots of gates. He would undo the wire ties, swing the gate wide and then jump on and ride it until it was fully open. Then he would wait for the horse and cart with its passengers to pass through the opening, ride the gate back to the closed position, fasten it and leap back to his seat beside his sister.

Once again, I tried to converse. 'Do all the gates have to be closed?' I enquired.

'If it's open, leave it open. If it's closed, leave it closed,' said Pask.

After Bob had opened and closed a number of gates, I turned to the silent little girl and said, 'That looks like fun. Is it your turn to do it soon?'

She shook her head. 'That's Bob's job.'

'So what do you do for fun?' I persisted.

'Nuffin.'

I gave up after that, and sat wondering how I was going to get through even three months at Orroroo. Brian was right, there was no shame in retreat. I wondered how long it was between trains. If I demanded that Pask turn the cart around now, would I wait a day, a week or a month for a train to come to take me back to Adelaide?

The little track ended at a stone farmhouse set in a dusty yard and surrounded by straggly gum trees. The stunted trees were bent almost double, all facing the same angle. They looked as if they had fought and lost a battle.

As we drove to the back of the house, Pask noticed that I was looking at the trees. 'Windbreak,' he said. 'Terrible winds out here.'

He opened the door, which didn't seem to have a lock, and we entered directly into the kitchen. Inside, the house smelled of boiled mutton, of dust and of despair. A kero lamp with blackened glass stood in the centre of a grimy table which was littered with this morning's breakfast detritus and possibly that of a few previous meals too. There was a wooden board on which sat a loaf of stale-looking bread, surrounded by crumbs and mouse droppings.

Long spider webs thickened with dust trailed from the ceiling to the kitchen dresser. A couple of stray blowflies traversed the kitchen aimlessly. They seemed to have given up the will to escape or indeed to live. Even their buzzing sounded half-hearted. It would be easy enough to swat them, but I seemed to be the only one to notice their presence. There was a coil of sticky yellow flypaper hanging from the ceiling. It must have been there a very long time because it was full of dehydrated black corpses. No standing room at all.

'Not much been done since the wife died,' said Pask, opening a window.

I watched as a couple more blowflies were blown in by the hot wind.

'Six months, it's been. I had my sister here for a bit, but she didn't like it much. Your room's through there. I'll get your bag. Sorry about the mess.'

He was right about the mess. I decided not to look at it until I had adjusted to my surroundings a little. One thing at a time, Rose, I told myself. That's what Michael would have said. Bloody Michael, dying like that and putting me in this situation. Bloody Pask's wife, doing the same thing.

Pask carried my bag into the room designated as mine and put it on the high iron-framed double bed. My room seemed to be a bit cleaner than the rest of the house. I wondered if he or his sister had decided to concentrate on tidying that one room, hoping that the rest of the place would go unnoticed. There were less cobwebs here, and the linen looked as if it might have been changed recently. I slapped at the once white, crocheted bedspread and watched a cloud of dust ascend into the still air.

'If you want a cup of tea,' Pascal called from the kitchen, 'the stove's on and there's wood just outside the back door. There's water in the kettle. The rainwater tank's out the back. But don't waste the water. We've got bore water for washing and that. You might have heard about the Pekina reservoir, but we don't get reservoir water out here. They use the water for the town and the dairy farms. The reservoir's pretty low anyway. We've got a bit of a drought at the moment.'

I heard the backdoor open, and I thought he'd gone, perhaps exhausted by the effort of putting so many words together, but then he stuck his head through the door into my room.

'We often have a bit of a drought out here. We're above Goyder's line, you know. Goyder was the government surveyor who worked out where the section of land that gets rain ends, and where the arid bit starts. We're classed as arid this side of Orroroo. We can still run a few sheep, though.'

He stepped back to leave. Then he stuck his head back through the door again. Must have got his second wind, I thought.

'I'm digging a dam at the moment so I'll be ready for the next time it rains. I'll just put the groceries on the table, and then I've got to go and chase a sheep.'

I jumped as a screech shattered the silence. It came from the corner of the kitchen, where what I had thought was a packing case stood. Bob went over to the corner and jerked a piece of canvas to uncover a large square cage containing a bird.

Intrigued, I walked over to look at it. The big white bird, which I recognised as a sulphur-crested cockatoo, glared at me, raised its yellow crest, spread its wings wide and shrieked again. It hurtled from the perch and flung itself against the wire. The cage shook and I thought the wire would collapse with the bird's fury. Then the thing began to hiss at me like a snake. I hate snakes. I was aghast. The cage looked too flimsy to contain so much anger. I looked at the kitchen door, wondering if I would have time to get away if the manic creature escaped.

'She doesn't like you,' said Bob, smirking at my horrified face. 'Dad's had her ever since he was a kid and she was an egg, so you're going to have to put up with her. They live a long time, cockies do.'

He gave a short laugh and ran out of the room after his father. Perhaps he, too, was needed to chase sheep. Or maybe he feared that I might ask him to carry in some wood or some water. Or perhaps, like the bird, he just couldn't stand the sight of me.

I flung the canvas back over the cage and there was silence, other than for the blowflies' buzzing. A white feather drifted out from under the canvas and joined the general debris in the room.

A white feather was what people gave men who weren't brave enough to leave home and go to war. I wished I had not joined this particular war. I found the cups and the pot and the tea and I made myself a good strong cuppa. It should have helped, but it didn't.

I sat at the kitchen table and I wished I was back home in Norwood, in my own nice clean kitchen. My kitchen might not gleam the way that Mrs Williams's kitchen did, but compared to this kitchen, mine was a paradise of hygiene. I wished I was wearing an apron. If I had been, I would have pulled it over my head and cried. But I didn't know where the apron was kept, or if indeed there was an apron in the house, and I doubted that an apron in this house would be clean enough to pull over my head if there was one. I had an apron in my bag, of course, but I hadn't unpacked my bag yet.

Unpacking my bag would mean that I really was going to stay here. I didn't want to unpack. I wanted to stamp my feet like Amy did when she was having a tantrum. I wanted to throw myself on the ground, and sob and scream at the top of my voice. I wanted to cry for my mother. I even wanted to sink into Michael's arms, or to hug his old woollen army coat I had burned.

Instead, I made a mental list of things to do. I could follow my mother's and grandmother's advice and clean the stove. It needed it badly. I wondered if there was any blacklead to clean it with, though. But I didn't think I was going to die just yet, and I didn't particularly want to die in this dirty kitchen anyway. One death in this house was probably enough.

I had had to wash the cup before I used it, so I decided that I would start by washing all the cutlery and crockery. The cups needed scouring with salt. They could have stood being soaked in bleach but I didn't know if there was any bleach in the house. When I went to Orroroo, probably next Friday, bleach would be at the top of my shopping list.

The girl, Annie, could help with the washing up. She might decide it was fun. The table needed a good scrub. I would have to find a brush and some soap and a bowl. I felt as if I could stand a good scrub myself after that train trip. I thought about my bathroom back home and sighed. I hadn't seen any sign of a bathroom in this house. The only sign of ablutions I had seen was the dunny, which was a long way up at the end of the backyard. There would probably be snakes out there.

I ought to find some food, if indeed there was any food in this godforsaken place, and work out what I was going to dish up to feed my new family. The groceries that Pask had put on the table seemed to consist mainly of potatoes and onions, tea and sugar. I should make some bread. I shook my head. This wasn't a family, it was a recipe for misery.

'Annie,' I called.

No answer.

'Annie!'

I went in search of her and found her sitting on her unmade bed with a grubby rag doll in her hands. There was a strong smell of urine in the room. That was another job, change Annie's sheets and make sure she went to the lavatory before she went to bed at night. Don't let her drink too much at night. I won't drink too much at night either, I thought. That long-drop privy was a long way down the backyard. It would be a dangerous trek in the dark. I wondered whether snakes slept at night.

Perhaps there might be some chamber pots in the house. I hadn't thought to look under my bed. If there were, they would probably need soaking in bleach as well. I didn't fancy using a chamber pot that someone had used and not cleaned properly afterwards. I could use a bit of kero, I supposed. Kero would clean anything.

'Right,' I said. 'This is what we are going to do.'

I led her out of the room and set her to work. She did as she was told, and eventually even mumbled a couple of words, but I could hardly hear what she said. I couldn't make up my mind whether she was shy or frightened or stupid, or if she had simply been taught not to talk. She was nothing like my Amy, who prattled away all day if you let her.

Perhaps Annie's parents believed that children should be seen and not heard. Or was it hereditary, as Mr Andrews had said Michael's heart problem was? Annie's father, after all, was a man of few words too.

The child and I sat and peeled potatoes and when I saw her looking at me, I smiled at her. She dropped her eyes immediately. Definitely nothing like Amy, I thought. No self-confidence at all. Not a patch on Amy or Mary to look at, either. Not that I was prejudiced or anything, but this kid with her drab sandy-coloured hair and her pale blue eyes was definitely not pretty.

That hair needed a good wash and cut and a brush too. It could even have nits in it. I wondered if I dare use a bit of the precious rainwater to wash the girl's hair. If there was a lemon tree, I could put lemon juice in the water. It might brighten her hair up a bit. There must be a lemon tree. Everyone has a lemon tree. I wasn't sure what that bore water would be like. It was probably full of minerals and would stink. It wouldn't do my own hair any good, either.

I sighed. Could I really stick this dump out for three months? Three months would at least pay off the council rates and give me a bit to put by. It would be a small nest egg to help the family. As soon as three months were up, I would be on the next train home. Maybe I could find work as a cleaner or a barmaid or something back in Adelaide. Mick wouldn't like that, but Mick was dead. Father Flaherty wouldn't approve either.

Come to think of it, Father Flaherty's housekeeper was getting a bit long in the tooth. She was always moaning about her arthritis. About time she retired. Could I stand working for Father Flaherty if it meant being home again? I would have to attend church, but at least Father Flaherty didn't keep a cockatoo, as far as I knew.

Of course I had been too hasty taking the first job I'd seen in the newspaper. I could have done better for myself than this. There must be dozens of jobs better than this one, out here in the sticks. I had rushed into this like a bull in a china shop. But I had had to do it. I couldn't let my boys go off to Broken Hill and get killed in the mines up there. Put up with it for a bit, Rose, I told myself. Just have a bit of intestinal fortitude.

I made a stew using some smelly, greenish mutton chops which

Annie got out of the Coolgardie safe that was hanging in the corner of the kitchen opposite the cocky's cage, the potatoes that we had peeled and some nasty mummified-looking dried vegetables that I found in a cupboard.

Those chops were definitely a bit past using, by my standards. I wouldn't have paid a butcher good money for them, but then I remembered Ada saying the ice man didn't deliver out here, so there was no way of keeping meat cool. She said when they killed a sheep you had to keep chewing on it until it was all gone. Apparently you would give half of any sheep you killed to your neighbour, and when they killed a sheep they would give half of theirs to you. That meant the meat was only half as rank as it would have been if you had to eat the entire animal yourself. I had thought she was exaggerating, but now I knew she was telling the truth.

I made a quick loaf of bread – more like damper really. I could make some real bread tomorrow. I had found some yeast that looked as if it still had a bit of life in it, in an earthenware crock next to the dripping tin on the kitchen dresser.

The meal was not something that you would find written up in the *Green and Gold Recipe Book*, but Pascal seemed delighted.

'I reckon you'll do, Mrs W,' he pronounced. 'Best bloody meal seen in this house for a long time. That bread is bloody marvellous. Isn't it, kids?'

The kids nodded. Annie smiled. Bob didn't say anything, but he reached for more damper, buttered it thickly, and then drizzled golden syrup over the top. I felt better about being there, knowing I had their approval. I wasn't sure why that mattered, but it did give me some satisfaction. Maybe I might stick out the three months. Maybe I would feel better in the morning. Things were usually better in the morning.

But how I dreaded going to bed without brushing Amy's hair, without reading her a story, without tucking her into her bed. Was Mavis being kind to my little girl? For the first time in my life I wished for a telephone. Just to hear Amy's voice would have helped so much, but of course that was impossible. I was so far away from her, from everyone I cared about. I might as well be on the moon as be at Orroroo.

'Goodnight, Amy,' I whispered in what I hoped was the direction of Adelaide as I undressed and got into the unfamiliar bed with the stiff sheets smelling of dust and mothballs.

'God bless you all and God keep all my children safe,' I prayed. Although I didn't really believe in God any more, I thought. If there was a God, why had He let so many rotten things happen to me? But it had been a long time since I had prayed fervently like that. I needed to have some vestige of faith and hope to cling to. If you are desperate enough you will cling to anything.

That night as I lay in bed waiting for sleep and the dreams of Molly to arrive, the wind came up and whistled and shrieked like an enraged banshee through the tortured trees. It beat relentlessly against the windows and I heard the door shaking. I hoped nothing nasty would get inside. Was it really the wind or was there something else, something unspeakable, out there in the darkness? I wondered how the house could stand the constant battering.

This was an old house, I told myself, and it had endured these winds for a long time, so it probably wouldn't fall down tonight. I lay in the unfamiliar bed in the darkness, listening to the windows rattle in their frames and wishing I was in my own bed at home.

The thought came to me that this was probably the bed in which Pascal's wife had died. Cancer, he had said. My mother had died of cancer, and in the end it was a relief for both of us when she died. Had Pask's wife died in agony, writhing and tossing on the mattress on which I now lay? Had she moaned as the wind in the trees was moaning now? I didn't even know her name, I realised. If her ghost hovered over me in the darkness, I wouldn't know what to call her, what to say.

The howling grew louder. Had the ghost come back from her grave to see who had invaded her bed? Was she angry, fearing that I had come to steal the memory of her from her children? Was it really the wind whistling in the chimney, or was it the ghost of Pask's wife shrieking in the darkness?

With relief I realised that some of the sounds were coming from Annie's room. I could cope with a crying child. I was used to that. It was much easier to deal with the distressed living than with the agonised dead. I lit my candle and groped my way to Annie's door. She was sitting up in bed, wide-eyed but completely unaware of this world.

'Mummy, Mummy, Mummy,' she wept. 'Don't leave me. Don't go away. I need you!' Her little body shook with sobs.

I wished that her mother could help her, answer her. I wished I knew what words her mother would use to soothe her so that I could use those words, too.

Was Amy crying for me just like this, at this very moment? Would Mavis comfort Amy? And how Mary must have wept in the night so many years ago, too, wanting me to hold her? Had anyone comforted Mary?

I sat on the bed and took Annie in my arms. There was a smell of fresh urine. I knew that she had wet the bed again.

'Annie, Annie, it's all right, Auntie Rose is here. Hop out of bed and I'll find a clean nightie for you.' I lifted her day clothes from the chair where she had hung them when she went to bed, steered her gently towards the chair and sat her down. 'You stay here and I'll get some more sheets and sort your bed out.'

There were no more sheets in the linen cupboard. Another job for tomorrow, I thought. Boil up the copper, find the scrubbing board and the bars of soap, and have a good wash day. At least with this wind, the sheets will dry quickly. Unless they blow away and find their way down to Adelaide. If I held tight to the sheets, they might carry me with them.

How I longed to be home. I wanted to sit and sob just as this little kiddie was sobbing. I was so tired, what with the journey and missing my family and the strangeness of the situation that I found myself in. God help me, I was even missing Mick, despite his fecklessness. But I would have to be the comforting grown-up lady. Someone had to be.

In the end I took Annie into my bed. She wouldn't be likely to wet another bed; she'd already done her dash in that department for the night. I felt a bit safer with her beside me. The wind didn't seem quite so savage now that I was not alone. Perhaps the mother's ghost was appeased because her child had been soothed.

In the morning the little girl woke and smiled at me shyly. 'Please don't tell Dad I wet the bed again, Auntie Rose. He gets so cross with me. I don't want to do it but I just can't help it.'

'It's our secret, love,' I said. 'Did I see some chooks out the back? Shall we go and get the eggs and fry some for breakfast with that bread that I made yesterday? That is, if your dad didn't eat it all last night.'

16

As Pask had said, not much had been done since his wife had died. A farmhouse is a busy place. I soon learned that there are a lot of things that you take for granted in the city that you have to do for yourself in the country. My homesickness abated a little with each passing day as new duties took over my life.

It was not that I stopped thinking of my family; I could never do that. It was just that as time passed, the pain grew a little less unbearable and I could think, with a smile instead of tears, of Charlie playing jazz on his trumpet, and I could wonder, without feeling panicked, how Mavis was coping with her pregnancy. I still hoped, though, that nothing would go wrong without me there to look after them. After a while I could even plait Annie's sandy hair without wishing it was Amy's auburn locks between my fingers. That one took a long time, though.

Pascal taught me how to milk their cow. At first I was terrified; the animal was so big and so solid. And the horns looked so sharp. The drool that dangled perpetually from the corner of the animal's mouth was a bit off-putting, too. And the smell of cow manure was different, stronger than the horse manure that we put on Michael's roses. I had to be careful not to step in the cow dung. It sticks to boots worse than mud. But Daisy had such huge, gentle brown eyes fringed with lashes that were longer and more elegant even than those of that English lady who was ravished by the sheik in the film. The cow's eyes captivated me. I immediately knew that Daisy and I would be friends.

It took a little while to learn how to milk. I had to discover the right sequence of squeezing and relaxing my stiff, arthritic fingers before Daisy would let her milk down.

'Milking will do your hands the world of good,' Pask told me. 'My old mother milked a cow every day of her life until the day she died. Even your crooked fingers will benefit, Mrs W.'

That first day when my milking lessons began, Pask sat behind me on a second milking stool. It was an unnervingly intimate experience, feeling the warmth of his body against mine in the cool of the morning. It didn't feel right. I didn't know him well enough to be this close to him. I wondered how I would look him in the eye after this. I had never been so close to a man who was not my husband before, and I wasn't sure if I liked it. Just as well Pask was no Rudolph Valentino. I might have disgraced myself.

Pask had his own particular smell. I noticed that when he was sitting behind me, almost embracing me, as he taught me how to milk the cow. His scent rose above the smell of the fresh milk and the odours that came from the cow, who seemed to pass a lot of wind from her backside, although her breath was sweet and smelled of grass.

The farmer smelled of tobacco and man-sweat and old boots and sheep, different to the way Michael had smelled. Michael's aroma was of sweat when he worked in the garden, and of the Velvet soap that I used to wash his clothes, and of course he smelled of cigarettes and often of whiskey. Somehow Pask's odour was more honest. I wasn't sure why, and I felt uncomfortable admitting I preferred Pask's smell, but it was true.

I don't know what would have happened if he had been an attractive man. Perhaps, I thought, it was just as well he had that missing eye. I'm not a woman who goes looking for sexual relations often, but I will admit Michael and I had had a reasonably good marriage in the intimate kind of way. Not that I had had any standards to compare our marital relations with, if you know what I mean. But there are some things a woman misses when her husband dies, even if there are others she doesn't.

Pask had to put his hands around mine to show me how to milk, and his hands were big and hard and calloused but surprisingly gentle. I felt a peculiar sensation, all quivery and embarrassing. I did my best to ignore that feeling. It wasn't decent. Especially with Michael just recently in his grave. And Pask's wife wasn't all that long in hers, either. I hoped Pask hadn't seen me blush at his touch. He couldn't have seen my face as he was sitting behind me. But had he felt my body flush? Most men wouldn't be able to perceive a woman's emotions,

I told myself. And I didn't think he was the sort of person to notice something like that. He was a farmer, after all. An insensitive sort of bloke, you could tell that just by looking at him.

When we met later in the day, at morning tea time, I tried to act normally. Nonchalant, that's the word. I smiled and poured tea and passed him a slice of cake. He grinned and accepted the cup and the plate in his usual manner. I was relieved that our earlier encounter was not mentioned. He probably hadn't even noticed that I had been discomforted by his touch.

But as he left he patted my hand, and asked if I felt I needed any more milking lessons. 'Just say the word, Mrs W, and I'll be there like a shot,' he said. 'It's no trouble at all.'

I blushed, and when I looked up again, Bob was scowling at me from the doorway. Why did that boy resent me so much?

'I think Daisy and I are getting along quite well now, thank you, Pask. But if I have any problems, I will let you know.'

Soon it became second nature to me to milk the cow. It was the highlight of my day to lean against the warm flanks of the beast and coax the thick milk from her udders. Not much else happened at Orroroo. The cow's calf was outside the milk shed, bawling for its mother, and I told the cow that as soon as she gave us our bucketful she would be reunited with her little one and she could give her the rest of her milk. Pask said the calf was lucky to be a female, because if it had been a boy it would be slaughtered. A bit like our men going off to the war, I suppose. Males are dispensable in many ways. It's the females who do the important stuff of breeding and nurturing.

There was something very elemental, very earthy about milking a cow. Until then, I had taken milk for granted. In Norwood, milk was a commodity the milkman delivered in the morning when he did his rounds with his horse and cart and he poured a measure in to the billy can which hung on a hook under the bougainvillea creeper on the veranda. You carried the milk indoors and boiled it to make sure all the germs were dead. You could get TB from milk if you weren't careful. Then, when the milk was cool, you skimmed off the thick cream and put it on a saucer in the icebox to thicken. Clotted cream, my mother called it.

My kids always fought over who was going to get that cream to go on their bread and jam. It drove me mad at the time, but how I missed those fights now! I hoped they were remembering to boil the milk back home. You have to bring it to the boil, let it rise to the top, then take it off the fire and do it again. Three times, it takes to boil milk properly, and you need that round pottery thing we all put into the bottom of the saucepan to stop it from catching. It helps to rinse out the saucepan with water before you put the milk in, too. Otherwise you have to scrub hard to get the milk solids off the pan.

And what if the lads back home forgot to bring in the billy in the morning before they went to work? Amy was at Harry's place just around the corner, but you couldn't expect a kiddy to remember things like that. The milk would go off if it was left outside all day. I wondered if it was as hot in Adelaide as it was at Orroroo. You would never get the smell of sour milk out of the billy if it stood outside all day and went off. I suppose you could try washing a sour billy with carb soda to clean it, but I wasn't sure that it would work.

But here milk was the part of the way of the life cycle. Here you got the full process. Grass to animal, to pail, to churn, to butter. Soon I knew it all. I had to get up early to milk the cow, but it was good to be outside before the sun came up and the heat began. The magpies that lived in the bent trees surrounding the farmhouse carolled their greetings to the pale morning sky, and the whole world seemed clean and new, and fresh as the foaming milk. A milky-pink sky gave way to a buttery-golden sun and suddenly the day was full of the sound of birds in ecstasy, early in the morning.

Then, too soon, the oven-like heat arrived with the implacable blue sky and the land baked, and the only bird sound was that of the crows lamenting. It was like being inside the wood oven when someone had over-filled it and kept the damper open.

I retreated to the darkened house, which gave at least the illusion of coolness, leaving the magpies to sit in the branches of the drooping trees, gasping with open beaks in the hot air. I began to leave a dish of water by the door for the birds. I couldn't let them suffer after I had enjoyed their glorious morning song.

A whole family of magpies lived and bred in those wind-tortured trees. Generations of them, Pask said.

He told me how the young magpies stayed with their parents and helped bring up the new fledglings. 'Some say the name Orroroo means the place where the magpies meet,' he told me. 'Other people say it means a windy place.'

'Both names seem right to me,' I said.

Gradually the seasons changed, and the mornings became crisper. The frost-covered grass crunched under my boots when I walked across to the cow shed and the cow's breath and my own breath steamed in the cold air. I was glad of the warmth of her body when I leaned against her side and squirted the white milk into the pail.

I made butter using a churn I had found in the dairy shed. It was hard work. Pask told me not to bother, we could get butter in Orroroo when we went in on a Friday afternoon for supplies. The town was even sending butter to Adelaide now that the dairy industry was in full swing. Once when we went into Orroroo he drove past the butter factory to show me the huge two-storey building with the milk cans standing around waiting to be taken back to be filled by the dairy farmers.

But I made butter because I had found a separator in the milking shed. Pask showed me how to get the cream from the milk, and how to use the churn. It was a challenge that I enjoyed, watching the cream changing colour from a pasty colour to a thick yellow as I worked the churn. It seemed silly to waste the cream and there was too much for the family to eat. Pask didn't like to take time away from his sheep and from the dam he was digging to go into town to buy supplies if he could avoid doing it, so by making butter we were saved purchasing it.

I put the butter in wooden forms and there was little rectangular wooden board with a pattern of a Scotch thistle to press it down with. That reminded me of those thistles that Ada, the lady on the train, had called roses. She was a nice enough woman, Ada Jenkins. I wondered how she was getting on with her dropsy.

Dropsy was a sign of a bad heart. My poor Dad had dropsy before he died. I remembered how Mum and I used to look after him. He was so grateful that he gave up the alcohol. Well, to be honest, he couldn't walk to the pub when his legs got bad, and we weren't going to fetch it for him, so he had to stop drinking.

I wondered if Ada's specialist in Adelaide had told her what to do. I should write to her and tell her to put cold compresses on her legs (though how would you make a cold compress out here, I wondered, when there was no ice chest and no man to bring the ice to put in it?). She should bandage her legs when she first woke up in the morning before the fluid went down into them.

How I wished I had her to talk to now. I would have liked a bit of company, to tell the truth. It was the isolation that go to you out here more than anything. Pask was a dead loss in the conversation stakes and the kids weren't much better.

I looked forward each week to our trips into Orroroo, although at first I felt an outsider there. After a few weeks, a few of the women began to nod and say hello to me, and I smiled back and eventually I got to know a few of them by sight. I knew it would take time before I would be fully accepted. Of course, I wondered whether they talked about me behind my back. I would have done, in their place.

Pask had introduced me as his housekeeper, but I knew our household was a little unusual and I wondered if they thought we were living in sin. I would have wondered about our domestic arrangements if I had been outside looking in, and I don't have the dirty mind that some people have. Besides, people are always suspicious of newcomers. I know it took me quite a long time to become really friendly with Mrs Williams, especially when I found out she was a Protestant.

None of the ladies I saw invited me around for a cup of tea, but I must admit since I didn't know how to drive a horse and cart I couldn't have visited them if they had invited me. So my social interactions in the town remained limited to a 'Good morning'. I thought I heard a lady say the words 'Stuck up' once as I passed her, but she was probably talking about someone else. I knew she couldn't have been referring to me.

Annie would say a few words now and then if she and I were alone together in the house, but she seemed afraid to talk to me if her brother was around. The little girl spent most of the day sitting in her tree house with her rag doll in her arms.

I watched her in the tree whenever I crossed the yard to go to the long-drop toilet or to get water from the tank, and I saw that she always appeared to be conducting long conversations with the doll. Sometimes she got quite carried away and I was afraid she would lose her balance and fall to the ground. The tree house itself looked a bit precarious to me and I was uneasy when I saw her heading out there each morning. It was not good for a child to be alone with only a rag doll and magpies for company.

I knew too that magpies could be vicious if they were nesting. Mick had been swooped on by magpies, back in Norwood a few times when he was out walking, and Mrs Williams had had trouble with them, too. I wondered whether Pask might not have lost his eye to the magpies rather than at war as I had supposed.

But they seemed tame enough, the magpies of Orroroo. Sometimes I saw them splashing in the dish of water by the backdoor, and sometimes they would take a piece of bread or a piece of meat from Annie's hand.

The tree house looked as if it had been there for a long time, and I wondered if Pask had played in it as a child, although it was hard to imagine Pask as a child. He seemed to have sprung full grown and tanned and wrinkled from the earth itself. If any man could be said to be part of this dry and empty landscape, Pask was that man.

Although Annie had grown to accept me, Bob seemed to resent my presence on the property. If I turned round quickly when he was sitting at the table, I would see him glaring at me for no apparent reason. I ignored him as much as I could. He didn't need me and I didn't need him. But he was never backward at coming forward when the food was on the table.

So I was alone a lot, really, and I would have enjoyed a bit of company. Even Mrs Williams would have been welcome if she had turned up on the doorstep. I imagined showing her how I could milk a cow and make butter. She wouldn't have known where to look, she would be so surprised. The butter was my pride and joy. I used some of it to make scones in the wood oven. They were nothing like those scones Mrs Williams had brought over the morning of Michael's funeral. Nothing anaemic about the fluffy scones I made.

There was an old fig tree in the garden that still had a few late figs on it. I made jam. That was better than Mrs Williams's jam too. I found ginger and almonds at the back of the pantry. The almonds were a bit soft but good enough for cooking. I put them in the fig jam and we ate the jam with the scones. Pask said it was the best jam he had ever had.

I was so busy that I lost track of the days. Although I had been scrupulous to always cook myself an egg for my Friday meal, much to the amusement of Pask and the kids, one day I realised that I had eaten a mutton chop on a Friday. I was horrified. Despite our weekly trip into town, somehow I had been convinced that it was Saturday, and I had chewed the meat and swallowed it before I remembered what day it was. I had committed a mortal sin without even knowing it. I was doomed, because there was no priest in the area I could confess my sin to.

Even in all the years when we had not gone to Mass, Michael and I had been careful not to eat meat on a Friday. Why, I wondered, were we so careful about that, when we had not had the human decency to look after our daughter better? Did we care more about the church laws than about family laws? But still I knew I had sinned and I felt guilty over this latest lapse from grace.

I wondered if I could write to Father Flaherty and make a long-distance confession. I wasn't sure if the Church allowed it, but it might be worth a try. How had Burke and Wills managed? Burke was an Irishman. Was he a Catholic or did he come from the north of Ireland? Perhaps God had special rules for people who lived in the outback. In the meantime, I would just have to do my best not to drop dead until I could figure out how to obtain absolution.

But should I confess the business with Mary while I was at it too? I was loath to go that far. And Mary had forgiven me, so perhaps I could forget about that particular sin. I had nothing else on my conscience, apart from Rudolph Valentino. If I found a priest, I would tell him about the mutton chop, even though it was an honest mistake. I would probably put Mary and the sheik off for another time, though.

The mail was delivered regularly and deposited in a kero tin on a post at the gate to the property, but Pask did not collect the mail all that often. It depended on when he happened to be around that side of the farm, so I was never sure when my next mail would come, but it was a great comfort when I did receive a letter.

I especially treasured the letters from Mary. I wept when I thought how long we had been apart. Now, when I saw her rounded handwriting on an envelope, I clutched the paper to my heart and dashed into my room to read it, no matter how busy I was. She wrote about Paddy, how well Fred's business was doing, how she loved the recipes I sent her. I always gave Mary the correct list of ingredients, though I admit I often leave things out when I give other people recipes.

My family would never know how I looked forward to those letters, how I would read and re-read them, and then read them again. Were there hidden messages between the lines telling me what was really happening at home? I always carefully re-folded the pages and put them into the envelopes they had come in lest the dust that pervaded everything in this house spoil them.

At first everyone wrote their own long letters, but after a while Joe and Brian seemed too busy and they just added a short PS – 'Hello, Mum – Hope you are well. We are well,' to the letters Charlie wrote.

Charlie was a great writer of letters. A real comfort. He wrote of the jazz band he had joined and how he had managed to get hold of a second-hand white jacket to wear for performances. He was paid a few quid when the band played at the Palais Royal. Once he had played on the Floating Palais on the River Torrens, and one of the band fell in and was pulled out dripping but still clutching his clarinet.

Charlie wouldn't give up his apprenticeship, though, he wrote, so I mustn't worry about trumpet-playing going to his head. Although jazz was all the rage now, he said, and it was a real pity I could not hear him play some of the new tunes he had learned. His favourite at the moment was 'Sweet Georgia Brown'. He knew even I would enjoy it.

He insisted everything was fine back home and that they were coping very well without me. The boys had learned to wash and iron (Joe was unhappy because he had scorched his best white shirt, but it was his own fault) and they could cook mashed potato and snags pretty well now. They were keeping the house clean enough. 'It might not be up to your standards, Mum, but it's not bad,' he insisted. He assured me that they would have a good clean up before I came home and that I would find the place sparkling, even the windows.

'They tried to keep Mrs Williams out of the place, although she kept offering help. She had brought some soup around a couple of times. Charlie swore it was not a patch on the soup I made, though. Not much meat, and the vegies were overcooked. There was no pepper and not enough salt.

Amy always added notes in her big round child's handwriting. Sister Mary Leon had smacked her over the fingers with a ruler for making mistakes with her piano scales, but Amy had managed not to cry. Amy wrote that she was not going to give the nun the satisfaction.

That made me smile, it was the sort of thing I would have told her to do. Teresa Tierney had had the mumps but was better now. Amy had learned all her twelve times tables and had finished reading her new primer ahead of most of the other girls in her class.

Mrs Williams's cat had had kittens and Charlie and Mavis both agreed that Amy could have one of them, as our old cat, Mulligatawny, had died. Amy had found the body on the back veranda with ants all over it. Charlie had buried it in the back yard and Amy had put roses on the grave. The new kitten was a boy cat so it wouldn't have babies. She had named it Ginger.

I should have been pleased to know they were coping very well, but actually I was a bit miffed that they could manage without me, although I really didn't want to admit it, even to myself. You put your heart and soul into bringing kids up and then they go and grow up and have independent lives.

It was a bit ungrateful of them, when you thought about it. When I went home, would they actually want me back or would I be in the way? Should I go back now before they forgot me entirely? But then the boys might go down the mines at Broken Hill, and I couldn't let that happen. I would stay at Orroroo for a while longer. Until our ship came in. But Orroroo was a very long way from the sea.

17

We ate early on the farm. By five p.m., Pask and Bob would come in with huge appetites worked up from whatever work they were doing with the sheep. I hadn't asked exactly what they were doing but it seemed to involve spending a lot of time touring the property on horseback. Pask said he was digging a dam too, and he wanted to get it finished before the rains came. He said by April or May there should be some rain.

I often saw him gaze upward with his good eye, an anxious look on his face when he went out of the kitchen door in the morning, then he would shake his head and mutter something about Goyder's line and impending ruin if it didn't rain soon.

On the days when he and Bob were busy digging, they were even dirtier and more tired and Bob's mood was even nastier than usual. I always had the meal ready on dam-digging days. Silently the two males would devour their food and then Bob would splash some water over himself and collapse on his bed.

In the evenings, Pask liked to play with the cockatoo, whose name, he had told me, was Solomon. I didn't like it much when he opened the cage door and let the thing out to strut around the kitchen, although Pask always cleaned up any bird poop that Solomon dropped. I kept well away from the side of the room where the nightly promenade occurred, aware of the baleful stares I received from Pask's pet as it stalked about the room, pecked at the chair legs, and then clambered up to sit on his shoulder, where it sat, preening itself. I decided the bird was a sort of avian Bob.

I found it was more pleasant, and probably safer, to sit outside in the cool of the evening and listen to the magpies singing sleepy trills. Much nicer birds than cockatoos, magpies are. Except perhaps in the mating season.

The cockatoo and I had established an uneasy truce during the day. I had learned that if I covered it with the canvas it was quiet. It had learned that one scream meant 'Goodnight, Cocky', so it no longer shrieked at the sight of me. Pask said the cocky was called Solomon because his father had suggested a biblical name for it, but later, when it laid an egg, they had realised it was a female. Just the one egg. It never did it again.

Solomon hadn't liked Pask's mother or Pask's wife much either, Pask told me. In fact, his wife, Elsie, had been terrified of the bird. That knowledge made me feel a bit better. It was Solomon who was the crazy one, not me.

Annie would help me with the dishes and the tidying up before she went to bed. She liked me to read her a story, and she would lie awake waiting until I came in with a book.

After Annie was in bed, I would sit on a bench just outside the kitchen door to watch the sun go down between the scrubby little trees. The magpies sang their lullabies and the last laments of the crows died away as the sun set. This was my private time, the time when I could relax and collect my thoughts, remember my family back in Adelaide, and wonder what they were doing.

One night Pask wandered out the door and stood looking down at me. He took his pipe out of his pocket and began to fill it with tobacco. He tamped the tobacco down, lit the pipe and sucked on it reflectively. He squinted up at the sky with his good eye. It's a pity he's only got one eye to look at this sunset with, I thought. A sky like this is too big even for two good eyes.

'I've put cocky away for the night,' he said. 'A penny for your thoughts, Mrs W. Would it disturb you if I come out here for a while? I wondered where you got to in the evenings. I thought maybe you went into your room for a bit of privacy. Do you mind if I sit here for a while too?'

'It's your bench, Pask. If you want to sit here, it's not for me to complain. I'm the housekeeper, remember?'

'Well, I suppose you are, Mrs W,' he said, settling down companionably beside me. 'But I reckon you would let a man know if he was in the way, and I wouldn't want to get in your way, or disturb you at all, if you know what I mean. So if you don't want me out here, just say the word. It's real pretty this time of day, though, isn't it? Makes a man glad to be alive, looking at the sky like this. No flies and not too many mozzies around.'

He took the pipe out his mouth and looked at it. He hesitated for a moment as if he wanted to say something but was not sure how to phrase the words. 'Is Bob bothering you at all, Mrs W?' he asked.

'Bothering me? No, not really. He's a very quiet boy. Doesn't talk much.' I wanted to say that he was a surly little bugger and needed a good kick up the backside, but it didn't seem appropriate to make a remark like that to the child's father, even if he did believe in my frankness on other matters.

'He took it real bad when his mum died. He was the one who found her, you know. Annie was out playing in her tree house like she does, and I was out with the sheep. Bob had been getting the eggs from the chooks and Elsie was washing up the breakfast dishes.' He knocked the pipe on the edge of the bench and began to refill it with tobacco.

I usually don't like the smell of tobacco, although of course there's no getting away from the stuff. Most men smoke. But there was something rich and fruity about Pask's tobacco that was almost attractive. A bit like the fruit cake I make. Everyone likes my fruit cake. I decided next time we went into Orroroo I would buy some mixed fruit so I could make fruit cake.

'Even when she was real crook,' Pask continued, 'she still kept trying to do things. I reckon she knew she was going, like, and she wanted to leave the place tidy. Not that it stayed tidy for long after she died.' He sighed. 'It wasn't much use, all her effort, when you think about it.'

I nodded my agreement. By the state of the place when I had arrived, all Elsie's efforts were in vain.

'Anyway,' Pask continued, 'Bob came in and found her on the floor by the wood stove, curled up in a ball and cold and stiff. It's pretty hard for a kiddie to see a thing like that. He's never been the same since. Withdrawn, that's what the local doctor says. In shock. A bit like some of the fellows got in the trenches when the bombs were going off around us.'

I wondered if he was going to tell me how he had lost his eye. He had never said much about the war. But Pask was more concerned about the present than the past.

'About time he got over it, I suppose,' he continued 'but the doctor says it has to take its time. Nothing anyone can do about it. So if he's a bit difficult, maybe you can just overlook it, like.'

'Yes, I can understand that finding his mum like that must have been awful for him. My children were upset when their father died. Even though it happened in Mount Gambier, and we didn't see it happen, it was dreadful. The boys tried not to show their feelings, but Amy took it very hard.'

'What did he die of, Mrs W?'

'He had a heart attack. It happened on a train and they brought him home for the funeral. It took me a long time to come to terms with things.' I decided I wouldn't mention the word axe. Some things are best kept private.

Pask nodded and sucked on his pipe. 'I reckon that was a bloody good way to go, if you don't mind me saying it, Mrs W. A heart attack is quick. Merciful, like. Elsie's death was real bad. We both knew she was dying, and there wasn't nothing anyone could do except wait. Eats you from the inside out, cancer does.'

He rubbed at his eye. 'I have to be careful of this eye. Only got the one, you know. I got a bit of shrapnel in the other one in France. They said I was lucky it wasn't worse. I have to watch the dust around here. I reckon I've got dust in my eye right now, the way it's watering. It's always windy at Orroroo.'

He blew his nose. 'It blew a gale the day we buried Elsie. Her doctor said it was the pancreas. He said it would take three months to kill her, and he was dead right. He said it would get into her liver and he was right about that, too. She lost a hell of a lot of weight and turned yellow and vomited all the time.'

He sighed. 'The pancreas, that's the sweetbread, if you're a sheep. Can't look at sweetbread any more now when I kill a sheep. I used to like offal, before Elsie died. Now I just chuck it out for the crows.'

I patted his hand. It was the least I could do. He moved a bit closer to me on the bench, then he seemed to think better of it. He moved away again and stared at the wind blown trees that surrounded the yard.

'I was a bit withdrawn, the same as Bob is, for a while after Elsie died. I didn't even feel like going into Orroroo, I didn't want to talk to anyone. When people spoke to me, the words just didn't seem to come. I suppose it takes a while to get over a death. I used to think about the fact I knew more dead people than live ones, if you count my mates from the war and my parents and Elsie.'

He sighed. 'I've felt better since you've been here. How long has it been since your husband died, Mrs W?'

'It's three months now,' I answered. 'Michael died on 16 February 1928. It was right in the middle of summer. I don't think I'll ever forget that date.'

'Yes, it's early days, yet,' said Pask nodding wisely. 'It takes a while to get used to being alone, when you've been married for a while. You'll come to terms with it, just like I did. And Bob will get over his mum's death eventually. Just give the lad a bit more time, Mrs W.' He grinned at me. 'I reckon he'll come good soon. Everything will be all right now you're here.'

Everything might be all right for him and his family, I thought, but what about me and my family? I had people back home who needed me and I had no intention of staying at Orroroo for longer than I had to stay. Once my finances improved, I'd be back to Adelaide like a shot, and Bob and the rest of them could jump in the lake. Or in the dam, if Pask ever finished digging it.

18

I hadn't realised how cold it could get at Orroroo. I thought the heat of summer would last forever, but suddenly my hands were white with chilblains and I welcomed the warmth of the wood stove as I stirred the mutton broth. We all huddled around the wood stove now in the evenings, our hard wooden kitchen chairs drawn in a circle around the glowing coals. A short time ago, I thought, we had sought the shade of the house to protect us from the heat, but now the frost laid siege to us. Even the magpies sat huddled in the trees, their warbling muted by the cold and the mist.

Pask's conversation was of shearers and of shearing. He talked of past shearings, the shearing that would soon take place, and shearings of the future.

I realised that four months had passed since Michael's death and funeral. I had got past the three months mark at Orroroo without even noticing it. I wondered if Pascal had realised my probation period was up. Now, I supposed, I could stay as long as I wanted to. But how long did I want to stay? How much money did my family need?

My employer hadn't said anything. He wrote my cheques every fortnight and I posted them back home. I didn't need much money out here. I had kept a few pounds back from the money I had found in Michael's sock drawer at home, just in case. I was keeping it for a rainy day but it didn't rain much at Orroroo and we only went into the town when we were running out of essential items like tea and sugar.

Bob continued to irritate me. He bickered with Annie and tried to pick fights with me. When he came in from working with his father, he sat on a chair in the kitchen and told me that I wasn't running the house properly, that his mum kept the furniture polished and the windows cleaner than I did, and that the tea wasn't strong enough or hot enough, or the porridge was lumpy. He needed to get out of the house, I decided. Preferably before I threw the rolling pin at him.

'Why don't the children go to school?' I asked Pask. 'There must be a school at Orroroo. Or at Pekina perhaps. Is Pekina nearer than Orroroo?'

'About the same distance. It'd take me an hour and a half to take them to school in the morning with the horse and cart and another hour and half to pick them up afterwards,' Pask protested. 'Then the horse has to be taken out of its harness and have a rub down and I wouldn't have time to get my work done with the sheep. I need young Bob to give me a hand with the dam anyway. That dam has to be finished before the rains start. We had really good rains in the early twenties, but there hasn't been much since, and I have to get every bit of water I can.'

I knew he was worried about the possibility of a bad drought. You never knew how long a drought would last, but you have to be ready for when it ended. Until now, I had not realised that sheep needed so much attention. I thought farmers just released the sheep out in the paddocks and caught them when they needed wool or meat from them.

'But have the kiddies never gone to school?' I asked. 'I'm sure education is compulsory. Kids need to be taught and they need time with other kiddies too. How are they going to get on in life if they can't read or write? If I could drive the cart, I'd take them, but I don't know how to manage the horse.'

'They did go to school when their mother was alive,' Pask admitted. 'Elsie learned to manage the horse and cart before the kiddies were born. But then they missed a lot of school when she was crook, because she couldn't take them, and I just haven't got around to organising for them to go back. I've got a lot of catching up to do. Everything went downhill when Elsie was sick.'

He looked at me over the rim of his teacup and I wondered if learning to manage the horse and cart was next on the agenda for me. I didn't feel enthusiastic about that. It was one thing to be a housekeeper and milk a cow, but it was another to go driving carts all over the countryside. I pretended to be busy filling my cup again, although I didn't really want more tea.

Pask sighed. 'Maybe when the dam's finished,' he said, 'I'll be able to spare the time to take them to school each day. If there were six kids around here, the government would give us a school teacher and we could have a school, but you have to have six kids in the area for that, and all the neighbours' kids have grown up and left school.'

'Well, are their school books still here?' I asked. 'What if I give them their lessons just until you sort things out here, so that they won't be too far behind when they do get back to school?'

The books were resurrected from the cupboard where they had been stored. I saw a few other books stacked in the cupboard as well and picked them up.

'Those are Elsie's books,' said Pask. 'I told you she liked books and music. A real lady she was. Didn't get much music out here, though. She brought those books with her when she first came up from Adelaide. You might like to read them, Mrs W.'

I looked at the titles. The Bible, of course. Every home had one of those. And Swift's *Gulliver's Travels*. Poor Elsie. Had she thought to find some exotic destination in Australia, but all she had found was Orroroo? There was a copy of the complete works of William Shakespeare too. Michael would have liked that. There was also a volume of Tennyson's poetry. I realised then just how much I had missed reading since I had come here. We always had books at home after I was married. Michael was a great reader.

'Thanks, Pask, I'll do that. It would be nice to have something to read in the evenings. Michael and I always used to read at night, and it's too cold to sit outside now.'

I saw a look of disappointment cross his face. Had he valued our evenings on the bench outside the kitchen door? Some nights we hardly spoke, especially if he had had a tiring day chasing sheep or digging the dam. But no matter how tired he was, he had always arrived on the bench, accepted the cup of tea I handed him, drank it and then lit his pipe and smoked it. I suppose it could be called a companionable silence, but at the end of each day, I was longing for a chat.

Feckless or not, Michael did have the gift of the gab. He had never been to Ireland of course, but you would swear he had kissed the Blarney Stone. His mother always said he was born talking. That was why he was such a good union man. A union man had to be persuasive. Michael could stand up there in front of a group of men and talk his head off. I once heard one of his mates say that Mick could charm the birds out of the trees. I wondered how he would have fared with the magpies of Orroroo. Mick could persuade the men to do almost anything he suggested, and the men loved him for it. They even forgave him when he was wrong about something. Which, Michael swore, wasn't often.

'It's not what you say, it's the way you say it' was Michael's motto. 'Silver-tongued Walsh' was his nickname.

I could have used Michael there when Pask and I told Bob he would be having lessons at home. Neither of us had Michael's powers of persuasion. The boy resented the suggestion that he needed education and he put up quite a fight.

'I'll just give you lessons for a while, Bob,' I said. 'Then when your father has time, when the shearing is over and the dam finished, he'll be able to take you back to proper school. At least you won't be quite so far behind the other kids if you do a few lessons at home.'

'I'm going to be a farmer like Dad, so I don't need book learning,' he protested. 'I'm not never going back to school.'

'If Auntie Rose says you're going to do school work at home then you are going to do it, or you'll cop a walloping from me,' thundered his father. 'And you're going back to school as soon as I get around to taking you there and there's no two ways about it.'

'If you are going to be a farmer, Bob,' I explained, 'you have to be able work out how many bales of wool you have and how much you're owed for the wool. Otherwise the people who buy them from you could pull the wool over your eyes, as they say. And you have to be able to read the labels on that stuff your dad dips the sheep in. You probably have to work out how much stuff each sheep gets.'

'Mrs W is dead right. Give the sheep too much of it and they get crook. It could even kill them. That stuff's got arsenic in it. It's the arsenic that kills the lice and ticks. And if you don't give them enough, you've wasted your time and money doing it. Complicated stuff, that is. If you can't read properly you'll never get it right. And you have to be able to write to keep your accounts and your stock journals.'

Reluctantly Bob agreed with this reasoning, and we spent part of the day doing basic lessons. Annie decided that she wanted to be able to read to her rag doll when they were in the tree house together. She said needed to be able to write too, so that she could write her name on her stuff in case Bob took it. I wasn't sure what she meant when she said that, because she didn't own much, but a few days later I saw that she had scrawled, 'ANNIE'S ROOM NO BOYS ALLOWED' across her door.

I'm a great believer in education. Just because I had to leave school early didn't mean I wanted to be ignorant all my life. Michael's mother used to say I wasn't good enough to marry Michael because I was stupid, and that had made me read books to show her that I was worthy of him. I am proud to say that I have read more books than Moira Walsh ever saw the outside of.

When Annie turned out to be a better student than her brother, it spurred Bob on to greater efforts with his studies. He didn't want to be outdone by a girl, especially by a girl younger than he was.

Annie was a new child now. She had lost her fear of me and of the world in general. Her bed wetting, which had been nightly, was now only rare. Perhaps it was because I settled her in with a bedtime story and a hug each night, but the nightmares that had plagued her had gone. The family slept much more peacefully now that Annie's cries no longer rent the night air. Now the only person in the house who had nightmares was me.

I had had nightmares for so long that I should have been used to them, but it's hard to spend night after night running as hard as you can to stop something that you know cannot be stopped. I hoped the others couldn't hear me. I worried about the noise I might be making. Michael always used to complain how I whimpered and made choking noises in my sleep and how my legs thrashed about. At Orroroo I always shut the door to my room tight to muffle my distress.

Maybe it was the changing seasons, or maybe I had shut it out, but I didn't hear the wind howling as loudly as it had that first night I was here. Or was Elsie's ghost resting now, in the knowledge that her children were being well cared for?

The farmhouse seemed much brighter, more homely now. I had

cleaned everything that didn't move, and one day I even bathed the oldest sheepdog, much to its and Pascal's disgust. The younger dogs evaded me, but the slow old kelpie was easier to catch and dunk in the tin bath. Afterwards, the dog hung its head in shame and glared at me from the edge of the yard.

'Don't worry, mate, just chase a few sheep and roll in a few dags and you'll smell normal again in no time,' I heard Pask tell the unhappy beast.

There was a wilted rose bush outside the kitchen door, and I threw the washing-up water from the tin dish on it each day. I gave the unhappy plant a good prune. I put some of Dobbin's manure on it. Michael always said horse manure was the best thing for roses. He had told the truth that time. The straggly leaves grew brighter and greener. New shoots appeared, and one morning I found a white rosebud on the bush.

'The wife loved roses,' said Pascal as we admired the rose. 'I reckoned that bush died when Elsie did. I never thought I'd see it look like this again. Looks like you've brought it back from the brink, Mrs W. That's a bloody Lazarus rose bush, like that bloke in the Bible.'

'My husband Michael grew roses,' I said. I still found it hard to mention Mick to Pascal. I don't know why it was, but I felt shy to talk about my husband to this man. It shouldn't be like that, I told myself. Pask had had a wife who had died and I had had a husband who had died. You can't deny the past and you shouldn't have to deny anything.

'He loved roses too. He used to call me his Rose of Tralee. That's an Irish song he used to sing. He was a good singer, my husband.'

'So he was an Irishman?' asked Pascal. 'I should have guessed that much, with a name like Michael Walsh.'

'He was as Australian as they come,' I said indignantly. 'His people were Irish, way back. He was second-generation Australian. Our kids are third-generation Australian now. I suppose the Irish do tend to hold on to their culture. It's only natural. People like to remember their background. You like to know where you came from and who your people were.'

'Elsie was an English girl,' said Pask, a little wistfully. 'I suppose I never should have brought her out here. I met her in Adelaide. She was a real lady. She liked books and music. She wilted in the heat up here, just like that rose bush. She and her dad came out from the old country, and her dad died just after they arrived. Lung problem, it was. TB, I suppose, though Elsie never said that.'

I knew what he was saying. Even people who definitely had it, and who coughed up blood continuously, tried to pass it off as pleurisy or bronchitis. Sometimes they called it consumption because that sounded better than tuberculosis or TB. There's a bit of a stigma about TB. Somehow you think of it in connection with the slums and dirty houses. A lot of soldiers came back from the war with it. Mick was lucky he didn't get it in the trenches; it was rife there.

'They'd come out to Australia for the climate because of his lungs,' Pask continued. 'The doctors told him it might help, but it was too late. After he died, she got a job as a waitress in Balfour's tea shop in Adelaide. Bit of a come down for her, but she needed the money. That's where I met her, when I was down in Adelaide once.'

He sighed. 'A real English rose, she was. That's why she planted the rose bush. The white rose of Lancashire. Or York. I forget which it was. One side had the white rose for an emblem and the other had a red rose. The War of the Roses, it was called. It sounds a bit silly to me. It happened back in England, I forget when.' He shrugged. 'Elsie knew all about it, though. She was interested in history. She must have missed the history. England's full of history. She always said you couldn't move in England without stepping in history. There's no history at Orroroo. All you step in here is sheep or cow shit. But she put up with it, never complained. Then she got the cancer of course.'

I nodded. I knew what he meant. It was hard to lose one's husband or wife. We had that in common, Pask and me. Harder for him, I suppose, with the two little kiddies. At least my kids were able to cope on their own. But sorrow lingered for a long time. I still missed Rudolph Valentino, too. Eventually you came to terms with loss, I supposed.

'We've got a few Irish around here,' said Pascal. 'There's lots of them over at Pekina. Little Ireland, they call it. Lots of Irish at Peterborough too. They work on the railway. They hold an Irish dance every now and then at Pekina. The St Pat's Day dance has been and gone, but they'll probably have another shindig in a month or two. Any excuse for a celebration if you're Irish.' He grinned at my frown. 'Not that they're not hard workers too. Pretty good mob, really. I'll keep an ear open for you in case they've got a dance coming up at Pekina. It's not that far to go in the horse and cart. It'd be real good to have a night out. Do us all good.'

The letters from home told me again that the family was managing quite well without me. Everyone was thriving. The garden at home was blooming, Charlie wrote. The roses had survived the heat of summer and now, possibly due to the chook droppings the boys had put on them, were having a late autumn flush of new blooms. Charlie reckoned that chook manure was just as good as horse shit. Dad would be thrilled if he saw those roses, Charlie said.

Joe and Brian had planted broad beans on Anzac Day because they remembered their father had told them that was when beans should be planted. It had rained on Anzac Day, just as it always did.

It hadn't rained at Orroroo, though, I recalled. Charlie said that the young plants were coming up nicely. I sniffed and tossed my head. I bet they forget to pick those beans when they are still young and tender, I told myself. I know they will forget to pull the strings off from the beans properly. They'll probably boil the guts out of them, too. Broad beans are really nasty if you overcook them. They go all grey and soggy.

It wasn't nice to know how well they were coping without me. I was not indispensable. I knew I'd told them they'd be all right but secretly I didn't think they would be. The money I was sending was helping a lot, Charlie said. Amy was doing well at school and Mavis thought the world of her. So she bloody should too, I thought. Amy deserved to be thought the world of by everyone.

And so did Mary. Poor little Mary. She seemed happy now. Happier than you would expect her to be, when you thought about what she had been through.

I wrote about Bob and Annie and the farm, but I didn't say much about Pask. There wasn't much to say about him anyway; he was always out chasing sheep. Somehow I felt that I needed to keep Pask and his family and my real family in two separate boxes. It would be dangerous to mix them up.

19

'Hooray!' yelled Bob. 'Hooray!' He leaped into the air, thrust his arms high and beat the air frantically.

On the other side of the dam, Pask was banging a stick against a piece of rusty corrugated iron and shouting at the top of his voice. Annie and I stood on the edge, shrieking, adding our voices to the general hubbub. I shook my apron and Annie held her rag doll aloft and waved it.

The excited dogs, puzzled by our mad behaviour but anxious to partake in the occasion, ran about beside us and barked as loudly as they could.

In the dry dam below us, a small flock of sheep that Pask and Bob had mustered for the purpose milled about, confused by the commotion and bleating piteously. Pask had explained that what we were doing was called puddling. The idea was to keep the beasts moving so that their hooves would compress the soil at the base of the dam and therefore make the soil impregnable to the rain that Pask hoped would soon arrive and fill the basin.

There was no sign of rain or of any water yet, though. The sheep's hooves raised a cloud of white dust that made Annie and me sneeze. The dust rose into the blue cloudless sky and hung motionless in the still air.

The youngest dog decided he was going to be the first to dive into the new dam. He leaped into the air and landed on the back of an unfortunate sheep, which skittered sideways and collided with its neighbour. Bob, not to be outdone, jumped in after the pup.

'Easy there, Bob!' yelled Pask. 'We want to keep those sheep turning gently.'

But the sheep were panicked. They streamed up the gentle slope of the far side of the dam and stampeded back to the edge of the paddock. The dogs tore off after the fleeing sheep and herded them into a tight bunch. The lead dog looked at Pask enquiringly.

'Let them go, Blue!' shouted Pask. 'The dam's solid enough now anyway.' He whistled and the dogs trotted back.

It's a pity Bob hasn't got as much sense as the dogs have, I thought.

'Bloody silly kid!' said Pask, echoing my thoughts. 'I reckon he does need to go to school. He could have broken a sheep's leg. He could have broken his own leg, if it comes to that. Anyway, the dam's finished now. As soon as the shearing's over, he can go to school. I hope his teacher has got a bloody big cane to use on him.'

Pask calmed down a bit. He turned to me. 'What do you think of the dam, though, Mrs W? She's a beauty, isn't she?'

As dams went, it didn't look very impressive to me. But I had not had the labour of digging it, so I nodded my appreciation and held my tongue on the matter of size. I told Pask how nicely shaped it was, and I offered to transplant some of the lilies that grew down by the creek to the edges to pretty it up. He shook his head and said once the dam was full, the stock would be trampling around the edges in order to drink, so landscaping would be waste of time.

'Tell you what, though, Mrs W.,' he said. 'When we've got some water in there, we'll toss in a few yabbies. I can get some from my mate's dam. Yabbies are like freshwater shrimps. Delicious, they are. They'll grow really well in the dam, and we'll catch them with a bit of meat on a string and have a feed. Bob will enjoy that.'

'I know what yabbies are.My kids used to catch them in the River Torrens.'

I grinned at the thought of Bob going to school and of me having a bit of peace and quiet, although I would miss having Annie around the house all day. And I didn't really want to turn Annie over to a teacher with a cane, if that was what education was like at Orroroo. I wondered if I could find a reason to keep Annie home for a bit longer, and just let Bob go to school.

I would talk it over with Pask tonight, I decided, after the children had gone to bed. We had begun to sit by the wood stove in the evenings now. The time for sitting outside on the bench had gone now that the autumn chill had begun, and although I missed the song of the crickets and of the magpies as the sun went down, and that feeling that if I reached up I could touch the thick heavy stars in the sky, there was something comforting in watching the flames flicker behind the grate of the stove. It was nice to sit, feeling the warmth on my face, holding a book in one hand and a cup of tea in the other.

'What is that boy doing now?' asked Pask, bringing me back to the present moment.

I looked around. Bob was nowhere to be seen. Annie was looking up into a tree and shaking her head.

'I told Bob not to climb that tree but he said he knew he was going to catch it from you, Dad, for jumping into the dam, so he's gone up there and now I think he's stuck. He's crying,' she added with satisfaction. She yelled up the tree. 'You're a cry baby, Bob.'

'Bob, you get down here now. Right now,' shouted Pask. 'I'm giving you two minutes to get out of that tree and if you don't, I'll belt hell out of you.'

'Calm down a bit, Pask,' I said. 'If you scare him, he might fall out of the tree, and it's pretty high.'

'I can't get down, Dad. I'm stuck. I can't see the branch I climbed up on. I'm scared, Dad.'

'Bloody kid thinks he's a possum. Except possums have got more sense than to climb up past where they can't get down from. I don't know what's got into that boy.'

'Dad, Dad, help me, Dad!' Bob's voice was becoming more and more frantic.

'I climbed worse trees than that when I was a kid but I never lost my nerve,' Pask muttered to me. 'I suppose I'm going to have to go up and get him down. My mum always said she hoped I'd have a son just like me. It looks like her wish has come true.'

He might have climbed worse trees than that when he was a kid, but had he climbed any since he had lost his eye, I wondered. But I wasn't going to go up the tree, it wasn't the sort of thing a woman did, and anyway it was Pask's kid, not mine. So it would have to be Pask who did the rescuing.

I watched as Pask swung himself up into the lower limbs of the gum tree. He was surprisingly agile for his age and, as he had said, he knew how to climb a tree. Annie and I watched from below as he made his way up to the level where Bob clung to a branch that had begun to creak ominously.

'I saw a big branch fall off that tree last summer,' whispered Annie. 'What if the branch Bob's on falls off now?'

'Bob will be in big trouble if it does,' I said. 'But I have heard that branches only fall off gum trees when it's hot. Maybe the branch won't break just yet.'

The dogs milled about under the tree, the oldest standing with his front legs on the trunk and peering up into the leaves. The pup who had caused the initial problem pushed his way in, trying to see what the old dog was looking at, and was nipped by his elders as a disciplinary measure. That's what Bob needs, I thought. Less threats and more action.

Pask reached Bob. He stretched out his hand to the boy but Bob was clinging hard to the branch on which he was sitting. He refused to let go of it to take his father's hand. I could hear the boy whimpering as Pask tried to persuade him to release his grip on the tree. In desperation, Pask grabbed a handful of Bob's trousers and dragged the lad towards him. Annie and I held our breaths as Pask guided Bob down the tree and then cheered when they reached the ground.

Pask shook Bob and then pulled him close and hugged him. Then he held him at arm's length and looked into the boy's eyes with his one eye. 'Don't you ever do such a stupid thing again, boy,' he thundered. He left the rest of the sentence unfinished so that Bob could imagine the dire consequences if he re-offended.

Bob broke free and ran off, sobbing, towards the house.

'I don't think he'll do that again in a hurry, Pask,' I said. 'Boys will be boys, though. It's that dam I'm worried about. What if he jumps in when it's full? Can he swim?'

'Yes, he can swim, but when the dam's full it'll be slippery around the edges and if he gets in he may not get out again. I'm going to have to put the fear of God into him about that dam. And you too, Annie,' Pask said, turning to his daughter. 'You remember how the Pearsons' kid was drowned in their dam?'

Annie nodded. She'll be all right, I thought. Girls have got more sense than boys in some ways. They get into trouble too, but they face different dangers.

20

The rains began and Annie and I were kept busy trying to keep the mud out of the house and cleaning it up when it did come in, mainly on Bob's feet and the dogs' paws. Four sets of clay-covered gumboots in various sizes now stood on a hessian bag just inside the kitchen door.

After the evening meal, Annie would go off to bed and I would tuck her in, read her a story and then come back to the fire to make more tea for Pask, Bob and myself. I had a chamber pot under my bed, so I wasn't worried about having a call of nature during the night. There was no way any of us wanted to go out to the long-drop lavatory in the cold. We emptied our pots on the lemon tree each morning. The tree was blooming. That's the best thing you can do for a lemon tree, empty a chamber pot on it.

Then Pask would order Bob to go to his bed. Bob usually cast a resentful glare at me which I always pretended not to see as he left the room. I wondered whether I was sitting in his mother's chair and if that was the cause of his anger. I tried changing my seating, but no matter where I sat he still left the room looking as if he hoped the fire would erupt from the stove and engulf me.

I had finished *Gulliver's Travels* and decided that I was right the first time I had read it, many years ago. Swift was not really to my taste, although he had been one of Michael's favourite authors until he discovered James Joyce. I'm not sure why I didn't enjoy Swift. Too fanciful, perhaps. I'm a more down-to-earth person than Jonathan Swift was.

I wondered which of the other books I might read next. I didn't quite feel up to Shakespeare after a day spent milking the cow and coping with Bob and the housework. All that 'raineth' and 'wilt thou' would be a bit too much after that. But the Tennyson was more attractive. I've always fancied Sir Lancelot. He was almost as romantic as the sheik.

I had left school at thirteen because I had to go out to work to help out when my father was ill and couldn't work. My parents didn't consider education important for a girl anyway. Patrick and Danny were made to stay at school longer than that, even though they were itching to get out and earn money. Michael's Mum always said I wasn't good enough for Michael. She said Michael could have done better than to marry me. Well, I showed her. I had more children than she ever managed to have. And they've turned out better than her kids too, come to think of it.

But I will admit that Michael was an educated man, and we always had books at home. Michael had bought *The Idylls of the King* for me when we were engaged. He said I needed my mind stimulated. All I had wanted at that stage was my body stimulated, but I knew I had to improve my education to be worthy of Michael.

Now I re-discovered Tennyson in Elsie's book. There were some bits about Sir Lancelot and King Arthur, and a lot of other poems I had never seen.

Pask read the Bible, peering at the pages with his good eye. I was bemused by this. It didn't quite fit with my idea of him. Sometimes I thought he was only reading because I was reading. I hoped the effort of reading by the smoky kero lamp wouldn't harm his eye. But he was determined. He began at the beginning of the enormous Bible, and worked his way patiently through the Old Testament. He even skimmed through the 'begat's, which intrigued me. I would have skipped those entirely. I only like those stories in the Bible where people are having battles or running off with other people's wives. I like a bit of excitement in my religion.

I looked over his shoulder as I put the teapot on the table and saw that he was reading about King David. I wondered if he was looking for the story of Bathsheba. But he seemed very intent and serious.

'Are you finding answers in the Bible?' I asked.

'I'm not sure what the questions are, to tell the truth,' he said. 'Funny stuff in this book. Funny peculiar, I mean. This David bloke was an interesting fellow, wasn't he? A real lad. Got up to all sorts of tricks. I probably shouldn't say it, but do you reckon maybe he was a bit too friendly with Saul's son, that Jonathan chap?'

'I'll have to re-read it. I don't remember anything about that.' I said.

'It's not bad reading,' he went on. 'I had no idea there were stories like this in the Bible. Of course, there's a lot of boring stuff too. Pads it out, I suppose.' He looked up at me and grinned. 'It might have been quite a short book otherwise. Elsie was fond of the Bible. She used to sit here at night reading it. I used to sit by the fire and watch her. I used to watch her a lot, after the doctor told us how crook she was. I knew there would be much time left to look at her. You can tell when time is running out.'

He closed the book, put it on the table and watched as it opened itself. 'See how it still falls open on the pages she used to read the most? She didn't read the old part much, she just read the New Testament. The Jesus bit. Stuff like the resurrection and life after death. She was fond of that part. I reckon it helped her a lot when she knew she was dying. Was your Michael a religious man?'

'He was and he wasn't,' I said. 'That was the trouble with Michael. He was a really complicated person. He could say one thing and sound as if he really believed what he was saying, and the next day he might say the complete opposite and he would sound just as convincing about that, too. He used to argue like a Jesuit. Jesuits are a sort of priest we Catholics have. They're supposed to be able to see both sides of an argument.'

I shook my head at the memory of the heated arguments, not always about religion, that had taken place around our table, then added hastily, 'I don't think Michael meant to tell lies. I think he just changed his mind about things from one day to the next and said whatever he believed on that particular day.'

'It sounds as if he wasn't a really reliable fellow, then,' said Pask. 'How could you trust a bloke like that? You wouldn't know where you stood with him.'

'To be honest, sometimes I wonder if Mick knew what he believed himself. There were some things that you couldn't change his mind about, though. He could be really stubborn when he wanted to be.

But how deep his religious ideas were, I couldn't say. I often wonder if he prayed before he died, or if he would have prayed if he knew he was dying.'

'It couldn't have been easy living with a bloke like that. At least with Elsie you knew where you stood.'

'But the Bible contradicts itself,' I argued. 'There are bits where it says turn the other cheek and there are other bits where it says an eye for an eye.' I could have bitten my tongue when I realised what I'd said, but Pask didn't flinch.

I changed the subject of authors quickly. 'Even Mr Tennyson contradicts himself. There's a poem in here that I'm trying to understand, it's called "In Memoriam" and it talks about God and at times it sounds really hopeful but then there's a line that says we know not anything, and the poem ends by saying life is futile and the poet seems to be asking if there really is anything beyond death.'

'There has to be something beyond death,' Pask said. 'It stands to reason. Otherwise what are we doing here, what's it all about? Why does anyone bother? You know what, Mrs W, we were better off when we were sitting out there on that bench looking at the sunset and seeing the stars come out. Maybe you shouldn't read that book if it upsets you. I didn't know Elsie was reading stuff like that. Don't read it if you don't like it.'

'Well, the point is, I really do enjoy the way Tennyson writes that poem but it's a bit frightening if a man as educated as he was doesn't know the answers.'

'Is he dead then?'

'Yes, he died in 1892.'

'I reckon he knows the answers now, then, one way or the other. We'll find out when it's our time. You got to admit, though, Mrs W, there's something very relaxing about being dead. You stop worrying about everything when you stop breathing.'

He opened the door of the wood stove and pushed another bit of wood into the fiery depths. 'Elsie and Michael found out the answers, I suppose. And we will when it comes our turn. I wouldn't worry about it until we get there. How about another cup of tea before we go to bed?'

I poured the tea and then looked at the book on the table. 'I think I'll go back to reading the poems he wrote about King Arthur and Sir Lancelot. They're easier to understand and I like them. There's one called "The Lady of Shalott" with Sir Lancelot in it that I really enjoy.'

'Aren't shallots those onion things?'

'Yes, you're right. Little brown ones. I always put them in the gravy at Christmas time. I like shallots. I wonder why Tennyson called her the Lady of Shalott. Maybe that's the place the onions originally came from. The spelling's different, though.'

We lingered over the tea. I felt that we were both reluctant to end the evening. It was becoming harder and harder to leave the fireside and say goodnight and go to our cold bedrooms. I told myself that it was because it was pleasant to be able to spend time with an adult without Bob interrupting our conversation.

I think we both noticed how the boy tried to distract his father whenever Pask and I sat together at the table eating or drinking tea. Suddenly Bob would burst into our discussions with irrelevant talk of pastoral matters, usually on subjects about which the boy knew I was ignorant. He could not seem to understand that his father and I were enjoying a simple, innocent adult friendship which was perfectly natural in the circumstances. We were, after all, two grown-up people isolated from other society and it was only natural that we should be drawn together to converse. The boy was unreasonable.

I refilled the teapot from the kettle a few times, but at last my bladder was bursting and I thought if I drank any more tea I would explode. There's a limit to how much a chamber pot will hold. Pask must have felt the same, because he closed the Bible and rose from his chair.

He patted my hand and grinned. 'Well, sleep well, Mrs W. Don't you go dreaming about that poet bloke. See you in the morning.'

I dreamed of Pask that night. He was standing on the wooden kitchen table wearing Sir Lancelot's gleaming silver armour. The visor of his helmet was open, showing his weather-beaten face with its black eye patch. His burnished armour shone in the light from the kerosene lamp.

Except for the area below his knees. I was surprised to see that

Pask was wearing his old muddy gumboots instead of the traditional grieves or whatever they were called on his legs. He'll get mud all over that table. And I hope no one thinks of using their sword on his legs, I worried. But no enemy was nigh.

Beneath and around the table swirled the waters of the dam which had miraculously filled, and I, languidly reclining in the tin tub we used for our Saturday night baths, drifted slowly past Sir Pask on his lofty platform. Roses of many hues and small brown onions floated beside me in the water. I wore only my black straw hat which was trimmed with blue roses.

Well, that was a change from dreams of Michael returning dead from Mount Gambier or nightmares of running vainly to save my little sister Molly, I thought, when I woke in the morning to the song of the magpies in the trees that ringed the farmhouse.

21

One day a hawker came to the farm. An Afghan chap with a horse and cart laden with wares.

Pask said the Afghans used to wear funny-looking jackets, little round hats, baggy trousers and sandals instead of boots in the old days, but now, after that shooting business at Broken Hill back in 1914, they wear ordinary clothes. They probably don't want to draw attention to themselves these days. A very nasty affair, that was. I still think of that young girl, Alma Cowie, her name was, who was on the picnic train the day the Afghans attacked and who was killed by those two mad men. I don't think anyone will ever forget that incident.

It just shows you that you can never take life for granted. There Alma was, all dressed up in her Sunday best, all white lace and frills and flounces, looking pretty as a picture, from the photos that they showed in *The Advertiser*, and sitting in an open train wagon, out for a Sunday school picnic, with her picnic luncheon packed, and half of the people of Broken Hill on the train too, and two insane Afghans who wanted to do their bit towards the war in Turkey came along with an ice cream cart and shot her dead.

I think there were a few other people killed as well as Alma, but it was the newspaper photos of that young girl that upset me. Such a pretty young thing she was. Dead for no good reason. People ought to leave their hatred and their silly ideas behind in their own country if they want to come to Australia. You just don't expect violence and hatred like that in this country. Those were the only shots fired in anger on Australian soil during the Great War.

So the Afghans wear ordinary clothes these days to fit in better. They seem a peaceable lot now. They still carry merchandise around the countryside and sell it. I haven't seen any selling ice cream, though.

Pask had pointed this particular chap out to me once when we were on the way to the town, and said he was an itinerant merchant. So I wasn't really worried when I saw him. Anyway, I knew Pask was working close to the house that day.

I knew it wasn't very nice of me to feel apprehensive about the Afghan just because he was an Arab, because after all the sheik in Rudolph Valentino's movie was an Arab. It was a bit different to seeing one on the silver screen, though. But of course Rudolph Valentino was really Italian or American, I'm not sure which. He just pretended to be an Arab for the film.

And the Afghans have done their bit over the years for Australia, when you think about it. I remember Michael telling me how they carry supplies right through the outback with their camels. Michael said that they opened up the country, carrying supplies to the navvies when the telegraph line was taken up to Alice Springs, and now they're carrying the sleepers for that new railway that's being built to the Alice. Michael said the train to Alice Springs should be running next year, 1929, and that it will be called the Ghan after the Afghans. Mick said the plan is to take it all the way to Darwin one day. Personally I don't think it will ever reach Alice Springs. I expect the whole thing is just one of Mick's daydreams.

This Afghan didn't have a camel and he wasn't carrying railway sleepers. He halted his horse and cart, jumped down and uncovered the wares he had laid out in the back of the cart.

Pask came out of the barn when he heard the cart arrive, and the children, who still hadn't started school yet, looked up from their lessons and ran outside. I followed them out into the yard to see what was happening.

The trader had brought blankets and rugs and saucepans, dishes and kitchen implements, and bolts of cloth in various colours. There was vanilla essence and tea, sugar and scissors and knives. Most of what he was selling was the sort of stuff that you could get from the general store in Orroroo, but it somehow seemed exciting to see the goods brought to our door.

The children began to finger some cheap toys that the man showed them, but Pascal told them to stop that at once.

'You don't need rubbish like that.'

I saw the disappointment in Annie's eyes. All she had to play with was that old rag doll in its dirty dress. Come to think of it, Annie's own clothes were getting shabby now, and much too tight. She was filling out nicely since she'd had some decent food to eat.

Bob was growing too. I would swear he was taller than he was when I first came to Orroroo. Funny kid, that Bob. Even though he sat with me to do his sums and his reading, he was always tense. I despaired of ever really reaching him.

A few months ago, I had resolved to ignore him, but now I felt sorry for this motherless boy and I wished that I could at least be his friend if not his Auntie. I couldn't hope for affection, but I would have liked acceptance. I wondered what I could do to show him that I cared about him.

'How much for this material?' I asked the hawker. I was looking at some blue cotton. The colour reminded me of the blue roses the lady on the train had shown me.

The man named a price and Pascal said it was too dear.

'What do you want that stuff for, anyway, Mrs W?'

'Annie needs a new dress and Bob could use a shirt or two.'

Pascal named the price he would pay, and the hawker said a slightly higher one. I was astounded. I had never seen people haggle like that. I had always gone into a shop and paid what ever was written on the price tag. People didn't haggle in John Martin's or David Jones's shops back home. Eventually agreement was reached, the money paid and the goods handed over.

'That's how it's done out here, Mrs W,' said Pascall, 'Hawkers expect that sort of thing. Makes their day, having a bit of a haggle. It's how they do business.'

He lifted the bolt of material from the cart, carried it in to the kitchen and dropped it onto the table. 'That sewing machine hasn't been used for a long time. It'll need oiling and sorting out. I'll fix it tonight. This colour's a bit unusual.'

I cut out a frock for Annie and a couple of shirts for Bob. The machine was old and noisy but the treadle worked well and when the kids woke in the morning and found their new clothes hanging on the chair by their beds, they were astounded. Annie acted as if all her Christmases had come at once.

Even Bob grinned and said, 'Thanks, Auntie Rose.'

There was a bit of material left over, so I made a new dress for Annie's rag doll and then, on impulse, I fashioned some roses from the off cuts. Blue roses like the ones I had worn on my hat in my dream. I pinned them on my black straw hat. It looked a bit garish, but this was Orroroo after all, not London, Paris or Rome.

I wished that Ada Jenkins, the lady from the train, could see my hat now. I wondered how she was, up in Hawker. I might write another letter to her, when I get time, I thought. She hadn't answered my last one, but it might have gone astray. Unless something had happened. Had Ada resented my advice on how to look after her dropsy, or had she succumbed to her bad heart? Or was it possible she couldn't read and write?

22

Every morning when the two roosters that lived with our hens out in the yard woke me with their commotion, I would get out of bed, throw on some warm clothes, find my boots and go out to milk the cow. I always avoided getting too close to the sparring birds. I didn't like the way those two roosters crowed and strutted. They were trying to outdo each other at showing off to the females. I had already seen minor scuffles in the dust of the yard.

It never pays to have two cocks in a hen house. There would be big trouble soon. I warned Pascal about it.

'I'll get round to giving the old bugger the chop one of these days,' he said. And went out to chase a sheep.

He was mulesing the young sheep. Mulesing involved using a sharp knife to cut the folds of flesh with the wool on it away from around the backside of the sheep. I had watched it once, and hated it. The poor sheep struggled and bleated in agony and bled copiously. Pascal slapped a bit of warm tar on the wound, hit the sheep on the backside, and sent it on its way. He said mulesing was a necessary evil. It was for the sheep's own good and was something you had to do for merino sheep.

'The blowflies are attracted by the dags hanging on the wool. They lay their eggs around the sheep's bums and the maggots burrow into the folds of flesh and eat their way into the poor animals' backsides,' Pask explained. 'You don't never want to see a flyblown sheep. Break your heart, that would.'

Each morning Annie went out to get the eggs. They were good layers, those chooks. Soon, I thought, I would let a couple of the hens sit on their eggs rather than take them all away.

Annie would enjoy seeing the little chicks running about, I thought. It would be a bit of fun for her. Bob enjoyed the mulesing, cruel little devil that he was, and Annie should have the pleasure of watching little chickens grow up. Girls liked that sort of thing.

It would be better if the eggs were fertilised by the young rooster rather than the old one, though. You got stronger chicks then. More of them survived. It was the genetics again, I supposed. The CSRI would know all about it, I expected.

I must get onto Pascal to kill the old rooster. Maybe when he had finished with the mulesing. Bob, eager to learn all the aspects of sheep farming, was helping his father. I suspected the little wretch enjoyed the process. Come to think of it, Bob was always eager to take part in the slaughter of a sheep when we needed meat, too.

I heard shrieks from the yard. The old rooster was chasing Annie, his red feathers shining, the long ones in his tail standing erect and his head with its savage beak extended towards her bare, bleeding legs.

The hens were raising a ruckus but most of the noise was coming from Annie, who screamed and ran, still clutching the egg basket, although the brown broken eggshells with their contents scrambled in the dust left a trail on the ground behind her.

I grabbed the tea towel and ran out in to the yard. I flapped the towel at the bird. He rose into the air and flew towards me. I beat at him with the rag. I pulled Annie away with the other hand.

'You rotten bastard!' I yelled. 'I'll have you in the stew pot tonight. Just you wait. You won't be cock of the bloody roost any more.'

I marched with the tear-streaked Annie down to the mustering yard where Pascal and Bob were slicing into the rear ends of the distressed young sheep. I averted my eyes from the blood and gore and tried not to hear their agonised bleating.

'Put that bloody knife down, Pascal,' I yelled. 'Leave those poor animals alone and come up to the yard and do your duty.'

Pascal seemed amused at my fury. 'What's Annie done now, Mrs W? Spilled the milk or burned the stew? If she needs a belting, you can give it to her. Go right ahead. You've got my permission.'

'It's not what she's done, it's what's been done to her. Look at her legs. All scratched and torn. It's your rotten old rooster. It's attacked her. Nearly killed her. Now you get back up to the house and cut its head off before it murders us all in our beds. Now!'

I had never shouted at a man like that before. In fact, I had never spoken to anyone like that. Not Mick, not even Mr Andrews when I wanted Mick's coffin opened. Not even to the insurance man when he said there was no money. But it worked.

Pascal put down the mulesing knife, wiped his hands on his pants and strode back to the house. Bob ran along beside him, eager to be part of the action, and Annie and I followed. She hid behind me until Bob dived for the bird. He rolled on the ground with the effort, but he caught the rooster and laid it on the chopping block.

The old rooster struggled, but Pascal swiftly chopped off his head. The blood spurted towards Bob, who laughed hysterically and jumped out of the way. The headless chook ran around the yard for a bit with the kids chasing it and laughing until the bird collapsed in a small heap.

'Heartless pair you are,' I told the children, but I was glad to see the creature dead. He wouldn't be attacking Annie again.

I hung the carcass on the clothes line to bleed and then I plunged him into boiling water to loosen the feathers. I pulled out the guts. Together Annie and I sat on the step outside the kitchen door and plucked the limp body. Little feathers rose from the bucket in which we put them and chased each other about the yard. It was always windy at Orroroo.

The dead rooster didn't look as big, now that he was dead, as he had been when alive. I've often noticed that people seem smaller when dead, too. I wonder whether a soul increases the size of a creature. Do animals have souls, though?

As he lay in my lap while Annie and I plucked him, it was hard to believe the bird could have terrorised anyone. She thought it was a great joke when I tied the tail feathers together and made a feather duster. She always did the dusting after that.

The broth I made from that rooster was wonderful. Everyone had second helpings.

'I would have killed the old bugger weeks ago if I knew you could make soup like that out of him, Mrs W,' grinned Pask.

23

On most Friday afternoons, we went into Orroroo for supplies. There had been no rain for a couple of weeks, and Pask was planning the shearing. He needed to get some sort of chemical to drench the sheep before they were shorn. The way he dosed those animals, I resolved that if I ever got back to Adelaide I would only ever eat beef or pork. Heaven knows what those chemicals were doing to our guts when we ate a sheep that Pask had killed. But probably the people who farm cows and pigs dose them too.

Pask said we might as well get some more flour and sugar and tea, and maybe some sultanas, raisins and spices and suchlike while we were there. I knew he was thinking of fruit cakes. But the main reason we were going to town was to hear the latest news. Pask was desperate to know about the latest feat of aviation.

All the way in he talked about Smithy's flight. To listen to the man, you would have thought that Pask himself had captained the first flight across the Pacific. I knew that all he had ever done was drive a horse and cart, but that didn't stop him from being an expert on all things aeronautical. Bob listened, enthralled. Annie and I were bored by it all. The conversation reminded me of Michael talking about trains. Perhaps only males were interested in technology.

'We've had planes here in Orroroo, you know, Mrs W,' Pask was saying. 'The first one landed on 11 February 1921. So I've seen a plane or two, apart from those ones that used to buzz about over the trenches in France, but that's nothing like that flight that Smithy just made.'

Captain Kingsford Smith and Mr Ulm, his relief pilot, had been due to arrive in Sydney yesterday. Pask wanted to hear whether their flight across the Pacific had been successful. People in the town would be bound to have heard the news about Smithy on the radio.

Pask did not own a radio. Even if he had one, he could not have used it. The electricity had not been extended out as far as his property, although Pask had hopes that it would come out that far in the near future. He was a great believer in the future and all the benefits it would confer.

I had less faith. I have never put my trust in technology, especially where transport is concerned. Look at that disaster in Sydney in November last year when the mail steamer struck that ferry boat, and more than sixty people were killed. Travelling too fast did that. I prefer to keep my feet on the ground. It's safer that way.

Trams are all right, of course, and I had coped with travelling in the hired car at Michael's funeral and on the train to Orroroo, but that was as far as I intended to go with motorised transport. The idea of sitting in a seat in a flimsy contraption that went through the clouds and over the water made me feel quite ill. I knew it was a very long way from England to Australia. I'd seen it on a map.

'Smithy and Ulm have flown all the way across the Pacific,' Pask said with relish. 'You have to hand it to them. They've got real guts. You wouldn't think it was possible. There's a bloke called Captain Lyon who's the navigator. Now that's a man who knows how to read a map. And they kept in touch all the way with radio. A chap called Warner did that. Look how many of them there were in that one plane! The whole thing is amazing. It's going to change the world, you mark my words, Mrs W.'

'Yes, but do you really think it's going to make any difference to people like us, Pask? I mean, who could afford to fly in a aeroplane even if they wanted to do it? And why would you want to anyway? What's the hurry to get from one place to another?'

I heard Bob groan from the back of the cart, but I wasn't about to stop because of his opinion.

'I felt quite sick when the train coming up here from Adelaide went fast,' I said. 'A plane would go even faster. I think it would be terrifying to be up in the air with the birds, travelling at the sort of speed aeroplanes go. I admire Captain Kingsford Smith and his friends, but I can't see what use it all is. You might as well think of flying to the moon.'

'Well, I want to fly in an aeroplane,' said Bob. 'Just because some old people don't like the idea doesn't mean it won't happen. I want to go in a train and a car and a boat too, some day. It would be great to ride in a car.'

'I've been in a car and I didn't think much of it,' I said, remembering Michael's funeral. 'Cars are more uncomfortable than a horse and cart. They rattle and shake and make nasty noises. At least you know where you are with a horse. And horses don't cost as much to feed either. They can eat grass. And you get manure from them.'

'You don't feed cars,' Bob said contemptuously.

'They have to be fed petrol,' said Pask. 'And yes, cars are more expensive to run than horses. So are aeroplanes. But it's the way of the future.'

He turned to look at Bob and Annie and then looked back at me and nodded gravely. 'Mrs W,' he continued, 'I bet these kids will travel in cars and aeroplanes one day. Or if they don't, their kids will.'

He reined in the horse as we approached the town. 'There's a new era coming, and we have to be ready for it. Things change. For example, look how wide the main street of Orroroo is. That was because they used to use bullock wagons and there had to be a lot of room to turn them around in. Bullocks can't manoeuvre as easily as horses and carts can. But we don't need that much space any more because since the train line has come up here we've moved on. The whole world is going to change in the next ten or twenty years, just mark my words.'

He drew the cart up to the general store and we climbed out. He tied the horse to the hitching rail. I reached into the cart for my basket.

'What's going on over there?' Pask said.

A small group of people had clustered around a very small, dark-skinned child with startlingly blonde hair. The girl was shrieking at the top of her voice. I couldn't understand her words, but I could tell that she was absolutely distraught. I have never seen a kiddie so hysterical. You would have thought they were going to skin her alive.

Two men were trying to drag her into a motor car, but the girl clung to the veranda post outside the general store with all her strength. A couple of the women in the crowd were remonstrating with the men, but you could see the women were intimidated by the men, who wore an air of authority that fitted them as well as their brown suits and their carefully brushed hats did. They looked like government flunkies, all bluff and bluster. They reminded me of an inspector of schools I once saw when I was picking up Mary from St Josephs, there to check that the nuns were following the government curriculum.

'It's the law,' one of the nuns had whispered to me. 'All the schools have to toe the line. Woe betide us if we upset the government inspector of schools. They could close us down.'

That inspector scared hell out of those poor nuns. I remember that even Mother Superior was bowing and scraping to the fellow, and she was a tough old biddy. These two men had that same officious air about them. I felt like knocking their fedora hats into the horse manure in the gutter.

'You wouldn't think a kiddie could be that strong,' one of the male onlookers told Pask. 'Those two blokes have caught a wild cat there.'

'How long before they belt her one and chuck her in the back of that car, do you reckon?' asked another.

Horrified, I turned to Pask. 'What's happening?' I asked.

'That'll be one of them Abo kids that they take down to Quorn,' said Pascal. 'The Protector of Aborigines says if the kiddies have got white blood in them, and quite a few of them do these days, they're better off in the institution there. Colebrook, it's called. They used to take them to Oodnadatta until a couple of years ago, but then they decided it was too easy for the kids to get away and see their relatives unless they moved them further away, so now they take them to Quorn.'

'That's right, Pask,' said one of the men. 'It was May 1927 they started putting them into Colebrook. They've got people there who look after them and teach them the sort of stuff they're capable of learning. You can't put kids like that in an ordinary school. They would never fit in.'

'The only way those young savages are going to learn anything is if they go to Colebrook,' agreed another one. 'It's for their own good. Look at that kiddie's blonde hair. She's got white blood. She has to be taken away.'

'But she's crying. She's really upset. She wants her mum,' said one of the women.

I recognised her and walked over to her. 'Do you know what the little one's saying, Mrs Pitman?' I asked.

She shook her head. 'I can't understand what she's yelling but I'm sure it's her mother she's crying for. They can't just take her away like that, can they, Mrs Walsh?'

Another woman, Mrs Clements, who I had often had a chat with in the general store, joined in. 'And look, she's dirty and cold and so thin. No shoes either, in this weather. It's a disgrace, treating a kiddie like that.'

'Like I say, she'll be better off in Colebrook,' said her husband. 'They've got these sisters, these Evangelical Missionaries, there. They look after the kids, teach them English and everything. Eventually the kiddies get jobs working for rich people, cleaning their houses, that sort of thing.'

I knew the sort of job he was talking about. I had cleaned rich people's houses when my dad got sick and lost his job. I had to leave school to work and earn money to help my parents out. And I had hated every moment of it.

I pushed through the crowd and went up to the man who seemed to be in charge. He gave me a filthy look. You could see he was not going to let an interfering busybody muck him about.

'Where is this child's mother?' I demanded. 'Look at her, she needs a hot bath and a good feed and some warm clothes. Can't you see she's shivering?'

'She'll get all those things at Quorn, missus,' the man snapped.

'How far is it to Quorn from here? Pask, how far is it to Quorn?'

'It's a fair distance. Not so far if you've got a car like that, I suppose. But it'll take a while to get there,' replied Pask, a faint smile playing about his mouth as he observed my mounting anger.

'So it's going to take a while to get there, and this little girl is cold and upset and probably hungry.' I turned back to the government man. 'What are you going to do about her in the meantime? Are you going to buy her some food and some warm clothes at least? You're standing in front of the shops here.'

'I'm not going to buy anything, missus. I'm paid to transport the brats, not feed them. This bloody kid's run away once already. What

I might do is tie her up so she can't run away again. She thinks she's going back to her mother but she's got another think coming.'

'And so have you!' I shouted. 'This is no way to treat any child. Pask, I want you to take me and this kiddie back home so I can bath her and feed her and dress her in something more suitable. Right now!' I glared at the two men again. 'Then, I suppose, we will have to allow these monsters to take her to Quorn, but not before then.'

'Geez, your missus has got a temper on her, mate,' said one of the officials. 'How far out do you live?'

'Not that far. About an hour by horse and cart. Less than that with your car, though. Well, if that's how it has to be, that's how it has to be.' Pask turned to me and asked meekly, 'Can we get the flour and stuff first, Mrs W?'

I noticed that Pascal had not denied that I was his missus. I also saw that Annie was stifling nervous giggles as she stood on the edge of the crowd. Bob, however, was gazing at the little stranger with what looked like disgust in his eyes.

'We'll follow you out to your place and your missus can feed the kid if that's what she wants, but then we're off to Quorn,' said the man.

I had won a small victory.

'Get the flour and stuff for the fruit cake,' I ordered Pask. 'And the chemicals. The little girl sits in our cart, though, with Bob and Annie. I don't trust these blokes not to take off as soon as I let them out of my sight.'

'Your kids might catch something,' the man warned. 'These Abo kids have got scabies something awful, and nits. And if she jumps out and gets away, it'll be on your head, not mine.'

'You better keep a good eye on her, missus,' said his companion, 'or the Protector will be after you, too.'

I glared at him.

'Don't look at me like that. I'm just doing my job,' he protested.

'She's not sitting next to me,' yelled Bob. 'I'm not catching her Aboriginal diseases. She stinks. I've seen kids like her when I used to go to school, before my Mum died. There was a camp not far from the school. I know what Abos are like. I'm not having nothing to do with her.'

'Shut your mouth, Bob, or you'll feel the back of my hand,' snapped his father. 'If your Auntie Rose says the kid's coming with us, the kid's coming with us and there's no two ways about it.'

'You've done the right thing there, Mrs Walsh,' said Mrs Clements. 'You showed those ruffians a thing or two.'

Mrs Pitman agreed. 'I reckon no one has ever given those fellows a piece of their mind like that before. Arrogant blokes, it'll do them good. I don't suppose you've got time for a cup of tea?'

'Not this time,' I said, taking hold of the little girl's arm. It was so cold and so thin. She looked to be about the same age as Annie, but she was so little. 'But next Friday I'll make sure that I do.'

'I'll get the supplies, Mrs W,' said Pask, heading for the shops. 'Oh, by the way, have you blokes heard how Smithy got on? Has the plane landed yet? Are they safe?'

We loaded the provisions. Bob groaned as he climbed up and sat on the seat. I noticed that he positioned himself on the other side of the cart so that Annie was in the middle and he was as far away from the Aboriginal child as he could get. From that position, he glared at the little girl, who appeared so surprised at her change in fortune that she didn't notice.

We took the little girl back to the homestead. The government men followed slowly behind our horse and cart. Bob sat backwards in the cart so he could watch the progress of the car.

Annie was more interested in the child, and spent the time unsuccessfully trying to coax a smile out of her new friend. 'There's a blanket here, Auntie Rose,' she said. 'It's the one Dad puts over Dobbin, but it's clean and it would keep the wind off of her. Do you think we should put it around her? She's shivering.'

Back at the house, I set the tin tub in front of the wood stove and filled it with hot water. I tried to undress the child, but she screamed blue murder as if I was going to drown her.

'There's almost as much water in her eyes as there is in the tub,' Annie said. 'And it's no wonder, if those men have taken her away from her mum.'

'I know, love,' I said.

Annie was right. This child had been torn from everything she knew and loved and she had no idea what these people intended to do with her. The men who had stolen her from her mother might believe she would be better off in an institution than in the place from which they had removed her, but I was sure there would be no joy for the kiddie where she was going. It was evil to cause a child such pain and sorrow. And I could do nothing to prevent it.

I shivered, although it was warm by the wood stove. I gave myself a shake. This would not do. I had to do whatever I could for the lost little girl. There wasn't much time to help her.

'You get in and have a splash, Annie. Show her it's fun. Then she might want to have a go.'

Annie stripped off her little frock and got into the hot water. Soon the Aboriginal child became interested and dipped her hand, then her toes, into the water. While the children played and splashed in the water, I found some warm clothes that Annie had outgrown.

Pascal and the two men who were to take the girl to Quorn had gone out to look at the barn. I knew that Pascal kept his beer supply there.

I disapprove of heavy drinking. I didn't like it when Michael had his whiskey binges, although I will admit Mick was never violent to me. When he was drunk he just sat and stared at the walls. I think he was seeing the trenches on the Somme and his dead mates, because sometimes he muttered the names of men I knew had died there beside him. Sometimes the tears would run down his cheeks but if you asked what was wrong he shook his head and said he was all right. He just had a touch of conjunctivitis.

Although I don't like drunkenness, I have never supported the Women's Christian Temperance Movement either. Mrs Williams is a member of the WCT and her poor husband isn't even allowed a beer on a hot day.

The WCT ladies' motto is Lips That Touch Liquor Shall Never Touch Mine. I wouldn't have thought that even Mr Williams would've wanted to touch Mrs Williams's lips, but there's no accounting for tastes. I do believe that a bit of a drink is good for a man. A beer or two might even mellow those officious government bastards, soften their hearts a bit.

I suspected that they would be a little while, so I heated some mutton stew up and by the time they returned the children were all sitting at the table eating. Bob sat at the end of the table and glared at our visitor, who was now clad in Annie's cast-off skirt and jumper and thick socks and some boots that Annie had outgrown, as she devoured the stew from the bowl I had put in front of her.

'She's got no table manners, either,' Bob muttered.

'Neither have you, Bob,' said Annie. 'Mum was always telling you not to talk with your mouth full. You're still doing it.'

'Well, she can't talk at all,' retorted Bob. 'Even with her mouth empty. At least not properly. I can't understand her and neither can you. You're acting as if you do, but you're just a girl, too, so you don't count. You can't fool me. This kid probably wouldn't say anything worth hearing even if she could talk.'

'Bob, you are not saying anything worth hearing either,' I snapped. I had lost all patience with him. 'The little girl may not understand what you're saying, but she can understand the way you're saying it. How would you feel if you'd lost your mum like she has?'

'I have lost my mum!' shouted Bob, flinging his spoon down on the table and standing up. 'And now you've come in and taken over and you're throwing your weight around and running everyone's lives and acting like you own the place.'

He ran towards the door, paused and glared at me. 'You've got Annie eating out of your hand and I've seen the way Dad looks at you. You think you're bloody clever, don't you? You think you can have Mum's house and Mum's things and even Mum's husband. And now you're bringing Abos into the house too. A bloody Abo that's getting a ride in a car!'

He choked back a sob, and I remembered that he had said he wanted a ride in a car. I had a sudden mad idea that perhaps the government men might be persuaded to take Bob to Quorn and leave the little girl here. I shook my head. Pask would never agree to that. A pity, really.

'You're just a bloody intruder, that's what you are,' Bob yelled. 'Just like your nigger! We managed all right before you came and we'll manage all right again when you go back to Adelaide! And you can't go soon enough for me.'

He ran out of the door, almost colliding with Pask and the two men on their way in. Pask tried to catch his son, but Bob eluded him and escaped. Pask, standing by the door, watched Bob run across the yard and into the shed. He shook his head slowly. I knew he had heard at least some of the boy's outburst, but I wasn't sure how much of it. I thought he hadn't quite believed the scene he had just witnessed. I didn't believe it either.

I stood by the table blinking back tears. I had known Bob didn't like me, but I had no idea of the depths of his resentment for me. And what was that about taking his mother's husband away? Where had he got that idea from? I admit I had felt the occasional tingle when Pask touched me. I did like it when he smiled at me, and I enjoyed our time spent on the bench watching the sun go down, but nothing had happened between us. The boy was mad.

'We've been having a bit of a talk out in the shed, missus,' said one the men, choosing to ignore the altercation he had interrupted. Perhaps he was used to that sort of thing in his line of work. He sat himself down in the chair that Bob had vacated and looked at the empty bowl Bob had left on the table.

I didn't know his name and I didn't want to know it, but I handed him a bowl of stew because he looked hungry. We had plenty to go round.

'Pask says you're upset about the kiddie being taken away from her mum,' he continued between slurps. 'She's going to be better off where she's going. We can't leave a child in the kind of conditions she was living in. Not a kiddie with a bit of white blood, anyway. And you can see the white in her. Look at that fair hair.'

'Yes, we have to take her to Quorn,' said the other chap, sitting down and reaching for a bowl and a spoon. 'We found her in what they call Perceived Harmful Surroundings, so it was our duty to remove her.'

'It is never right to take a child away from her mother,' I said.

The words caught in my throat as I remembered what Michael and I had done to Mary when we discovered that she was pregnant. We had locked her in the back bedroom, kept her out of sight of the neighbours, imprisoned her for the term of her pregnancy. We told everyone that Mary had rheumatic fever and must stay in bed. She was contagious. That kept them away. Even Mrs Williams. I had worn a small cushion at first around my belly, then a bigger and bigger one, until the night that Mary went into labour and I delivered her baby.

Mary had demanded to see her baby when it was born although I told her it was better that she didn't.

'No!' Mary had screamed. She leaped out of the bed then, even though she had just given birth and was still bleeding and hurting, and she snatched the baby from me. You could tell by the way she grabbed that baby she had no idea how to hold a child or care for a child. Not a clue. How could she, when she was only a child herself? There was no way I could permit Mary to get anywhere near a newborn baby. I just couldn't let it happen. It takes practice to raise children. She would have killed the poor little mite with her ignorance.

But I still recall how Mary clung to Amy, baptising her with her tears, and how she begged Michael and me to let her keep her child. Or if she could not acknowledge that she was its mother, if she had to pretend for the sake of decency, in order to stop people gossiping, that the baby was mine, to be allowed to live in the same house with her child and watch her grow. Just to be near the little one.

'I can be her sister if I can't be her mother. But don't send me away from her. I can't live without her. She's my whole life. I didn't know it until I saw her. I'll die if I can't see her.'

We kept Mary in that room for a week with the windows shut so the neighbours wouldn't hear her howling. She was locked in there until we felt it was safe for her to travel. I put cabbage leaves on her breasts to stop the milk coming in, and I fed Amy from a bottle. We kept the door locked so Mary couldn't grab the baby and run away. Michael spent a lot of time talking to her. He said it was best if he spoke to her and set her right.

At times I heard her voice raised but he managed to calm her down. He wasn't known as Walsh the Silver-tongued for nothing.

Once, I swear I heard her shriek, 'If you don't let me keep my baby I'll tell Mum everything.'

I've always wondered what it was that she wanted to tell me. I should have insisted on hearing what she had to say. But Michael said

I must stay out of her room, that he would deal with her ravings. He told me that Mary was demented. He said it was due to the pain of childbirth, that some women were driven mad by labour pains, and that Mary was saying dreadful untrue things that would only upset me. It wasn't right that I, her mother, should hear the sort of language that the girl was using. Mary would regret her words later when her sanity returned.

Now that Michael was gone, perhaps I could ask Mary what it was she wanted to tell me. She hadn't seemed demented when she stayed with us after Michael's funeral. She had seemed perfectly sensible and sane. Perhaps Fred's love and support had cured her insanity. It did seem peculiar that Mary should have gone mad after just one birth. I've had five children and I never went mad.

Mary hadn't raved when we took her to the railway station and put her on the train with a one-way ticket to Mount Gambier. She seemed resigned to her fate. She had sobbed, but that was understandable, poor little mite.

Michael had friends who would meet her at the other end, give her a roof over her head and find her a job. It was her chance for a new life without anyone knowing about her dishonour and her sin. It was the right thing, the honourable thing to do.

We said she must never come back to Norwood, back to Adelaide, again. She had no parents, no family and, above all, no baby. We would not accept the shame of it all. The baby was better off with us. It would be brought up in a loving home.

I dolloped stew into Pask's bowl, and then I scraped the bottom of the saucepan and filled the dark little girl's dish again.

Was our home a Place of Perceived Harmful Surroundings, I wondered? What irrevocable harm had we done to Mary? How could she ever forgive us? I would never have ever forgiven that sort of treatment. I'm not the forgiving kind. Thank God Mary survived. Thank God she has turned out all right. Thank God I have her back.

I put the teapot in the middle of the table and set out the cups and the milk and sugar. I poured tea into the sugar basin. Pask looked at me, took charge of the pot and handed the cups around.

These men were using the same rationale that Michael and I

had used, I thought. I sat down and put my hands over my eyes and wondered how many crimes are committed against innocent children with no voices and no one to defend them.

The government man was still talking. I hadn't heard most his reasoning, but it probably wasn't worth hearing anyway. I looked at the dark-eyed child, who was rubbing her full belly. But a full belly doesn't replace a lost family.

'You must take her back to her mother,' I implored. 'Her mother will be frantic. She must be thinking she'll never see her daughter again.'

'That's probably true. But you can't change the past and you can't change the present. All you can change is the future, and none of us know what the future holds. Maybe she'll grow up and find her mother again. But probably she won't want to. She won't speak the same lingo as her mother does after a few years with the sisters, so she won't be able to talk to her mum even if she does find her.'

His mate nodded his agreement. 'These kids tend to lose their culture when you put a whole pile of them from different tribes together. It's the government policy. They assimilate better that way.'

'Have you ever heard the song "Galway Bay"?' I asked him. 'I'll sing it to you. Just the bit that I think fits the situation.'

Pask and the other men looked a bit alarmed as I broke into song. Annie and the Aboriginal child watched in amusement.

> 'The strangers came and tried to teach us their ways,
> They blamed us too, for being what we are,
> But they might as well go try to catch a moonbeam,
> Or light a penny candle from a star.'

'I don't think she's ever heard that song, Auntie Rose,' said Annie, looking at her friend.

'It's a nice song, Mrs W, but what's it got to do with anything?' asked Pask.

'It occurs to me that the English invaded Ireland in much the same way as they invaded Australia, and that they're treating the people here just as they did my people back home,' I said.

'I'm not English,' protested the government official.

'No, but the laws you're enforcing are English,' I said. 'Or if the laws aren't, the reasoning behind them is.'

'We make our own laws in Australia now,' interjected the other man. 'We've got Federation and everything.'

'Laws are laws,' said the official, reaching for his hat. 'And we have to enforce them.' He patted my arm patronisingly. 'The kiddie's got a full belly, and she's got some warm clothes, so she's better off now than when you first saw her, missus. I reckon we'll all just have to live with the rest of it. You've done what you think is right and now I have to do what I think is right. And we can't ask the kiddie because she doesn't speak English.'

Annie and the little dark girl had moved while we were talking. They were now sitting on the floor in front of the wood stove, basking in its warmth. Annie had brought out her rag doll and was showing it to the girl, who seemed fascinated by it. When the man went to pull the little stranger to her feet to take her away, the child quickly passed the doll back to Annie.

Annie shook her head and put it in her new friend's arms. 'I reckon you need her more than I do,' she said.

The child said something unintelligible. She shook her head, smiled suddenly showing very white teeth, wiped away the tears that had begun to roll down her cheeks again, and thrust the doll back in Annie's hands.

We watched as the men lifted their small prisoner into their car. They drove off leaving a cloud of dust which lingered in the air like a white wraith, like a half-remembered song, or like the memories that I had tried for ten years to forget.

24

I was down in the dumps for quite a few days after that. I tried not to show it, but they all sensed it. Annie did her best to cheer me up. Bob was chastened by the thrashing he had received from Pask out in the shed after the visitors had left. I think he was also embarrassed by his outburst and was more polite to me for a while. Both children suddenly became very enthusiastic about their lessons, and insisted that I listen to them read, that I check their times tables and look at their writing exercises.

I took care not spend time alone with Pask or to look in his direction too often if Bob was in the room, or to share too many jokes or confidences. I didn't want to upset the boy if I could help it. There was no need to add to the tense atmosphere that prevailed in the house.

Pask took me on one side when the children were out of the room and asked if I was angry with him. 'Did you think I should have done more about that little black girl?' he asked.

'I know there was nothing we could have done, Pask,' I said. 'I'm just upset about the system that lets things like that happen. Maybe things will be different in a few years' time, like you were saying the other day.'

The children took me for walks around the property and showed me things I had seen a hundred times before although it was really getting too cold to be outdoors much. Pask was predicting more rain. He had high hopes of the new dam filling soon.

None of us spoke of the little Aboriginal girl, but I felt the thought of her lingered in everyone's mind.

'We did try to help her,' said Annie at last, trying to lift the teapot.

'I know, dear. But sometimes everything we do goes wrong. Put that teapot down, love. It's too heavy for you. Get the knitting needles out and I'll teach you how to knit. We could make you a new jumper.'

I kept wondering how the Aboriginal girl was faring at Quorn and how her mother was coping with her grief. And I wondered how on earth Mary had managed when she was exiled to Mount Gambier at the age of barely fifteen, just a week after childbirth. I had never been to Mount Gambier but Michael said it was cold there. Had the people she had boarded with given her warm pullovers to wear? Had she cried herself to sleep every night?

These were things I could never ask her, any more than I could ask, after all these years, who was the boy who had fathered Amy. I had given up my right to ask those questions when I had sent her away. It was difficult for a mother and daughter, separated for years, to ever recapture what was lost. It might be impossible. Like the Aboriginal child and her mother, Mary and I no longer fully spoke the same language. People are changed by the experiences they live through, and different places alter the way you think.

You can't change the past or the future, the Protector of Aborigines man had said. But you could change the present. And if you did do something about the present, then you must change the future. It stood to reason. If I had not come to Orroroo, my family might have been thrown out on the street, declared bankrupt for not paying the council rates and the other bills. And if I had not come to Orroroo, what would have happened to Annie and Bob and Pask?

But what would happen to them when I went back to my own family, as go back I must, some day? Was Bob right, that they had been all right before I came and they would be all right again when I left? They hadn't looked all right to me when I arrived. I felt that they had benefited by my presence, even if Bob didn't share my opinion.

It was no good worrying about it now. I would just take one day at a time. That was another of my mother's sayings. It probably made as much sense as the one about cleaning the oven.

'I know what would cheer Auntie Rose up,' said Annie. 'Why don't we take her to see the Poem before it really starts raining? We won't be able to get in there once the ground's wet and the creek's full, but right now would be a perfect time.'

Pask scratched his head. 'Yes, why not? The shearers are still working on Carmichael's property and they can't come until next week, the sheep are already mustered in the top paddock, and the dam is finished. I reckon we could spare a day to have a look at the Poem.'

'We have to do it before we go back to school,' said Annie, 'because we won't have time afterwards. We ought to see if it's still there.'

'Of course it's still there,' said Bob scornfully. 'That Poem will be there forever. Even after we're all dead. I bet one day people will drive a car to see it. I don't think Auntie Rose can walk that far, though. She's a bit too old and a bit too fat to be able to climb around that track.'

'We can help her,' Annie insisted. 'We can have a picnic, can't we, Dad?'

I was intrigued. The only poems I had ever encountered were on the pages of a book, and there was no climbing or walking involved in inspecting them.

'Where is this poem?' I asked. 'What's it about?'

'You'll see tomorrow,' said Pask with a grin. 'It's one of Orroroo's best-kept secrets.'

The next day we all climbed into the cart and Pask shook the reins lightly. The horse headed off towards Orroroo. Perhaps the Poem was in the institute building in the main street, I thought. But why, then, had the children insisted I pack a picnic lunch and why had Annie told me to wear my stoutest boots and my oldest clothes?

We tied the horse to a tree and Bob ran ahead down a narrow path beside the creek. Annie took my hand and Pask followed behind us.

'Look, Auntie Rose, there's some old carvings here,' Annie said. She pointed to a rock face which had been engraved with circles.

'What on earth is that?' I asked Pask. 'Is this the Poem?'

'Well, it could be a poem,' said Pask. 'No one knows what it means. That little Aboriginal girl might have been able to tell us, but then she couldn't speak English, could she?' He ran his hand over the rock. 'Feel how warm it is,' he invited me.

'It feels as if it's alive,' I said.

'I've heard it's really old. The people who carved it are all dead. I doubt that the present-day Aboriginals would know what it says, not that there's many of them left here now. It must have been something pretty important for them to have spent so much time carving it, though. But the Poem we want to see is quite a long way from here. We've got a fair old walk ahead of us, Mrs W.'

I stood and watched the light play over the rock face. The meaning had vanished, just as the people who had carved it had vanished. And those few people who might be able to understand it had been driven away from here, away from their own land and culture, forced to assimilate into an acceptable way of life by the government. These strange carvings would soon be eroded and gone, just as the language of the little black girl would be lost to her next generation.

I traced the circles on the rock face with my finger. 'Pask, where did the people go to, the people who did this carving?'

'I don't really know,' said Pask, turning back. 'Those carvings were here when I was a boy. I remember how we kids used to sit on hessian bags and slide down that rock. Most of the old people were gone by then. There were big problems with them spearing sheep when my dad was a boy.'

'Well, there would have been less kangaroos for them to hunt if the sheep were eating the grass. But what did they get for the land your people took?'

'I don't reckon they got anything. The blacks just wandered away off up north when the farmers came in and brought the sheep. They'd have had to have kept moving north, though, because then the graziers started moving their cattle up there, too.'

'So it was a lot like Ireland,' I said. 'Except when the English moved us Irish out of our homes, some of us went to America and some of us came to Australia. We were looking for a last refuge, somewhere safe. But the black people didn't have any Australia to go to. They were already here.'

'Come on, Auntie Rose,' said Annie, tugging at my hand. 'We have to follow Bob or he'll go and jump in the reservoir.'

We scrambled down the path beside the creek, always hearing Bob's whooping and shouting just ahead of us, but never catching up with him. Pask, burdened with the picnic basket, still managed to give me a welcome hand over the most difficult places.

I began to believe Bob's judgement that I was too old and too fat to undertake a trek of this nature. I was worn out when we arrived at a place where we could see the blue water of the reservoir stretched out before us. Down by the water's edge, Bob was extending a bare foot into the water.

'Bob, you get back up here this minute!' shouted Pask. 'Otherwise you're going to catch a belting like none you've ever had in your life. You just come back now!'

Bob climbed back up the track, scattering a small flock of sheep which were grazing on the lush grass by the water. This, I thought, looked more like the green pastures that the Lord was meant to lead his flocks through.

I wondered if the land beside the railway track I had come through on the way to Orroroo had been transformed by the little rain we had had. Then I wondered if it was raining back in Adelaide and that made me think of Amy and the boys, and I wondered what they would think of this countryside.

'We'll have the picnic here and then go on to the Poem,' said Pask.

'You mean it's further on than this?' I asked in dismay. I really had had enough walking for one day, and we still had to make the return journey.

'It'll be worth the effort, Mrs W,' Pask assured me. 'It'll bring tears to your eyes. It's a real bit of history, that Poem is. The only real history we've got in Orroroo, so you have to see it. It must have taken Mr McDonald ages to carve that stone. It's pretty impressive.'

'That other carving was pretty impressive too,' I said, but Pask didn't seem to hear me.

My feet hurt, my back ached and I was exhausted by the time we reached the place where the Poem was carved on a sheet of rock above the creek. I had to admit it was a pretty place, a secluded glade above the creek. I sank down on a fallen tree trunk and looked about me.

There was the Poem, carved into a black rock, the words white against the slate. There was a lot of it. Mr McDonald must have spent ages on it. I wondered whether he had been inspired in his effort by the carvings done by the earlier, vanished people.

'Did you ever slide down this rock on a hessian bag?' I asked.

Pask shook his head. 'We wouldn't have dared. The whole community would have had our hides.'

He explained that Mr McDonald carved it because he wanted to celebrate the friendship he shared with the other lads and the secluded place by the creek where they spent so much time. 'McDonald invented some sort of bicycle, and he went to America patent his invention. He carved the first bit of the Poem before he went. When he came back he found out that the other two chaps had died. That's when he carved the second part of the Poem as a memorial to them as well as a sort of celebration of the good times they had here. What do you think of it?'

Annie and Bob stood expectant beside him.

'It's a beautiful place,' I said. I looked at bit more closely at the words on the rock face. Suddenly I had a vision of Moses scrambling down the side of Sinai with the tablets of the Commandments in his arms. Words of truth written in stone.

'It must have taken him hours to do all this work,' said Bob. 'He must have written it on a bit of paper first because he couldn't just make it up as he went along. He might have made a mistake otherwise.'

'You would have to be sure that every word was right,' I agreed. 'And it's a lovely poem. Do you understand his message?'

'Yes,' said Bob indignantly. 'I can read.'

'Actually, he's saying the same as that old carving on the other side of the creek.' I said.

'Bullshit,' said Bob. 'You can read Abo now, can you?'

'Both carvings say, "I was here and I loved this place. Please look after it when I am gone." What do you think Mr McDonald and his friends did here, apart from write poems?'

'I think they listened to the birds and picked flowers,' said Annie. 'And I reckon they ate grapes, and spat out the seeds, because look at that grapevine there. It must have grown from the seeds.' She pointed to a vine that was tangled among the gum trees.

'I reckon they caught yabbies in the creek and cooked them and smoked cigarettes they had pinched from their dads,' said Bob. 'And yarned about what they were going to do when they grew up. Only not all of them did grow up, did they?'

Bob looked both defiant and wistful, and I shuddered as I realised that his expression reminded me of the expression on the face of my brother, Danny, in that photo with his ostrich-plume-bedecked slouch hat that hangs over my mantle-piece back home. But Bob would never go to war, there could never be war again, the League of Nations would not allow it.

'I think they wondered how long it would take them to get back,' said Pask. 'And if the horse would be still be waiting for them when they got back to the beginning of the track.'

'No, they didn't,' said Bob. 'They rode bicycles, remember?'

'Whatever,' said Pask. 'Come on, everyone, we'd better get going. Mrs W looks as if she's ready for a cup of tea.'

25

'There's going to be a dance at Pekina!' announced Pask triumphantly as he tossed the mail he had collected from the letter box on the edge of the property. 'I was talking to Ian Anderson, the postie, and he told me. Now, that will get you out of the doldrums, won't it, Mrs W?'

'When?' asked Annie.

'Do we get to go too?' asked Bob, giving me a furtive, jealous glance.

I could see he was worried that his father might intend to take me out on the town and leave him and Annie at home. Perhaps he was worried about what we might get up to unless he was there as chaperon.

'It's next week. Next Saturday night. And yes, we're all going. I told Ian to get our tickets from Pat McGuiness. It's a basket supper, so I reckon you could take some of them beaut scones you make, Mrs W, or maybe even a fruit cake. Bloody nice, that fruit cake is.'

'What will I wear?' I asked.

'What's wrong with that hat with the blue roses on it? I reckon that'll knock them Irish for six. It's not a real dress-up affair, everyone just wears the best they've got. I might clean me boots, though.'

I got the hat with the blue roses on it down from the shelf. Was this a hat for every occasion? I asked myself. It would have to be, because it was the only hat I had.

What would the people at Pekina be like? Pask had said Pekina was called Little Ireland. Would people would be suspicious of me, a lone widow woman, living with a single man? I had become friendly with the ladies in Orroroo now, but these folk were Irish Catholics, and their morals were stricter than the Protestants of Orroroo. Or would they judge me as stuck-up because I came from Adelaide?

Maybe I should make some sort of excuse and stay at home in

the farmhouse and let Pask and the children go alone. I could have a headache on the night, or develop a stomach problem. But perhaps it would rain and the roads would be impassable and none of us would be able to go.

You are being silly, Rose, I told myself. I was acting like Pask's cocky. Sometimes the bird didn't want to come out of her cage and had to be coaxed out for her exercise. It might do me good to see some other people. And if they were unpleasant, I could sit in a corner and talk to Annie. Pask wasn't a very social sort of man, anyway. He would probably want to sit in a corner as well. Probably this Pat McGuiness was the only person he knew at Pekina.

I made a fruit cake and packed it carefully in a kero tin that Pask had cut in halves for the purpose.

We took turns to have baths in the tin tub in front of the wood stove. I brushed Pask's suit, which I suspected had not been worn since Elsie's funeral, and probably only worn for his wedding before that. Bob shone everyone's boots. He even shone mine, which surprised me.

We donned thick coats on top of our best clothes. The wind was blowing cold. It felt as if it was blowing straight from the South Pole. We had plenty of tarpaulin to cover us as we sat on the cart, in case the rain Pask was hoping for began.

'It snows sometimes at Peterborough,' said Annie, rubbing her hands together to warm them. 'I've never seen it, but a girl I know in Orroroo says her auntie saw it once. Mum used to talk about winter in England when it snowed. I'd love to see snow.'

'I'll just settle for a bit of rain,' said Pask, 'but not until after the shearers have been and gone.'

A farmer is never happy, I thought.

'But what will the sheep do without their wool if it rains after they've been shorn?' I asked.

Bob looked at me scornfully. 'They'll just have to grow some more, won't they?'

Pekina is a smaller settlement than Orroroo, but it has a big Catholic church and a presbytery for the priests. Next door there was a convent for the nuns who taught at the school. The Pekina pub was conveniently situated opposite the church.

'My mate Tim sneaks out of church and hides in the pub to get out of listening to the sermon,' confided Pask as he halted the horse and cart outside the institute building. 'Although Father Travers isn't a bad sort of bloke.'

We could hear the music even before we got out of the cart. There were two fiddles and an accordion, a couple of flutes and a drum. The hall was packed with revellers and Pask seemed to know everyone, because he strode into the hall, shook hands all round and began to introduce me to people. He slapped men on the back and was slapped on his back in return. There were a lot of 'G'days' said. Pask was affable and a bit loud, friendly and popular. I was amazed. This was not the Pask I knew.

I looked for Ada Jenkins, the lady I had met on the train, the one who had told me about the blue roses and her health problems, but she was not there. Probably her dropsy was worse. Of course she wasn't Irish, and I didn't think she was Catholic, but Pask had said almost everyone from miles around would be there.

Pask had told me that Black Rock was not far from Pekina, and Ada had said she lived near Black Rock. I had hoped and half expected her to see her there. But a dance is probably not very interesting to a woman with bad legs and dropsy. I was a bit disappointed not to see her, and I made up my mind to find a corner and sit in it.

'This is Mrs W,' Pask announced to a couple who had come to greet him. 'She's staying with us right now. She's marvellous with the kiddies. They worship the ground she walks on. She's Mrs Rose Walsh if you want to be formal. Mrs W, this is my old mate, Tim O'Halloran, and this is his wife Anastasia.'

Pask thrust the half kero tin at Mrs O'Halloran. 'Anastasia, I know your fruit cake is famous, but you haven't tried this yet. You've got a new rival in the district as far as fruit cake goes. You'll have to ask Mrs W for the recipe. Where are we depositing the goodies?'

Anastasia took the cake from Pask. I was a bit worried that she might resent me for being a competitor at fruit cake baking, but she smiled at me and shook my hand.

'We'll have to get together, Rose. You must be sick of only hearing sheep talk day in and day out. Get Pask to bring you over for the day soon.'

A tall man with red hair who wore a dark suit, a smile and a clerical collar approached.

'Father Travers, this is Rose Walsh, Pask's housekeeper,' said Anastasia.

A priest at last, I thought.

'Father, could I have a quick word with you?' I asked, grabbing his arm urgently.

'So you ate a mutton chop by accident on a Friday, did you?' said the priest softly.

We were standing in the kitchen at the back of the hall.

'Well, I can't give you absolution here and now, because this isn't a confessional and I'm not wearing my vestments, but if that's the worst thing you've done at Orroroo, I wouldn't think the Lord will be too concerned about your soul. Say three Hail Marys and come and see me in the church some time when there's a bit less celebration happening, my child.'

Flattered at being called 'my child' by a man half my age, and feeling as if I had had my soul soaked in bleach and hung out to dry in a warm breeze, I thanked the good priest and joined Pask, who was deep in conversation with a short, stout man.

'Mrs W, this is Angus McKenzie. Angus is a Scot but the Irish don't mind. They let me in too, as you will have noticed, and I'm not even halfway Irish. Not sure what I am really, and don't much care.'

I had never seen him so effusive. I wondered if he'd had a swig of something before we had left home, but I hadn't smelled any alcohol on his breath when he had helped me into the cart, and Pask, like me, drank very little anyway.

His mood was contagious. My spirits lifted when he asked me to do him the honour of a dance. I hoped Bob wasn't watching. But Bob, too, was infected by the ambience and he was talking animatedly to some lads his own age.

The band did not seem to have heard of that awful jazz that obsesses Charlie. They played the lovely old dance music that Michael and I had danced to when we were courting. They were playing my favourite, 'The Pride of Erin', when Pask and I got up to dance. As we moved around the floor, I caught a glimpse of Bob and Annie sitting on a bale of straw eating some greasy-looking cream cake.

'I hope they won't get upset tummies from that stuff,' I said to Pask. 'You can't trust cream unless you've milked the cow yourself.'

'Can't hear you, Mrs W. What did you say? This music is a bit loud and I'm a bit deaf.'

'Probably from chasing sheep,' I said. 'They're noisy buggers.' I moved a bit closer and repeated what I had said.

He grinned. 'Those kids'll be all right. Got cast-iron guts. You should have seen the stuff they had to eat before you came up here. I'm not much of a cook and my sister's worse.' He twirled me around and drew me close again. 'They're not bad kiddies. A lot happier now that you're here, Mrs W. Don't pay too much attention to anything Bob says. He's a bit hot-headed, but I reckon he's learned his lesson. Spare the rod and spoil the child, as they say.'

We danced a military two step and then a progressive waltz. There's nothing like a progressive waltz to get you acquainted with every other dancer on the floor. Well, with the male dancers, anyway.

I was amazed that I could still remember the steps, and even more amazed to discover that Pask was a surprisingly good dancer. He was very light on his feet, and never stepped on my toes once. Michael liked to dance, but after a few rounds with him my feet were usually sore and aching.

We were thirsty and I asked for a lemonade, but Pask pressed a beer on me.

'Do you the world of good, that will,' he insisted.

He had a couple of beers himself. Then we danced again. Then we had another drink. I told myself that I had better be careful about the alcohol. Michael was the drinker in our house; I only ever had the occasional sip. Mrs Williams would have been horrified if she saw me now. But one or two drinks couldn't do any harm, surely.

'I think we have had enough alcohol, Pask,' I suggested. 'We've got a long way to go home.'

'I wouldn't worry about it, Mrs W. The horse is only drinking water and he knows the way in the dark.'

I told myself that when I'd had some supper I'd feel a little less dizzy, but supper didn't make much difference. I must be coming down with something, I decided. I hoped that the Spanish flu hadn't started up again. Perhaps my dizziness was just because of all that unaccustomed whirling and twirling, or perhaps my newly shriven soul was reacting to a lack of sin.

Of course, I was not as young as I used to be, I reminded myself. I hadn't danced like this since Michael and I were courting. And it was warm in the institute building with all those people crammed in to it.

After supper, an entertainment was announced. We all sat on hard chairs around the edge of the hall and listened to a tenor give a quite reasonable rendition of 'Danny Boy' and then of 'Trotting to the Fair'. Not as good as my Charlie's voice, but pretty good nonetheless.

Next, a group of girls came out dressed in traditional dress just like the outfit Mary used to wear for her Irish dancing. I remembered the hours I had spent embroidering shamrocks on that stiff green tunic she wore for performances in the church hall. The girls did a jig, their arms stiff down the sides of their bodies and their legs moving like the needles on sewing machines.

It brought tears to my eyes to remember the days when Mary danced. She won a couple of medals for it. Michael and I were so proud of her.

Pask noticed my expression and asked what was wrong, and I told him that I was thinking of my daughter, so he went and got me another drink to cheer me up. I didn't really want it, but he insisted and I didn't want to insult him.

'And now, ladies and gentlemen, we will call for volunteers from the floor. Is there anyone out there who can give us a genuine Irish song?'

'Auntie Rose knows an Irish song. She knows 'Phil the Fluter's Ball'. She sings it when she's scrubbing the floors.'

Oh, Annie, Annie, what have you done? I thought to myself.

'Well, so you have hidden talents, Mrs W,' said Pask, propelling me out the middle of the floor. 'I knew about that Galway Bay song, but I didn't know there were other ones too.'

'It'll be grand to hear the "Fluter's Ball" again. I haven't heard it sung since I left Dublin,' said the beaming MC.

Father Travers, standing beside him, nodded agreement.

I protested, but to no avail. There was an anticipatory clapping and stamping of feet from the audience. Pask thrust another glass into my hand and I had a quick sip. I gasped as the fluid burned my throat. I held the glass up to the light. Amber-coloured, and there was no mistaking the flavour. This was whiskey. Irish whiskey. I remembered the taste from when Michael used to drink it. He used to call it the water of life. I have never been a whiskey drinker. I had only tried the stuff once out of curiosity, wanting to know why Mick enjoyed it so much. Afterwards I still didn't understand why he liked it. More fire than flavour, really. I passed the glass back to Pask. This was going too far.

I began to sing, my voice trembling a little, but I seemed to improve as I went on. Or maybe it was the fumes of the whiskey…

> 'Have you heard of Phil the Fluter from the town of Ballymuck –
> Well, the times were going hard for him, in fact the man was broke –
> So he just sent out a notice to his neighbours one and all
> As how he'd like their company that evening at a ball.'

By the time I reached the refrain, all of the audience were singing with me, and a few of them were jigging about the floor. The fiddler and the chap on the flute had taken up the melody. The applause afterwards was thunderous.

Pask came and got me and hugged me. I was so amazed I couldn't speak. Annie was jumping up and down and telling her friends that this was her very own Auntie Rose. Even Bob was applauding. He didn't seem to have noticed his father hugging me. Perhaps he was confused by all the general excitement. I certainly was. Over the noise, I heard Tim O'Halloran tell Pask that I was a fine figure of a woman.

Eventually, everyone sat down again and listened to a lament played on the Irish bagpipes. Worse than the Scotch bagpipes, the Irish pipes are, for utter gloom. That's the Irish, I thought. Happy one moment, miserable the next. Maybe not just the Irish were like that. It might be a universal thing, something that defines humanity.

I remembered hearing Father Flaherty, back in the days when we all attended Mass every Sunday, once giving a sermon about what he called the Human Condition. He must have been in a philosophical mood that day. I remember how the priest contrasted life and death, hope and despair, light and darkness. He said it was a universal trait. At the time, I put it down to typical Flaherty blathering.

Maybe it was the alcohol, but tonight, in retrospect, I seemed to understand that long-ago sermon a bit better. I remember Michael often believed he could solve the problems of the world after he'd had a few drinks. I remember now that I knew the solution to everything that night, but the next day all I had was problems.

But the band struck up and we danced again. I looked for Bob and Annie and saw them asleep together on a bale of hay. Someone had draped a blanket over them.

'They're all right, Mrs W,' whispered Pask into my ear. 'I'll carry them out to the buggy and they'll sleep all the way home.'

I must have slept all the way home too. I do remember climbing into the cart, and I remember it was raining quite hard when we set out home, because I was concerned whether the children were properly covered with tarpaulin so that they would not catch their deaths of cold. Unfortunately I can't remember a lot of what happened after that.

The next morning I woke in my bed, clad only in my petticoat. I couldn't remember getting undressed although my clothes were neatly draped over my bedside chair.

Dimly I remember dreaming that Michael and I were making love, but in my dream it was the muscular hard body of Rudolph Valentino who arched high and thrust himself into me with more gusto than Michael had ever mustered. The memory of the dream made my body glow. It must have been because of the sheik's smouldering eyes, I thought. I had a vague recollection of receiving and giving more pleasure than I had ever experienced in Michael's arms. The sheik seemed to know what he was about more than my husband had done.

That was probably quite a sinful dream I just had, I thought, when I woke up. It was not the sort of dream a newly confessed woman should have. And there was a certain stickiness between my legs that was familiar and yet surely impossible.

I turned over and saw Pask's naked back showing above the blanket beside me.

He woke and grinned at me. 'Reckon we slept in, Mrs W. We'd both better hope that Bob's still asleep. I have to go out and chase a sheep or two. They'll be wondering where I am.'

26

My head throbbed, but I realised that if the sheep were wondering where Pask was, Daisy would be wondering even more where I was. A cow with a full udder doesn't take kindly to a tardy milkmaid. Not that I was exactly a maiden. I heated some water and had a quick wash before I headed out the cow shed. At least I was too old to get pregnant.

The cow had already made her own way to the milking stall and she looked at me accusingly.

'It's all right for you, Daisy,' I said. 'You didn't spend the night getting drunk with a lot of mad Irishmen. And a lecherous shepherd. And to think I used to imagine Mick had no morals. Talk about the pot calling the kettle black. An old widow woman like me! I have sinned grievously. Mea culpa, mea culpa, mea maxima culpa and all the rest of it. I should be ashamed of myself.'

But I wasn't. I felt absolutely shameless and I spent the day thinking about Pask and wondering if he was thinking about me. He came in as I was serving the porridge. Bob was seated at the table complaining that breakfast was late and the porridge lumpy.

'It looks all right to me,' said Pask, adding golden syrup to his serve. He grinned at me and gulped his breakfast down.

'This is the worst porridge I have ever seen,' insisted Bob.

I smiled sweetly at him, picked up the jar of golden syrup and poured it over Bob's head.

Pask sniggered, put down his spoon and stood up. 'I'll be off to see the sheep,' he said. 'You'd better wash your hair before you come out, Bob, or some ewe might lick the syrup off you. Mrs W, remind me later to tell you what Tim O'Halloran and his wife suggested we ought to do.'

'What sort of suggestion would that be?' I asked, but he had gone. I wondered if I dare suggest a repeat of last night's behaviour. Would Pask ask me to share his bed again tonight? It was a pity Bob had been up at breakfast time. I had been hoping he would sleep in that morning, as Annie had done.

I took lunch out to the shearing shed where Pask and Bob were setting up for the shearing. Bob watched us like a hawk circling its prey. Pask and I hardly exchanged two words under that steely gaze, although the weather seemed to be worrying Pask more than his son was. He kept looking up at the sky apprehensively.

I didn't remind him of Tim O'Halloran's suggestion, or make any suggestions myself. Pask was preoccupied and seemed exhausted when he sat down to eat. Even the children went to bed early, saying they felt cold, although the wood stove was heating the room. They were probably exhausted after their night out at Pekina, I thought.

That night Pask didn't even linger to read the Bible. 'G'night Mrs W,' he said, 'I'm real tired tonight. I reckon the rain's on its way. Don't know what's going to happen to the shearing.'

And he went off to his room alone. I went and read to Annie for a while and then I too went off to my bed. That night it rained heavily. I lay in my bed and listened to the rain drumming on the tin roof and I worried about the shearing and I wished I had been more aware of our lovemaking the previous night.

How sad to have an experience that you would like to remember, but you were in a condition when it happened that prevented you remembering it. Would Pask come to my bed again soon? And if so, how should I welcome him? Should I be coy? Should I be seductive? How would I do that? I had never really been seductive with my husband, and I wasn't sure I knew how to do that sort of thing. I don't think Mick would have been happy if I had tried. He always took the lead in our lovemaking.

Would Pask think me shameless if I invited him to join me in my bed or, perish the thought, if I went to his? I had no experience in this field, and no idea what to do in this situation. I racked my brains to think what would happen if this was a film.

Perhaps I should find my cotton paisley scarf and flick it about in a shameless manner. That was the sort of thing that English lady did in the Valentino film. Pask would probably think I was shooing flies or mosquitoes away.

I might unbutton the top buttons of my dress and display my breasts a little. But the weather was a bit too cold to do that at present, and my breasts did tend to sag somewhat. Pask would have noticed that already, though, as soon as my corsets came off last night. He knew I was no spring chicken after all.

But we arn't living in a film, and he's not Rudolph Valentino. We're not even lords and ladies in a poem by Tennyson. This is me, Rose Walsh, and I'm an elderly widow woman with all those children to support, and he's Pask the sheep farmer with two children aged six and ten years, and we are real people and this is Orroroo. And I think I am falling in love with him and I know I should not do this.

My husband is hardly cold in his grave, I admonished myself, even if he was a complete and utter bastard. I wondered idly if it was much colder in a grave than it would be when I had to get up to milk the cow in the morning.

I haven't waited a year as any decent woman would have done. And his wife hasn't been dead all that long either. But that's how I feel and that is what's happening. I can't help it. I want Pask to come to my bed and make mad passionate love even though I know it's very wrong, and Father Flaherty would excommunicate me for being so sinful, and Michael would murder me if they both knew what was going on, but Father Flaherty is a long way away and Michael and I have committed worse sins and kept worse secrets than this from Father Flaherty. I didn't want to tell this one to Father Travers. And Michael, thank God, is dead.

I shook my head. This was one sin compounding another possible or probable sin. Here I am committing mental adultery with Rudolph Valentino as well as actual adultery with Pask if Michael isn't really dead (but Michael is dead, Mr Andrews said he was dead and every one agreed with him, and I had seen the coffin lowered into the grave). And now here I was feeling glad that Mick was dead.

Wishing another person dead was probably almost as bad as killing them. At least I think it might be. There is that command 'Do not covert thy neighbour's goods' as well as 'Do not steal'. That had to mean that intent to sin was as bad as committing a sin.

Damn theology and damn everything. I'm alive and Pask is alive and life is short, and one night soon he will come to my bed again. And I hope and I pray that it will be very, very soon.

But if it rains and the shearing is ruined will Pask be able to afford to keep me at Orroroo? What if I have to go home just when I've really begun to want to stay here?

27

I'm not the jealous type. I have always maintained that I haven't got a jealous bone in my body. Even so, after spending that night with Pask in my bed I began to wonder what Pask's wife, Elsie, had been like. It was natural enough, I reasoned, to wonder about the woman who had been married to a man who had made love to you. I had been comparing Pask to Michael. Was Pask comparing me to his dead wife?

While Pask and Bob were out chasing sheep, and Annie worked quietly at her arithmetic, I drank tea and added up the sum of my knowledge about the woman I was supplanting.

I knew she was English and didn't take too well to the heat. She came either from Lancashire or Yorkshire, so she must have had a funny accent. I thought about the way the kiddies spoke and realised there was just a tinge of something exotic about their speech. Not quite enough twang to be authentically Australian.

Pask's wife must have been little and blonde like Annie. Bob was darker than his sister. He resembled his father, with big bones and big feet. You could see he would be tall when he grew up. You can tell how big a puppy will be by the size of its paws. Boys are the same. Annie, on the other hand, was different. She had a small delicate frame and flaxen hair and blue eyes. Now that I was washing her hair and brushing it, it shone in the sunlight. She was a pretty little thing, really. I had to watch her or she became sunburned easily. Bob, like Pask, could spend hours outside and never go red. So Annie must take after her mother.

I also knew Pask's wife's name was Elsie and that she had died of cancer. Cancer in the pancreas and the liver, Pask had said. My mother's cancer was in her womb. It had eaten her from the inside out.

Mum always said her cancer was a judgement from God because

she hadn't cared for her children well enough. She blamed herself because Molly had died as a baby, and then later she felt guilty because she hadn't stopped her sons from going to the Great War to fight for the English. I told her that was nonsense. Her cancer was just bad luck. Some people got it, and some didn't.

But my Mum had been sixty years old when she got cancer. Pask's poor Elsie must have been only thirty-five or forty. How she must have worried about her children and what would happen to them after her death. She would have died with their names on her lips.

It had torn my heart to leave my children, but I knew that I could get on a train and go back to them. Elsie left her children with the knowledge that she would never come back. Never to be able to help them when they were sad or sick, never be able to make sure they were not hungry or cold or lonely, that must have been more agony than the pain of the cancer.

Perhaps it had been Elsie's spirit lamenting in the trees that first night I spent at Orroroo.

It made you wonder what sort of God could do things like that to a family. And the priests say that God is a loving father. I looked over at Annie working at her lessons, and shook my head.

She looked up at me and smiled. 'Is everything all right, Auntie Rose? Am I taking too long to do this? Is there something you want me to do?'

'No, love, I'm just thinking about a few things. You finish your sums and go on with that geography, and when you finish we might bake a cake. One of those sultana cakes that your dad likes. Not the fruit cake this time. I've noticed he has a lot of wind lately. I'm just going to go and make your father's bed and tidy up his room.'

I went into Pask's room and looked at his narrow bed. I punched the mattress. It was very hard. He didn't seem to have a lot of blankets on the bed either. He must have been much more comfortable in the bed in my room where we had slept and presumably made passionate love the night before last. I wished I had not tasted that whiskey. Terrible stuff, whiskey. I might have had more memory of that night if I had stuck to the beer.

I straightened the sheets and plumped up the pillows. I decided that the furniture could stand a bit of dusting, so I went and got the feather duster that Annie was fond of using and flicked it over the dressing table.

You would expect that a widower would keep a photo of his dead wife on the dressing table, but Pask's dressing table held only a copy of the *Stock Journal*, a comb for his rather sparse hair, and a tin of talc powder. A bit callous, really. A man should keep some remembrance of his wife. Would Michael have wanted to remember my face if I had died before he did?

I remembered guiltily how I had put Michael's photo in the shed at home. But there was a good reason for that, I reminded myself. It was all Michael's fault. Everything that had happened was Michael's fault. Including my sleeping with Pask.

If Michael hadn't died and left us insolvent, I would never have come to Orroroo and I wouldn't have sipped that whiskey and I would never have committed the sin of fornication. And I wouldn't be standing here wishing I could remember more about the sinning part of it right now.

Pask didn't even have a wedding photo in his room. Perhaps it was in an album in one of the drawers, an album that he might open from time to time to look at his wife's face and recall the past. He wasn't a brute, after all. He did have feelings. Quite a sensitive chap, really. At the Irish dance, people had been friendly to him, everyone had liked him. Perhaps Pask found it painful to look at his wife's photo and that was why it wasn't beside his bed. Or perhaps Bob was right, and he would rather look at me. Which would mean that he was a rather fickle person.

I opened the top drawer. Socks and underpants. The second drawer held singlets and some yellowed woollen long winter underclothing. Surely he must have a photo of Elsie. The kiddies would want to know what their mother looked like, especially when they grew up a bit. It was unfair to them if there was no photo of their mother in the house. Why was it not on display in the front room?

Not that anyone used the front room. It was little and poky and dark and contained only a couple of uncomfortable straight backed chairs and a sofa that sank in the middle and which smelled of mice. It was hot in summer and cold in winter. I kept out of that front room. It looked haunted, somehow. The kitchen was the centre of this household.

What had he done with all Elsie's belongings? Bob had accused me of using her things, but apart from a bit of crockery and the books in the cupboard there wasn't much of her stuff around the place. There was no silver, no pretty crockery, no fancy linen. She had only been dead for six months. Had he got rid of all her clothes already?

Perhaps he was so heartbroken he couldn't bear to keep anything that reminded him of her. If I could see her clothes I could get some idea of what sort of person she was. Did she wear the frilly, flouncy sort of dresses that I imagined an English girl from Yorkshire would wear? Was she slim like that lady whom Valentino had abducted on his horse or was she a bit on the plump side like me? Had Pask's mysterious sister, the one who didn't like Orroroo, taken all Elsie's belongings when she returned to wherever it was she lived? Was that why Bob resented women?

I opened the bottom drawer and there it was, lying on top of a green hand-knitted jumper that I had never seen Pask wear. Had Elsie knitted that jumper? If so, she had not made much of a job of it. Even without picking it up, I could see dropped stitches. Perhaps he kept it to remind him of her. Perhaps he was more sentimental than I had believed.

The photograph was of a young woman with luxuriant curls of blonde hair. Eyes that resembled Annie's eyes looked back at me from the portrait which lay on its woollen bed, next to some old shaving gear and some spare cartridges for Pask's rifle. I picked up the photo and studied it.

Elsie was pretty, in an English sort of way. Delicate and frail-looking. The sort of girl who would read Tennyson and Swift and Shakespeare and the Bible, and who would have looked elegant while she did it. Not the sort of person who would put her elbows on the table to prop herself up while she read.

Her elbows probably weren't red and her hands would not have been as work-worn as mine were, either. She would not have slurped her tea. I could imagine her sipping her Earl Grey tea delicately and nibbling at thin cucumber sandwiches without crusts. Pask was right;

he should never have brought a girl like that out here to this country. She didn't have the stamina for it. You could see that in the shape of her face, in the way her hair curled around her ears, in the hesitant smile she gave the photographer. Elsie belonged in a green and pleasant land, not in the hot, dry mid-north of South Australia.

Pask said Elsie liked history, but Orroroo had none to offer her. Looking at this photo, you could see Elsie needed to be amongst old stone buildings and the swirling mists of Britain where men played cricket on emerald grass, not in the harsh light of the Antipodes.

Like the white rosebush by the kitchen door, Elsie needed care and nurturing. Poor girl, she couldn't possibly adapt to life out here in the bush. But she probably would have got the cancer whether she had been in the town or in the country, in England or Australia. As with my poor mother, it was the luck of the draw.

But what I wanted to know was how did I compare with Elsie in the love department? And would Pask make comparisons? Did he really want me, a much older woman, after he had been married to this much younger, prettier girl? Was it just that I was available and she was no longer here?

Would any woman have done when he was desperate for sexual congress? Was he regretting what he had done in the heat of the moment? Even worse (and I beat my fist on his hard mattress when I thought about it), had he only made love to me because he was drunk and would it never happen again?

Shameless hussy that I was, I wanted it to happen again. More than want, I needed it to happen again. Every fibre of my being shouted that love was the reason for life. Forget faith, forget hope, let's just have the charity part of it. And not the anaemic 'love thy neighbour' sort of charity either.

I suddenly realised that it wasn't necessarily Pask I wanted, it was the sexual act. I wanted Pask because he was there, but if it had been another man, he would probably have done just as well. I had become some sort of female tomcat. Father Flaherty would definitely have excommunicated me for harbouring thoughts like these! Probably even the mild Father Travers would condemn me for my desires. And I had to admit, rightly so.

My body was crying out for the full-blown lust sort of love. Could I somehow get Pask drunk and lure him into my bed to repeat the episode, but this time with me sober and him inebriated? Was there any whiskey in the house and, if not, could I purchase some next time we went to Orroroo and could I lace his tea with it without him or Bob noticing? How could I go alone into the pub to buy the whiskey, though? It was not the sort of thing a lady would do.

I put the photo back and closed the drawer. I would have to wait and see what happened. I didn't want to rush into anything. If I was too forward, I might frighten him off and he might even decide that it was not a good idea to keep me here. He might decide that he would be better off without me at Orroroo. I wanted to stay just a bit longer. I couldn't lose him now that I had found him. I wanted him to make love to me again, and I wanted to be totally stone cold sober next time. I wanted to experience the whole thing, and not imagine it was Valentino or Michael or Lancelot of the lake.

And the kiddies needed me, too, I reasoned. They'd be very upset if their Auntie Rose went away. Even Bob, who might be glad to see the back of me, would certainly miss his three square meals a day if I wasn't there. I owed it to the kiddies not to rush matters. I owed it to Elsie's spirit to stay a bit longer and take care of her children.

Although what Elsie would think of the housekeeper sharing a bed with her husband didn't bear thinking about.

But most of all, I owed it to me. I deserved a bit of fun in my life after all the problems I'd had lately.

I should be more concerned about my own children, not thinking of Elsie's. I'd have to go back to Adelaide one day. Mary had written to say that she was expecting again. I'd soon be a grandmother once more.

But there'd be no harm in staying a bit longer at Orroroo. I had already committed the sin, if sin it was, and you can only be condemned to go to hell for eternity once.

Pask might not look like Valentino, but nevertheless I had been rushed off my feet, even if I couldn't remember much about it. It wasn't something that happened often to a woman of my age. This was something to be relished, something to be savoured.

Perhaps I should let nature take its course and just wait until Pask had the urge again. He wasn't a young man, when you thought about it. Younger than I was, but not really in his prime. Perhaps he needed a bit of rest between sexual encounters, a bit of time to recuperate.

Maybe when the moon was full, or when it was mating season for the sheep, or when the shearing was over, he might decide the time was ripe again for love. I would just have to sit tight and wait until then. And keep cooking. My mum always said the way to a man's heart was through his stomach. It might be time to make another fruit cake, even if it did play havoc with his bowels.

28

'That rain came at the wrong time. Now we can't start the shearing until the sheep dry out,' said Pask. 'The shearers won't touch wet sheep. So I reckon we'll take Tim O'Halloran up on his offer.'

'What was that?' I asked.

'You must remember that place that Tim was talking about at the Pekina dance the other night. Tim calls it Magnetic Hill. Some of the other blokes around here call it Bullshit Hill.'

'I don't remember anything about this at all, Pask,' I said, frowning with the effort to recollect the events of the Pekina dance night.

'Well, that might have been when you started feeling a bit crook, and Anastasia took you out the back for a bit of fresh air. Anyway, Tim's got one those Ford cars,' said Pask. 'A model T, he calls it.'

Bob interrupted his father. 'Why can't we get a Ford car?'

'Because we can't afford it. Tim's sons are grown-up and help him around the farm. When you are a bit bigger and can do a bit more work, maybe we'll get a car too.'

'That's not fair, Pask,' I said. 'Bob helps you a lot.'

'All right, Mrs W. I know he does his best. Well, maybe if we have a couple of good wool cheques and if the drought isn't too bad in the next couple of years, we might be able to think about a car.'

'When your ship comes in,' I said.

'Not many ships around here, Mrs W,' Pask grinned. 'It's a bit too far inland for that. Anyway, Tim said if we get out to his place early he'll take us out to Bull— I mean Magnetic Hill and show us something really strange.'

'Will we have a ride in the car?' demanded Bob. 'I really want to ride in Mr O'Halloran's car. You will ask him, Dad, won't you?'

*

Tim and Pask sat in the front of the car with Bob squeezed between them. I was glad he was in the front. I couldn't have put up with the way he was squirming with excitement. I half expected Pask to give him a clip in the ear, but Pask was doing his best to ignore the boy. Anastasia, Annie and I sat in the back.

'My daughter Mary wrote to me and said she's in the family way again,' I told Anastasia proudly. Pask and the kids had heard the news so often that every time I mentioned it they groaned. I was itching to tell someone else. 'We're hoping for a little girl this time. Every mother should have at least one daughter. Mary said in her letter that they'll call the baby Rose if it's a girl.'

'When my daughter was pregnant, we wanted to know ahead of time what it would be. That way you can knit pink things or blue things instead of all white,' said Anastasia. 'So we used her wedding ring on a cotton thread to predict whether it would be a boy or a girl, but it didn't work. The ring spun round and round, and we were absolutely certain the baby would be a girl, and then she went and had a boy.'

'It's just an old wives' tale, that business with the wedding ring. You can never really predict what a baby will be,' I said. 'I remember that I broke the spout of the teapot when I was expecting Charlie, and my husband Michael said I'd have a girl, but it wasn't. It was Charlie.'

'Just about here,' said Tim. 'I'll turn off the engine, put the brake on so it comes to a dead stop, then I'll take the brake off, and you'll see that the car will roll up that hill in front of us. Somehow it'll be dragged up the hill without the motor working.'

Pask was dubious. 'Have you tried it before?' he asked. 'It sounds a bit queer to me.'

'Yes, I did it last week. I did it twice because I didn't believe it the first time. It definitely does happen.'

'How did you find out about this, Mr O'Halloran?' asked Bob.

'Old Steve Finlay came up here, and had to stop for a call of nature,' said Tim, turning off the ignition. 'He got out of the car and when he'd finished, he turned around and saw his car going up the hill. He had to chase after it. He said he hadn't bothered to put the brake on because he didn't think the car would move because it was at the bottom of one hill and at the start of another. But it went straight up, all on its own. He thought he was seeing things. He says the devil pulled it up the hill. You can't get him to come within cooee of this place now.'

'I don't like it here,' said Anastasia. 'I reckon Steve Finlay's right. I reckon the devil lives here. Those hills over there are a funny shape. There's something about this place that doesn't feel right.'

She gave a little scream and clutched the seat in front of her as the stationary car began slowly to move of its own volition up the hill. Tim gripped the steering wheel tightly, Bob whooped in delight, and I grabbed Annie as she squealed in terror.

After travelling a short distance, the car slowed and stopped at the beginning of the next hill.

Tim put the brake on and looked at Pask. 'So what do you think causes it?'

Pask shook his head in disbelief. He got out of the car and looked up the road, and then down the road behind us. He gazed at the surrounding low hills where the green flush of new grass was breaking through the grey stubble. Then he got back into the car and shook his head again. 'I've seen it and I still don't believe it,' Pask said. 'Can we have another go at it?'

Tim turned the car around and went back down the hill. Anastasia and I clutched at the side of the vehicle in case some demonic force should snatch us through the open windows.

Tim halted at the bottom of the hill and looked around at everyone. 'Right,' he said. 'Do you all want to try it again? I've done it a few times now, and I still don't understand how it happens.'

'Yes! Yes, Mr O'Halloran. Do it again, do it again!' yelled Bob.

'I'm getting out, Tim,' said Anastasia. 'And Rose is getting out with me.'

'Let me out too,' said Annie, scrambling over me to get at the door. 'I don't like riding in a carriage without a horse anyway.'

'Do you think there are leprechauns in this country, Rose?' Anastasia asked me as we watched the car ascend the hill with no visible means of propulsion. 'Could it be leprechauns pulling the car up the hill like that?'

'No, leprechauns wouldn't be happy in Australia,' I said. 'It's not green enough. And the snakes would worry them. I don't think leprechauns would be interested in cars anyway. They specialise in pots of gold, don't they?'

'Oh, I forgot about the snakes,' said Anastasia. 'Of course, there are no snakes in Ireland.'

I smiled. It must be nice to live in a country with no snakes. I was always worried when I went out to the lavatory that a snake might be curled up just inside the door. The wood heap, that was another place where they lurked.

'To tell the truth,' I told Anastasia, 'I'm not sure there are leprechauns in Ireland, although my mother swore they were there. But there is something peculiar about this place. I can feel it.'

We both gazed up the hill. The car had completed its journey and had halted in the very same place it had stopped the first time. Tim and Pask were standing outside the vehicle talking animatedly. Bob was on his knees, looking carefully at the wheels, caressing the tyres. Perhaps he was praying, if Bob believed in God, that his father would somehow become the owner of such a vehicle.

'Maybe it is magnetism,' I continued, 'as Pask and Tim were saying. The car's made of metal, so perhaps there is something in the ground that pulls it up to the top of the hill. Some rock or something up there.'

'It has to be something supernatural,' said Anastasia, looking around at the low hills that surrounded us. 'If it's not leprechauns, probably it's something to do with the old people who lived here before us. Maybe the Aboriginals put a spell on the place.'

'They did make those carvings down by the creek,' I said. 'Perhaps Orroroo is the centre of something special. I remember Michael read a book last year called *Ulysses*. I don't mean that old Greek story about the chap sailing around the Mediterranean Sea, this was a new one by an Irishman, so it must be true. The fellow who wrote it was called James Joyce.'

'I've never heard of him,' said Anastasia. 'But I don't think I've heard about the Greek fellow either.'

'The new book was a novel and it was banned in a lot of places. I think there was a lot of dirty stuff in it, and probably some anti-English bits, too. That was probably why it was banned. I don't know how Michael got hold of a copy. I didn't bother reading it. Even Michael said it was a strange book. But he said it talked about a special place called the Navel of the World. A place where the usual rules didn't apply and strange things could happen. Maybe Orroroo is one of those places.'

'Where was the navel place in the book?'

'The one in the book was in Dublin. Well, it would have to be Dublin because the writer was an Irishman. But maybe everyone thinks the place they live in is special and that their feelings can influence the way things happen.'

Annie was climbing over the fence and I called her back.

'There are probably snakes in that long grass, Annie. A place like this, there could be anything lurking.'

She came back and stood beside me, fidgeting. She was getting bored, I knew, but I also knew there would be no hurrying up the men, who were still engrossed in their discussion at the top of the hill. I turned to Anastasia.

'Dublin is special to Irish people, and Rome is special to Italians and Catholics, and Greece is special to Greeks. Even England must be special to English people. I suppose miracles could happen if enough people feel that way about a place. The power of thought or something.'

'So is this business with the car a miracle, then, Rose? But what's the difference in believing in leprechauns or magnetism or navel places or miracles, anyway? We ought to ask Father Travers about it.'

'I don't know. Maybe there is something important and unusual about Orroroo, some spiritual and magnetic force that pulls at people's souls. I don't know if the church would approve of that idea, though. Father Travers would probably say we shouldn't meddle in stuff we don't understand. Michael always said the church says that sort of thing to stop people thinking for themselves.'

'So did you believe everything that your Michael said?' Anastasia asked.

'I did when we were first married,' I said. 'But now I know that most of the time he lied to me. I'm still coming to terms with some of the lies he told.'

Anastasia sighed. 'That's how life is, Rose. Men are animals. I know Tim is a good man, but he went and bought that car without talking to me about it, even though he knew I don't like cars. I'm sure he'll have an accident and hit a tree or a cow and get hurt or killed driving it. Most of the time, men live their own lives and women just have to pick up the pieces.'

She looked at me. 'You've managed to survive without your Michael pretty well, though. Are you going to stay in Orroroo or will you go back to your family in Adelaide? Pask thinks very highly of you, you know. And you really feel there is something special about Orroroo?'

'I certainly didn't like the place at first,' I said. 'But something has happened since I've been here. I'm not sure whether I've changed, or Orroroo has changed. Yes, I do feel differently about Orroroo now.'

'I feel hungry,' said Annie. 'Is it nearly lunch time? Why are men so keen on cars? Are we going to your house to eat, Auntie Anastasia? How long are those men going to play silly games up on that hill?'

29

A letter came from Charlie. It was a much thicker packet than the usual missives he sent. The first document I opened was a letter from my son, saying that Mr Andrews had received a box from Mount Gambier with Michael's personal effects in it. The box had gone missing until now. Apparently it had been taken to the police station by the proprietor of the hotel where Michael usually stayed.

When Michael had died, the railway people had delivered his stuff to the hotel because that was where they always sent his luggage, and in all the confusion surrounding his death, it had been put in a back room and forgotten for a few months. Then the hotel had a bit of a clean out, found Michael's possessions, and sent them on the police station. Eventually, the police got around to contacting Mr Andrews, and in due course Mr Andrews brought it to our home in Norwood.

Charlie said the box contained his father's briefcase and hand luggage with shaving gear and the like. When the boys opened the briefcase, they had found a sealed stamped envelope addressed to me. It was probably nothing important. The family were all a bit worried about sending me a letter from beyond the grave, as it were, but they felt they had no option but to forward it. They hoped it would not upset me too much. But it was obvious that their father had intended me to read the letter.

Charlie regretted that he could not be there with me when I opened it. He knew it would be a shock, after all these months. He expected it was probably just a note telling me to pay bills or to buy a shirt for Dad at the sales.

I held the letter in my hands and saw that it was indeed Michael's writing. Why would he write to me from Mount Gambier? He was never gone more than a week. Why would he waste the cost of a stamp to write to me? He had never done that before, not in all the years he'd been going up and down from Adelaide. Perhaps he really had run off – perhaps I was right and it wasn't Mick in the coffin after all! He had run off with another woman and this was the letter breaking the news to me.

And if he was still alive, then I had committed adultery with Pask. And with every inch of my body I was longing to commit adultery with Pask again. It was not just a sin of commission, it was a sin of intent to commit it again. And again, and again, and again. The penance for that would be much more than three Hail Marys.

I put the letter in my room. I didn't want to have anyone around when I opened it. God alone knew what I would learn when I read it. I somehow got through the day, cooked and washed and put Annie to bed and read to her, said goodnight to Pask and Bob. I told them that I was tired and was having an early night for a change.

I tried not to appear hurried when I went to my room. Pask raised his eyebrows and put down the Bible (I noticed he was reading the Song of Solomon and that he seemed to be quite engrossed in it).

Bob shrugged and poured a cup of tea for himself and his father. 'She's been in a funny mood all day, Dad,' I heard him tell Pask. 'Ever since she opened that letter. Do you reckon she's planning to go home soon?'

I thought I detected a hopeful note in Bob's voice. I ignored them both and shut the door behind me. I had to know what Michael had written so long ago. Suddenly the past was more important than the present. This letter might bear news that would have important consequences for my future.

I put the candle down on the little bedside table, sat on the bed, and tore open the envelope.

'Dear Rose,' Michael wrote. 'You will never know how difficult it is for me to write this letter. My heart is breaking, as I know yours will be when you read what I am about to write.'

Bastard! I thought. He really has gone off with another woman. I knew it. I always knew it. That's what he wanted the insurance money for. To set up a new home with some floozie at Mount Gambier or Melbourne or maybe even Sydney.

And to think of the tears I'd shed because of him. I ought to rip this letter up and put it in the chamber pot and piss on it. That would show him what I thought of him and his letters. But I didn't do that, because I wanted to see what sort of excuses the mealy-mouthed bugger was going to make. I would read the letter first and destroy it afterwards.

I read on, my hands shaking so much I could hardly read the words on the page.

I am writing this letter because I finally got the courage to go to confession (I went to another priest because I couldn't bear to tell Father Flaherty what I had done). The priest said he couldn't absolve me until I have asked forgiveness from Mary and from you. I have sinned against God and I have sinned against Mary and I have sinned against you, too, my beloved Rose.'

'Yes, I agree with that bit about sinning, Michael, but if you think I'm going to forgive you, you've got another think coming,' I said aloud, trying to resist the urge to spit on the page, and forcing myself to look at the words Michael had written.

I have been having pains in my chest for months and the doctor says I have angina and may not live long, so I have to confess this now or burn in hell forever.

I am afraid, Rose, very afraid. I know you and the children have always put me on a pedestal and you all think I am brave because I went to the war. I do not deny that, but in this instance I have to admit I am a coward.

What you and I did to Mary was a terrible thing, but it is nothing compared to what I did to Mary and to you. I have betrayed your trust and I betrayed a father's duty.

When you were out at the Ladies Guild at the church one night, I drank more whiskey than I should have done, and I seduced, indeed I raped, our lovely daughter Mary.

It was rape, for although I used honeyed words to persuade her to my desire, she was a child, indeed she was my own child and so the sin was compounded. I HAVE COMMITTED THE SIN OF INCEST, ROSE! [Michael had written that bit in capitals and underlined it heavily.]

Mary was innocent, helpless and absolutely unable to defend herself.

Nor can I use the defence of drunkenness to defend my self for my actions. I chose to drink the whiskey, and therefore I must be responsible for what occurred when I was under its influence.

I am the father of Mary's baby. I am the destroyer of her innocence. I have sinned grievously, in thought, word and deed.

I began to shake uncontrollably when I read his words. I pulled the chamber pot out from under the bed because I felt the vomit rising in my throat. As I heaved and vomited my last cup of tea into the pot, the thought came to me that this could not possibly be true. Surely Michael must have written these disgusting words when he was drunk or mad or was having delusions of some kind.

I shuddered and vomited again. The whole idea was revolting. This must be a mistake or a lie. He could not have done this to Mary and to me. Something had to be wrong. Perhaps the letter was a forgery.

I put down the chamber pot, wiped my mouth with the edge of the bed sheet and looked at the handwriting again. This definitely was Michael's writing. That was the way he sloped his letters, and that was the distinctive way he wrote the letter 'I'. The page misted as my eyes filled with tears. This was not a forgery; this filth had been written by my dead husband. How had I lived with such an evil man for so many years and not seen what he was really like? I must have been a blind fool.

I wiped my eyes with the bed sheet, not knowing or caring if it was the same bit of cloth that I had used to wipe the vomit from my mouth. There was another page to read. Disgusting or not, I must finish this letter.

And then I allowed you to blame her for what I had done, I caused her to suffer exile and loneliness and prevented her from ever seeing her child again. My shame was greater than my compassion for my own daughter. I have no excuses. There can be no excuses for what I did.

She, poor child, has forgiven me. I will admit that I used all my powers of persuasion to beg her forgiveness.

I know the irreparable harm I have done. I pray that Mary can rise above the harm done to her. I do not know how she has managed to find forgiveness in her heart for me.

I pray that you can also forgive me. I write this letter to you because I cannot bear to look at your face and tell you these dreadful things. I am writing it on the train to Mount Gambier and I will post it when I arrive there.

You should get it on Thursday. If you can forgive me, phone me at the Mount Gambier Hotel on Friday night (remember, it is always cheaper to ring at night) and I will come back to you on the morning train on Saturday.

I know that death is close. The doctor told me that my heart will fail soon. I beg your pardon for what I have done so that I will not spend all eternity in the fires of hell.

If you cannot bear to see me again, and if I do not receive your phone call, I will throw myself into the Blue Lake and become a suicide, mortal sin though that is. It is better to die quickly than to suffer slowly. I know that I deserve hell for all that I have done.

Yours faithfully

Michael E Walsh.'

There was a postscript. What more could he find to write after penning this, I wondered.

PS If I am dead you will have found my bankbook. There is not much in it. I used the money to set Mary's husband up in his butcher shop. It was the least I could do. I hoped that would help ease Mary's heartache, give her a feeling of worth and of value if she knew she was the wife of a successful business man. Money cannot not heal the hurt or absolve my sin, but I hope it will make Mary's life more comfortable.

So that was one mystery solved, I thought. I couldn't see that any amount of money could salve the hurt Michael had caused, but if that was where his money had gone, it was the only decent thing he had ever done for his daughter. I saw indentations on the page, and realised that the postscript continued on the other side of the page. Michael always did like to have the last say. If he had thrown himself into the Blue Lake, the water would have gurgled with his last words as he sank below the waves.

There is another bankbook under the copper in the laundry with enough money in to see you through until the boys have finished their apprenticeships.

M.E.W.

I put the letter down. I was angry. I was astounded. I was confused. I was disgusted. So that was why Mary would never say who the father of her baby was. Poor, poor Mary. Of course I had heard of incest, I had read about poor little Saint Dymphna. I knew what men, even Irishmen, were capable of doing. But you never expected that sort of goings on to happen in your own family. Our home was probably the worst example of Perceived Harmful Surroundings in all of Australia. Except that I had not perceived what was going on under my own nose.

I beat at the pillow, wishing it was Michael's face. I was glad he was dead. I was happy to know that he had died without fulfilling the penance the priest had given him. I relished the thought that because he had not performed his penance, he was burning in hell at this very moment, even as I read his letter from beyond the grave. Father Flaherty had always been adamant on that point. No penance meant no absolution of sin, and therefore no hope of redemption.

Part of Michael's penance had been to obtain my forgiveness. I would not forgive Michael. I had not forgiven him while he lived, and I would never forgive him as long as I lived. I hope Mick despaired when the angina gripped his heart for that last time, knowing he would face his Saviour unforgiven, unshriven, and utterly without hope of salvation.

My poor, poor Mary. Her sad little heart had suffered more than Michael had with his pathetic angina. Mary had been tormented beyond human comprehension by her father's abuse and then by my rejection as well. How bravely Mary had borne her cross!

Why did I not realise what was happening? How could I have been so monumentally stupid? How much did her brothers know or suspect? Harry and Brian were old enough to see what was happening. They might be able to keep secrets, but why would they do that? Were they so afraid of Michael that they couldn't tell me what was happening to their sister?

Let's face it, my whole family had learnt deception early, partially as a means of self-protection from Michael. Often it was easier to hide the truth than to suffer the consequences. But surely Charlie and Joe would not hide something like this from me if they knew. But they were so young at the time, just little boys. They couldn't possibly have realised the awful truth. And Mary had kept the shameful secret for ten long years. Was she protecting herself, or her father?

Suddenly I realised that she was protecting me. She must have believed that I couldn't deal with the truth about my husband and my marriage, and therefore she had kept the truth from me. She was much stronger than I had ever thought possible. Strong and stubborn, that's my Mary.

The only decent thing that Michael had done was to finance Fred's shop. At least now I knew where the money had gone. Not that money would recompense Mary for the harm she had suffered.

And Amy. What of my little Amy? What effect would this have on her? Of course she must never know. It would be a terrible thing for her to learn the truth about her birth. How could she ever live with that knowledge? She had worshipped Michael. Thank God he had died before he could have his wicked way with her as well. Who knew what would have happened if he had lived? What else could have happened? Would he have ravished another innocent little girl?

But what effects would there be from the incest? Amy had a double dose of Michael's blood. There was that hereditary business to consider. They say incest can cause all sorts of things. Madness, for example. And Michael must have been mad to have done such a thing to Mary.

Come to think of it, his mother wasn't a very nice person either. My mother never liked her. Mum always said Moira Murphy was a nasty piece of work. Mum said Moira had ideas above her station, and that the whole family should go back to the bog they had crawled out of.

Mick's dad drank, even more than my dad did, although Mick's mum said it was only on special occasions. They had a lot of special occasions in that family. And I just can't get along with his sister, Bridget, and I can get along with most people. That whole family is tainted.

But Amy isn't mad. She is a lovely, gentle little thing. A bit too pliant perhaps. A little too anxious to please those around her. Just like Mary was most of the time, when she wasn't being a stubborn little devil. How had Michael done this to Mary? It had to be his accursed silver tongue, that voice that could bend people to his will, his devilish Irish charm and persuasion.

Was the girls' shared trait of wanting to please people a weakness that would later show up as insanity? But Mary and Amy have got my blood too, and I'm not mad. I'm as sane as the next person. I'm definitely not crazy. I will admit I was stupid not to have seen what was happening under my own nose, but stupid is not mad.

That heart problem, now; that was hereditary. The union man had mentioned that it was. I would have to take Amy to a doctor to check her heart when I got back home. I would have to go home soon. Pask or no Pask, I must go home. I must write to Mary and get her to have a medical check-up too, I decided.

And the boys, I mustn't forget the boys. They had Michael's blood, too. Thank God they had my blood to add some stability to them, mind and body. I know my father died of the dropsy, but that was probably because of his drinking. My grandparents had lived to a good age; they were both at least seventy years old when they died.

But I couldn't say anything about this other unspeakable business to Mary. If she wanted to talk about it, I would listen, but I couldn't be the one to bring it up. It was just all too horrible to be true.

Had I dreamed the whole thing? I looked at the letter in my hand. It was true.

'To hell with you, Michael,' I said aloud. 'I don't forgive you. I will never forgive you. I hope God Himself never forgives you. I hope you're burning in the fires of hell right now. In fact, I hope you're burning in the very deepest depths of hell where the sun never shines and never will shine. May you burn for all eternity! I hope the furnaces are blazing and your flesh is melting from your bones and that then it grows back and is burned off again.'

I blew my nose on the edge of the bed sheet, then continued berating my dead husband. 'I wish you'd jumped into the Blue Lake. That would have cooled your ardour.'

There was a gentle knock at the door.

'Mrs W, did I hear you say you wanted me to cool my ardour? If so, I could go and chase a sheep. Although it's raining out there and I would rather stay indoors with you if you don't mind.'

Pask wanted to come to my bed. I had forgotten about Pask. Could I tell him about the awful news I had just received? It would be so good to unburden myself, to tell another person of my agony, my sorrow. But what on earth would Pask think of me and of my family if I told him the family secrets? This was an unspeakable thing.

I could tell no one; I must bear this burden alone, as Mary had borne her burden alone at Mount Gambier. The shame of it all prevented me from talking about this to Pask or to anyone.

I bent and stuffed the letter beneath the chamber pot under the bed. It should be safe there. Pask didn't use chamber pots. It's easier for a man. They can wee anywhere they like. Out the window, or on the lemon tree. It does a lemon tree a lot of good to have a man wee on it. It's the urea in the wee, I've heard it said.

Come to think of it, most things were easier for a man. I felt bitter towards all men, but I decided to be nice to Pask even if he was a man. Because right now I needed to have someone's arms around me, I had to have a good cuddle, a good seeing-to. I needed to know that I could be loved by a man. I had been betrayed and rejected, and I needed the reassurance of knowing that I was still attractive, still desirable.

A little doubt niggled in the back of my mind. Why was Pask so obsessed with sheep? Was he a New Zealander? I had never asked where his family came from. Who cared? He was here and I was here. The past was the past and I would deal with it when I had to. Right now I was here, and now I was going to make the most of it.

There was another soft knock on the door. Bugger you, Pask, you'll just have to wait.

'Just a minute,' I said. A lady shouldn't appear too eager to admit a lover to her boudoir, I reminded myself. I had learned that much from the films.

Bugger Michael. Bugger life, in fact. I blew my nose and rose to my feet and I washed my face in the cold water in the dish on the washstand. I looked into the still water and it reminded me of sheep. Sheep! That was what was wrong with the world, wrong with everything. We women acted like sheep being led beside the still waters. The men decided everything and we let them lead us.

My mother, and me, and Mary. Even the Virgin Mary, when you

thought about it. What say did she have in becoming Jesus' mother? The Archangel Gabriel came along and told her that she was going to give birth to God's son, and the unfortunate Blessed Virgin just had to go along with things.

And then there was that lady in the film, *The Sheik*, carried off into the desert against her will, when all she wanted was an independent life. And the Lady of Shalott in Tennyson's poem, dying for love of Sir Lancelot.

We were always the passive ones. Even when we were dancing, we never took the lead. It was time that women in general, and this woman in particular, stood up for herself and managed her own life.

I took a deep breath. I took a number of deep breaths. I felt a bit dizzy, the way I'd felt at the Irish dance.

I was an independent widow woman now, I told myself, and if I wanted to change the way things were done, I could change them. But I have needs and desires, and I am going to satisfy them.

'Hello, Mrs W,' Pask said softly through the door as he knocked again. He sounded a bit like his cocky, Solomon, muttering under the canvas in the kitchen.

'Damn you, Michael,' I thought. 'I'm really glad that now I know for certain that you're dead. At least I'm not committing adultery. You committed adultery and incest and all I'm doing is a bit of fornication, and I am going to enjoy it with all my body and soul, but I'm not as evil as you were. If God didn't intend me to enjoy sexual relations, He wouldn't have made it as good as it was last time. And this time it will be even better.'

'Mrs W, are you in there?' Pask was calling plaintively. Now he sounded a bit like one of his sheep, but that didn't matter.

I ran the comb through my hair and pinched my cheeks to make them red. I felt a bit better after that, so I walked to the door and opened it a just a crack.

I looked through it, smiling seductively. 'Come in Pask, I was just saying my prayers. I'm finished now. You can chase the sheep tomorrow.'

'You're a very good, religious woman, Mrs W,' said Pask. 'It's a joy and a privilege to have you here.'

'Michael,' I whispered aloud, hoping my dead husband, wherever he was, would hear me. It wasn't a very loud whisper though. I didn't want Pask to hear. 'I'm going to live life to the full from now on. To hell with you and with everything. I'll worry about any other problems in the morning. I'll take one day at a time. Maybe I'll clean the stove tomorrow, and maybe I will die and go to hell too, but I'm not going to die for a while yet, so you'll have a long wait if you're looking for me down there.'

I threw the door open wide and rushed into Pask's arms, tearing at his clothing and at my own. I dragged him into the room and kissed him hard on his startled lips and I ran my hands over his hard naked torso. I pushed him towards the bed and threw him onto it, and I leaped onto his body.

The bed springs crashed loudly. The little bedside table teetered and almost fell but Pask managed to disengage one arm momentarily to save it toppling. The alarm clock fell to the floor and began to make whirring noises as if in protest at its treatment. I was past caring about the clock or the time or the noise.

The bed springs began to creak rhythmically. I had never been in the dominant position when Michael made love to me; he had always had that honour. It was nice to have a change. A change is as good as a holiday and this was better than a holiday. It was much better than my honeymoon at Victor Harbor. I knew we were making a lot of noise but it didn't seem important.

The tempo of the creaking grew faster and louder. The cockatoo out in the kitchen woke up and began to screech angrily.

'Maybe the tarp has fallen off her,' whispered Pask. 'Let me up and I'll go and put it back.'

'Don't worry. She'll give up in a minute.'

'But she might wake the kids,' protested Pask.

'Then they can put the tarp back,' I said.

'Bugger you, Bob, if you are awake and listening,' I thought. 'About time you learned the facts of life.'

'Steady on, Mrs W,' Pask protested weakly. 'A man's not that energetic after a hard day chasing sheep.'

His protests were in vain. I had needs and I intended to satisfy them, sheep or no sheep.

30

I didn't clean the stove the next day. After a night in Pask's arms (well, we didn't exactly spend the whole night in each other's arms, we were both too old for that, and after the initial surprisingly passionate episode we both turned around and went to sleep), but after a night in his company the whole sorry episode of Michael seemed a little less dramatic.

Perhaps not less dramatic, but more bearable somehow. I felt better about myself, anyway. It occurred to me that I was alive, Mary was alive, Amy was alive, and the world had somehow gone on turning and the sun had come up each morning and gone down each night and even though awful things had happened, life, for us, had moved on. And it was good to know that Michael was really dead and his body was rotting in his coffin while I was in bed and enjoying life and love.

As Pask got out of bed, I suddenly realised there was quite a disparity in our ages. I was a widow woman nearing fifty and he could not have been more than… I had no idea. The kids were ten and six years old and he would probably have married at about thirty, give or take a year or so, so he must be about forty now.

'Have you ever thought about my age, Pask?' I asked.

'What are you on about, Mrs W?'

'Well, it's just that I'm a good deal older than you are.'

'That old rooster made bloody good broth, didn't he?' my lover grinned. 'I've got to…'

'I know, you have to chase a sheep.' I said.

I gave him breakfast, and he left. The sheep awaited.

It is amazing how the small tasks of domestic living can calm a person down. I realised that was what my mother meant when she recommended cleaning the stove when you thought you were dying.

The hard work would take your mind off your troubles, and by the time the grease was removed and the blackening paste applied and polished off, you would have worked out a solution to whatever was the problem, and things wouldn't look quite so bad.

I was still appalled, still dismayed, still furiously angry with Michael, still nauseated when I thought about the details of the crime, but I realised that a lot of time had passed since the actual act had been committed, and time somehow had a mitigating effect even though the horror lingered.

I was not sure why old evils should be less than new evils, but Mary seemed to have survived with her sanity more or less intact, and there was dear little Amy to cherish and to be thankful for. I know it was selfish of me to think that, but if Michael had not done what he did, Amy would never have been born. And poor little Mary would have kept her innocence longer, I reminded myself. I remembered Julius Caesar's funeral, and I decided that both good and evil had survived Michael's demise.

After Pask and Bob had gone out to chase sheep (which was a full time occupation at the moment), I would have time to reread the letter. The shearing was to begin next week, and so the sheep chasing was more frantic than usual. The sheep had to be rounded up and penned in preparation. I had packed a cut lunch (cold mutton and pickle sandwiches and a flask of tea) for my two shepherds, so they would not be back for a while.

I set Annie some fairly hard sums to work on and I went back into my room to reread the letter. It was still under the chamber pot, and was only a little damp around the edges. I moved the chair closer to the window so I could read Michael's words in a better light.

The magpies were practising their musical scales in the trees around the house. My bed was still rumpled from our lovemaking. I would have to wash those sheets after their hard usage last night. It would be nice to have them fresh and sweet for our next sexual encounter. As soon as I had read Michael's words again, I would go and fire up the copper to boil the linen.

The morning sun streamed through the window, and the trees were tossing in the wind, so I knew the washing would be dry in no time. The weather looked good for shearing. No matter what evil was in the letter, there was some good in the world, I reminded myself.

I looked at the crumpled paper in my hand. So Michael had asked the priest for absolution but was told that absolution was conditional on my forgiving his sins. Therefore, if the priests were right, Michael must be suffering in the depths of hell. I hoped that the church had got it right. The Pope had decreed it thus, and the Pope was infallible. A bloody good thing if Mick is suffering the torments of the damned, the fire and brimstone, the gnashing of teeth, the being doomed to the outer darkness for eternity, the whole kit and caboodle. Michael deserved it.

Him and his whiskey. If only I hadn't gone to the Ladies Fellowship that night. I wondered what was on their agenda ten years ago, but it was too long ago to know. I always went if there was a talk about diphtheria, after the way Molly had died.

Certainly Michael had had an agenda of his own. Had he forced himself on Mary, had he used violence? I hadn't seen any marks on her, but of course I hadn't looked too closely because I hadn't expected any.

But Michael was never a violent man. I will give him that. He was all for the weapon of tongue-lashing. He was good at that. But he was always pretty half-hearted about belting the boys. Even when they deserved it. Not like Mr Thomas down the street, who was always dragging his sons out to the woodshed for a good hard stropping.

The whiskey was a more likely culprit. Fond of his whiskey, Michael was, as Mr Anderson had remarked. Had he plied Mary with whiskey? I felt guilty when I remembered how Pask had given me whiskey the night of the Irish dance and how as a result I readily surrendered to his charms. It was the same thing, when you thought about it. Not Mary's fault at all. Or mine.

It was the demon drink, as Mrs Williams and the Women's Christian Temperance Union would have said. And Michael had another weapon as well as alcohol. In his letter, he admitted he had used honeyed words. He would have used persuasion. Michael was a master at persuasion.

And he believed that Mary had forgiven him. I recalled how, back in Balfour's café, Mary had told me she hadn't really forgiven Mick, she had come back for the funeral for my sake, not for her father's sake. Poor Mary had lied. For the sake of peace, and perhaps for the sake of the money for the butcher's shop, she had told Michael she had forgiven him. I had given way to Michael myself, many times, for the sake of peace. And Mary, poor innocent child that she was, Mary would have been more easily persuaded than I could ever be.

Amy must be a lot like Mary. That was why she was so easily led. I would have to give Amy more confidence somehow. Charlie was right, I did mollycoddle her too much.

I suddenly realised that the fact that I had left home must have made Amy grow up a bit. So perhaps something good had come out of my coming to Orroroo. Apart from meeting Pask, that is. After last night, my appreciation for Pask was growing fast.

It was a good thing Michael hadn't jumped into the Blue Lake, when I came to think about it. The union would not have paid for the funeral if he had committed suicide. And rightly so, too. And there would have been such a scandal. I would have been so ashamed, I wouldn't have been able to look Mrs Williams in the face.

People might probably have thought I had driven Mick to kill himself. That was a stupid idea, of course, but people love to gossip. Especially about something meaty, like a suicide. Father Flaherty might have refused to bury him in sacred ground. Michael would have had to be buried with the Protestants, I supposed. Serve him right. Or would even the Protestants have refused him entry?

I wasn't sure what people did with suicides these days. Once, I think, they were buried at the crossroads with a stake through their hearts. I had read that somewhere. But that was a long time ago and it probably not in Australia. We're more enlightened, more modern, more liberal here, especially now in 1928.

As for Mary. Well, that was a dilemma. Should I, could I, write to her and say I knew who Amy's father was? How could I apologise for going to the Ladies Guild that night and leaving her with her father? I didn't know the bastard would get drunk and rape her. It wasn't my fault. Or was it? Had I neglected my duty to Mary by going out gallivanting with the Ladies Guild at the church?

It all came down to trust. You had to have some trust in your husband's morals. Perhaps I could write to her and drop a hint or two? Maybe I could mention what a strong resemblance Amy had to Michael? Would that work? Would it open the floodgates and give Mary the opportunity to unburden herself? Or would it drive her away from me again?

I could not bear to lose my daughter again. I could not risk upsetting her, especially now that she was in a delicate condition, pregnant with a baby that might be a little girl to be named Rose after me.

Was I thinking of Mary's welfare or of my own, though? It was a bit like that business with Hamlet that Michael used to like to spout: 'To be or not to be?' In my case it would be 'To enquire or not to enquire?' To drag up the past when it was buried or not to drag it up. What was the moral position here? I wondered. What would a Jesuit say? But what do Jesuits really know about life anyway? How many priests lived through the sort of experiences I had lived through despite their reading about the theory of morality?

And what about your own morals, Rose Walsh, I asked myself. Jumping into bed with a younger man? And looking forward to tonight and hoping that he'll come knocking on the door again? And if he didn't come, I just might go and knock on his door. He wasn't going to get away from me now.

I can't write to Mary about Amy, I decided. What if her husband read the letter? It was one thing to accept that your wife had borne a child before you married her, but surely even a Methodist or a Presbyterian, or whatever Fred was, would baulk at the idea of incest. Especially if you had welcomed the perpetrator of that incest into your home, had a few beers with him (but did Methodists drink? I had never seen Fred down a beer while he was in my house) and made the trip from Mount Gambier to Adelaide for his funeral.

No, perhaps I would have to wait until I saw Mary again before I broached the subject, and then, gently, very gently, tell her that I knew the worst. But would I have the courage to talk to her, mother to daughter, about such a delicate subject? Perhaps one day I would think of some way to phrase the right words. But perhaps, like the little Aboriginal girl and her mother, separated by time and place, I no longer really spoke the same language as my daughter did.

But then there was that really important paragraph that lurked at the end of the letter and kept insinuating itself into my mind even while I was agonising over Mary's sufferings. I knew I shouldn't be thinking in such a mercenary way, but that bankbook under the copper loomed large in my thoughts. What a bloody silly place to put it! What if the fire from the copper had burned it, or if the water from the copper had overflowed and it was a soggy mess? Just like Michael, I thought. I hope he'd had the sense to wrap it in oilskin at least. Of course, rats would chew oilskin. Had he at least found a tin to put it in as well?

If that silly bastard Michael had not been so bloody secretive, the whole family would not have been put in the position in which we'd found ourselves. Why was he keeping that money separate from the rest of our assets? Did he have another plan for it? A separate agenda all of his own? It depended on how much was in that bankbook of course.

But it must be a substantial sum if it was enough to see us through until the boys finish their apprenticeships. Had he intended to keep the money to use for his own dirty purposes? Had he planned to run off with some floozie as I had suspected he had done when the news of his death came from Mount Gambier all those months ago?

And where had Michael got the money? I knew he had the occasional flutter on the horses, but I thought he usually lost. I remember he was excited when Spearfelt won the Melbourne Cup last year. He was out with his mates all night on 2 November Maybe that was the origin of the money. Or perhaps he'd won Tats and hadn't told me. Or it was insurance money not spent on Fred's shop. Put it under the copper until he needed it for some vile purpose of his own. Somehow Mick's ship had come in and he hadn't told me it had berthed.

I wiped the urine and some tears that I had shed from the letter and put it back in the envelope it had come in. I put the envelope under the mattress and pulled the dirty sheets off so that I could wash them.

What would I put in the letter to Charlie? The mail would be going tomorrow when Pask went to town to phone the shearers, so I'd have to write today. Pask had to give the shearers a couple of days' notice about when the sheep were all rounded up and ready, and he was bringing the last of the animals in today to put in the holding pens.

Tomorrow he would go into the town, send a message to the shearers and collect any supplies we needed to feed the men. He could take my letter to the post office while he was there. I must tell Pask to bring back more flour from the shop in Orroroo too, I remembered. I'll need to make a lot of bread for those shearers, Pask says they're hungry buggers.

I went out into the kitchen. Annie had finished her sums and was flicking at the dust on the dresser with the feather duster, humming the tune of 'Phil the Fluter's Ball' as she did so. I made a cup of tea and sat down to write to Charlie.

Dear Charlie,

I hope this finds you as it leaves me. We are busy up here preparing for the shearing. The kids are fine.

I have read the letter from your father. Not much in it of interest, but he mentioned there is a bankbook under the copper in the laundry. I hope it is not scorched from the fire.

Could you dig it out and see how much money is in it? Let me know by return post asap.

Love to everyone from your mother,

Yours faithfully,

Rose M. Walsh.

31

The letter had gone and the shearers had come. I thought of my letter sitting in the mailbag on the train steaming down to Adelaide and wondered whether the blue roses still bloomed beside the railway tracks. I didn't know anything about the natural history of Scotch thistles, but I supposed that they must die down and spring up in their season just as everything else does. A time to be born and a time to die, as Father Flaherty had said at Michael's funeral.

A time to be born. As I made bread for the shearers, I remembered the night of Amy's birth. As soon as I knew the birth was impending, I removed the cumbersome cushions that I wore to deceive the neighbours. I wouldn't be opening the door to anyone when I was meant to be writhing in childbirth.

Mary's waters had broken and she was moaning with pain and panic in the back bedroom. Mick had taken the boys to stay the night with Mrs Williams, telling her my labour had begun. He sat in the front room with the whiskey bottle and Mary and I got on with the business of birthing.

She was terrified when the pain grew stronger. Poor little creature, she was only a kiddie herself. Her body wasn't ready for this sort of thing. She had no idea of what was about to happen. I will admit I wasn't as sympathetic as I should have been. I still blamed her for getting herself pregnant. Now I felt guilty remembering how I had berated her, how unsympathetic I was to her.

She sobbed on her bed in the back room and I boiled water and fetched towels and rags, a knife to cut the cord and some string to tie the cord off.

Mick watched me go back and forth but didn't offer to help. 'Life would be a lot simpler if it was a stillbirth,' he said, between sips of whiskey.

At the time, I ignored his words. There was enough to do coping with the task ahead without listening to his whiskey-inspired blathering. Now, as I kneaded the bread dough in the kitchen at Orroroo, it suddenly came to me that he must have been suggesting that I should not try too hard to deliver a live baby. Was he suggesting that I should have neglected to immediately tie the umbilical cord and allow the baby to bleed to death, or perhaps that I should have accidentally dropped the child into the bucket of warm water that stood beside the bed?

I had heard of that sort of thing happening. It was the sort of thing that was whispered around a kitchen table over cups of tea, a tale that had always happened to the family of some cousin of a cousin in some dreadful dark house out in the back blocks of the country.

I slapped the dough hard on the board when I thought of this. If I was right in my interpretation of his words, I thought, then may the circle of hell in which Michael was incarcerated grow deeper and hotter.

I opened the door of the wood stove beside me and flung more fuel into it, despite the fact that it was burning perfectly well already. I looked into the flames, envisaging Michael's face in the fire.

What punishment did God hand out for incest, adultery, attempted murder and abandonment of one's daughter? For allowing an innocent child to take the blame for one's own sin? For lies and deception and pushing people to despair?

Could there be a worse sin than wishing the death of an innocent newborn child? And what of my sin, that of stealing another mother's babe? My own child's child, at that?

For when Mary's first agony was over and the tiny red-faced child had emerged into the world, I held her to my breast and I knew that this baby was mine and that I was never going to relinquish her.

Mary pleaded to see her baby. Although beforehand Michael and I had agreed that we would not let her see the child, eventually, and probably because I was so enthralled by the perfection of the new little creature that I had to show it to someone, I gave in and let Mary hold her daughter.

Just for a moment, Mary clasped her newborn. She kissed and crooned to her. She wanted to put the babe to her breast, but I tore

Amy away and carried her out to the arms of the grandfather who I now knew was also her father. Michael held the baby while I tore leaves from a cabbage. I carried them to the room where Mary lay weeping and bound them to her breasts to stop the milk coming in. Cabbage leaves work well for that purpose. In retrospect I knew that I should never have let that monster, Michael, touch Amy.

I slapped the dough again and cut it into pieces to put aside for the second rise. I looked at the knife in my hand. That's what I should have used on Michael. But maybe not a kitchen knife. What was needed was a castrating knife like the one Pask used on the young male lambs. If only I'd had one of those while Michael was alive!

And then, while Michael was holding Amy and I was standing beside his chair gazing at the child, nosey Mrs Williams burst in through my front door without even knocking and saw me there.

'So it's all over already, is it? Well, aren't you the tough one, Mrs Walsh? I heard all the noise, and then it went so quiet, so I thought it must be finished. But surely you can't have given birth a minute or two ago and be out of bed already? You know you're supposed to lie in and rest for at least two weeks. It's dangerous to get up as quickly as this, even for an Irishwoman. Can I make a cup of tea for you perhaps?'

I would swear the damned woman suspected something peculiar was happening in our house. She never stopped snooping around, that woman. I had to sink down in a chair immediately and pretend to have a fit of the vapours and allow her to make me a cup of tea in my own house.

When she brought the cup to me, Michael remarked that the tide had gone out, as he always used to say if a cup wasn't full to the brim.

Mrs Williams glared at him. She had never liked Michael. In retrospect, I have to admit she was a better judge of character than I was where he was concerned. But I suspect it was Michael's refusal to take the pledge to abjure alcohol that was the main cause of her dislike for him.

A week later we smuggled Mary out at night and took her to the railway station. We waited hours before the train came to take her away. And all the while Mary cried, and Amy cried and I tried to hide my tears and Mick and I tried to ignore the whole thing.

Annie brought me back to the present moment. 'Auntie Rose, Dad says can you bring some morning tea down the shearing shed? It's smoko time and everyone's starving.'

I left the bread for the second rise. The stew for the shearers' lunch was simmering nicely on the back of the stove, filling the kitchen with its fragrance. I checked that the food wouldn't get caught on the bottom of the saucepan, added a bit more flour and water, and put the lid back on.

I handed the basket of mutton and chutney sandwiches to Bob and the fruit cake to Annie, and lifted the flasks of tea I had prepared. Pask said shearers were hungry buggers and you had to keep them happy or the sheep suffered.

The cacophony of the shearing shed was overwhelming. I knew what sheep sounded like, I could not have spent seven months on a sheep property without hearing the constant background bleating the animals made, but now there were hundreds of the woolly beasts huddled in the holding yards loudly protesting their imprisonment and the treatment they were receiving.

'It's a good thing that sheep don't have a union,' I told Annie as we approached the shearing shed, 'or they'd be on strike for sure.'

Pask must have chased up every sheep for miles around. The animals were objecting in unison. Those sheep who had been shorn and ejected from the shed slid, surprised expressions on their faces, down the wooden chutes. They milled about shivering in the dust, complaining even louder than their mates who stood in the fenced queue waiting their turn.

Inside the shed, the bleating was almost drowned out by the incomprehensible shouts of the shearers who jostled each other as they grabbed the protesting sheep and dragged them across the slippery floor, the commands from their boss who sounded as if he had been a sergeant major in the Great War, Pask's anxious interjections as he watched his flock being manhandled, the excited shrieks from Bob and Annie and the yelping of half a dozen kelpie dogs. I put my hands over my ears.

This cacophony was overlaid by the shrieks of the corellas who obviously resented the intrusion of man and beast into their territory, the carolling of the ever-present magpies who had had their peaceful roosting in the trees around the shearing shed disturbed, and the usual miserable laments of the crows. It was like being in a madhouse. But the noise at least distracted me from my inner turmoil.

The smells were almost as overpowering as the sounds. The men's sweat, the animal smell of the assembled sheep and the occasional acrid scent of blood when a shearer cut too deep hit my nostrils.

Dust filled the shearing shed and slanted the rays of light. One of the wool classers stood outside the shed smoking. He had apparently decided that smoko began now, not when the boss said it did. I began to sneeze and nearly dropped my load.

Pask came over to me and relieved me of my burden. 'Well, what do you think, Mrs W? Have you ever seen anything like this in your life?'

'Never,' I said.

'Bloody beautiful, this is. This is what life is all about. Makes chasing sheep worthwhile, this does.'

'That cake looks good,' said a large hairy man wearing a sweat-stained singlet. 'Smells bonza, too. Reckon it's worth washin' me hands for a bit of that.' He turned and dipped his hands ceremoniously into an enamel basin of suds that stood by the door. He wiped his hands on his grubby trousers.

Pask cut a large slice of the cake and put it in the man's hand. 'Best bloody cake this side of Orroroo,' he said. 'In fact, it's the best bloody cake in the whole mid-north of South Australia. And wait until you get Mrs W's stew inside you. That'll be for lunch today. And what's for tea tonight, Mrs W?'

'You shouldn't think about the next meal until you've had the one you're about to have,' I scolded. 'But if you must know, it's roast mutton and spuds and fresh greens. That silverbeet that's been growing up the back by the long-drop. Annie picked it just this morning. And plum pudding to follow.'

Pask took me to see the wool that had already been shorn from the sheep. Piles of fleece were being pressed into the bales, and as I watched another fleece was thrown, tossed high into the air with effortless grace, the wool turned to gold as the airborne dust caught the sun that poured through the open doors, the whole gleaming mass of wool seeming to vault of its own will onto the sorting table.

The grader's hands were slick with lanolin as he checked the quality of the wool. He looked up at me. 'You want to get a bit of this stuff on your hands, missus. Does yer skin the world of good. Watch out, though. The floor's slippery with the grease.'

'We've got a pretty good crew here this year,' Pask told me as he led me out of the shed and helped me down the steps. 'And it's going to be a good cheque this year too, when the wool's sold,' he added.

'So you can afford to keep me on for a bit longer, can you?' I teased.

'I'm never going to let you get away, Mrs W,' he said. 'By the way, do you reckon you and Annie could look after these lambs that have got separated from their mothers? If you haven't time, I'll have to knock them on the head and you can make soup out of them. Seems a pity, though.'

He showed me three tiny lambs with short, tightly curled wool, their withered umbilical cords still hanging from their bellies. They bleated piteously as they huddled together in a wire pen. I picked one up and it nestled against my chest and tried to find a nipple.

'Elsie always looked after the orphaned lambs,' Pask said, grinning. 'I knew you wouldn't say no when you saw them. But it'll be a full-time job. You'll have to feed them every two hours if you want them to survive. There's bottles with teats for them up at the house, Annie will show you where. You'll have to water the cow's milk down quite a bit. It'll be too rich otherwise. Their bellies won't take too much cream.'

Bob, Annie and I carried the little orphans back to the house, and Annie and I found the bottles.

For weeks after that, the babies tugged at the milk and at our hearts until their milk-teeth grew and they learned to eat grass. Annie loved to cuddle them, and I fell in love with the way they skipped about when they saw us coming and fell over each other's legs as they scrambled for food.

Seeing Pask's elated mood, I half expected that he'd come to my bed, that first night of the shearing. But by the time the work of the day had been done, we were all exhausted.

I glanced out the kitchen door as the sun slid down the horizon and thought it, too, looked as though it was greased with lanolin.

32

When we had time to go to Orroroo again to replenish the supplies exhausted by the hungry shearers, there was a letter from Charlie waiting in the mailbox at the post office. We had beaten the postal delivery this time. I tore it open while Pask was putting the last of the bags of flour on to the buggy.

'Dear Mum,' Charlie began, 'We looked under the copper boiler out in the laundry and underneath it there was a tin in it with Dad's bankbook wrapped in oilskin, just like you said there would be. It was just as well he had done that, because rats had been nesting under the copper and they would have chewed the book up otherwise. We put some rat bait down and we will have to keep the cats out of the laundry in case they eat it. Amy will be devastated if her new kitten gets poisoned.'

For Christ's sake, Charlie, I thought, bugger the rats and the cats. Get to the point. How much money is there? Did Michael tell the truth for once? Are there enough funds to keep us going as he said there was?

> I don't know where Dad got the money, Mum, but there is fair bit there. Over a thousand pounds. We can't do anything about it until you come back, because of course the money goes to you in his will. You have to go to the bank and make the withdrawal.
>
> But we'll be on easy street while the money lasts. A thousand pounds should last quite a while. I wonder where the old devil got the money? I hope he didn't pinch it. Maybe it's from that insurance policy that he cashed in. Or maybe he finally won money on the horses. Anyway, it looks as if our ship has come in after all. When are you coming back?
>
> Yours faithfully,
>
> Charles R. Walsh.

'Good news or bad news, Mrs W?' asked Pask. He was trying to look over my shoulder at the letter while doing his best not show that he was being nosey.

'Hard to say, really. I'm a bit confused.' I said.

Pask shrugged and walked across the road.

I couldn't go back just yet, I reasoned. Although ewes always dropped the occasional lamb, the official lambing would be in the spring. And spring wasn't far away; I had seen the buds swelling on the almond trees down near the long-drop lavatory. Pask would need me there to care for the children while he was busy chasing the ewes. And what would become of Annie and Bob if I left?

Annie had a cold just now. She did tend to bronchitis. I had a feeling that she might be asthmatic, actually. She had that shovel-shaped chest that you see in asthmatic kiddies. I needed to be there until the winter ended to make her inhale steam made with Friar's Balsam to ward off pneumonia if her cold got worse.

And Bob was improving so much at his school work that I hated to leave him without a teacher. Pask had promised to make the time to take the children to school after he'd finished mending fences, but Pask seemed to be taking his time about finishing those maintenance jobs.

Michael's money would be safe in the bank for the time being, although I admit I've never really trusted banks. And the family back home was surviving pretty well on the money I was sending back and the bit the boys earned.

But I would go home soon and sort things out. When summer came, there would be Christmas to think about. I would have to go back to Adelaide for Christmas. But could I desert Pask and the kids at Christmas time?

Pask had gone off to talk to one of his farming mates, while I went into the general store. I had filled my basket and was chatting to the shop lady when Pask came into the shop looking grim.

'They've got diphtheria at Hawker,' he said. 'I've just heard that it's been all through the mid-north. Four kiddies have died at Carrieton and two at Peterborough. It's a real epidemic.'

Diphtheria. How I hated and feared that word. My little sister Molly had died of diphtheria when she was two years old and I was six. I remembered how she had wheezed and coughed and choked and how I had been sent for the doctor, and how I came back to find her dying on the kitchen table and how my mother had been hysterical with grief.

My mother never really recovered from Molly's death. When the boys died, it pushed her over the edge, but she had never really been the same after Molly died. I suppose I've never recovered from those events when I was six years old, either. I've seen many deaths since then and lain out quite a few bodies, but Molly's death was the first death I'd seen.

'Maybe it won't come to us,' Pask was saying. 'Maybe we'll be all right. We're a fair way out of town, after all. Maybe it will pass us by.'

I thought of the angel of death with his wings spread wide, flying like Smithy through the mid-north, hovering over a home that he'd selected at random, and pausing to snatch the first-born (though my poor mother had lost Molly, her last-born) and then moving on to the next doomed household to inflict agony on the mother in that home, too. What criterion did the angel use to choose the children he took? I prayed that Pask's home would be spared. Pask had lost enough already. Although I was not their mother, I could not bear to lose Annie and I didn't even want to lose the bitter Bob.

Actually, the boy's mood hadn't been as unpleasant lately. Perhaps the ride in Tim's car had helped. Perhaps the magnetism at Magnetic Hill had drawn out some of the anger from his young soul.

I looked for the children and found them with a group of their friends, children who lived in the town and who went to the local school.

'Auntie Rose, Bertie says there's a new teacher at the school. He says she's really nice. Do you think Dad would be able to take us to school again soon?' Annie asked.

'Dad's finished the shearing and he ought to have more time now,' Bob said hopefully. 'He promised when he had more time he would take us back to school. I do miss my mates, and there's a proper football team now that I could join. I used to like kicking a football, when we went to school, before Mum died. Will you ask Dad about it, Auntie Rose? Please?'

'We'll have to see what he says. He's a bit worried because there's sickness about at the moment and he doesn't want you two to catch it. Perhaps in a couple of weeks' time we might think about school. When the sickness is gone.'

I bought some syrup of ginger and some compound tincture of cinchona bark from the chemist. Just in case, I thought. I remembered that during the diphtheria epidemic back in 1885 when Molly had died, people were using that. It hadn't helped Molly, but perhaps it had helped me, because I didn't die. I didn't know of anything better, so it would have to do if the angel of death called on us. I prayed again that he would pass us by.

We went back to the farmhouse and we decided to stay there. We would try not to go too far afield until we felt that the epidemic was over. We had plenty of supplies. We would put ourselves into quarantine until it seemed safe to emerge again. We didn't erect any barricades, but we stayed behind our fences.

Letters from Adelaide kept arriving in the kero tin by the gate, brought erratically by the postman. On days when there was no mail delivered, we wondered if the postman was ill. Or was there diphtheria in Adelaide, too, and my family were sick? Or had the train drivers died and mail could not be delivered?

I hoped there were no diphtheria germs on those letters. Did the postman visit homes where people had diphtheria? Did he wash his hands after he touched their letter boxes? Was the postman allied with the angel of death? I burned the envelopes in the wood stove just in case, and I washed my hands after I'd read the letters. You couldn't be too careful.

When mail came, I learned that the family in Adelaide was growing impatient for my return. They'd had a headstone made for Michael's grave and the stonemason wanted his money. It was wrong to keep him waiting, Charlie said, when we had all that money in Dad's bank account. Charlie had been to see the bank manager and there would be no problem for me to get hold of the funds. As Michael's wife, I had inherited everything, and it was my signature that was needed to release the money. They could not understand, Charlie wrote angrily, the pen digging holes into the paper, why I did not come home immediately. What was keeping me at Orroroo, anyway?

33

The tin bath full of tepid water in which we had been dunking Bob stood in front of the wood stove. The water reeked of vinegar because I had remembered that vinegar will often bring a fever down. When Bob's temperature rose, we put him into the water. When he cooled, we took him out and swaddled his shivering body in towels that we had heated by hanging them in front of the wood stove.

I knew it was late by the shadows that were lengthening outside. I could hear the cow lowing desperately too, calling me to milk her. Pask and I had lost track of the time because we were too busy with Bob. I knew I had milked Daisy this morning. The pail of milk was still standing on the kitchen table where I'd put it when I came back from the milking stall and found Bob slumped on the floor by the stove.

Occasionally Pask or I would grab a hunk of bread, spread with mutton fat from the tin by the stove, to stave off our hunger, but meals seemed irrelevant now. We had pushed the same unappetising food towards Annie when she whimpered that her tummy hurt and she needed to eat something. In the end we sent her snivelling to her bed, just to get her out of the way.

The kerosene lamp had burned out while Pask and I laboured to lower the boy's fever. I had no time to clean the blackened glass and replenish the fuel. Now the only light came from the flickering flames through the grille of the wood stove. There was kindling in the basket beside the stove and we fed the fire with that. The supply was dwindling, but neither of us wanted to leave Bob long enough to go out and get wood from the heap on the back veranda.

Bob lay now, limp and wrapped in a thick blanket, across Pask's knees. I was reminded of a picture I had once seen of that statue called

The Pietà by Michelangelo, the one where Mary is holding the corpse of Jesus newly taken from the Cross. The expression on Pask's face was similar to Mary's, exhausted and resigned to grief.

The boy hadn't moved or spoken for such a long time and we were both wondering how much longer he could endure this fever. I felt that any minute Pask would say something like 'Maybe it's time to let him go. We can't let him suffer any more.'

But I had no intention of giving in. I'm not a quitter. I checked the hot vinegar compress that I'd put around Bob's throat, and then I tried to spoon brandy mixed with water into his mouth. I had already tried the ginger and the cinchona but I wasn't sure if it had worked. Bob had vomited it, anyway.

That was the trouble. I had no idea how much to give the kiddie or how often. I didn't want to make him worse than he already was. But when you're desperate you'll take desperate measures.

'We should have taken him to the doctor when we first knew he was sick,' I said, knowing that I had already said that dozens of times. I wasn't sure if I was blaming Pask or blaming myself. Both of us were to blame. Or God, or the angel of death, or politicians. Most things were politicians' or God's fault when it came right down to it.

'But we kept hoping that it wasn't the diphtheria, didn't we?' Pask insisted. 'And what if it had only been a bit of a cold and we took him to the hospital and he caught it there from the kiddies who already had the diphtheria?'

Bob coughed and spluttered and pleaded with me to leave him alone. 'I just want to go to sleep. Or maybe I want to die,' he whimpered.

'You're not going to bloody well die, Bob,' said his father, rousing himself from his torpor at the sound of his son's voice, weak though it was. 'We've had enough dying in this house. You are going to get better and that's all there is to it. It's just a bit of a cold you've got.'

I knew it wasn't just a bit of a cold. I had shone Pask's new electric torch down Bob's throat and I had seen the little white spots there. Later they changed to grey patches. This wasn't croup. It wasn't quinsy. This was diphtheria. Again I berated myself for not standing up to Pask, for not demanding that we rush Bob to the doctor.

'I've raised six children and I've never lost a child and I'm not going to lose you, Bob. Here, swallow this.'

I had remembered a remedy my father swore by. He said it would cure anything. Dad insisted that his cure was better than snake oil. I got a teaspoon of sugar, and dribbled two drops of kerosene on to it. I grew up with that remedy. I used to hate it when my father dosed me with it, but it always fixed my sore throats when I was a youngster. 'Kill or cure,' my dad used to say.

A gargle of glycerine and water and some sort of soda was supposed to be good too, I remembered. But I couldn't remember the exact measurements and anyway I didn't have the soda. Did sheep dip contain soda? And I remembered Pask saying sheep dip contained arsenic. That wouldn't help at all. Bob looked past gargling, anyway. It would have to be the kero.

Bob gagged and struggled. I was sure he thought I wanted to murder him. But after he had swallowed the kerosene on sugar and I had given him a glass of warm water to wash it down, he looked at me gratefully although wordlessly, and patted my hand. He couldn't talk. Kero does that to you. You become speechless for a while after you've swallowed it. But perhaps he did realise I was trying to save him, I thought. I bent and kissed his brow.

Pask and I sat there all night with Bob. My face got scorched every time I opened the door to put more sticks into it, and I wondered idly if that was what it was like in hell, and if Michael was still burning. I hoped he was roasted and basted and crisp and brown on the outside, and that his intestines were boiling on the inside.

When you considered how much pain a parent suffers to have children and raise them, you realise what a precious trust a young life is. First there was the discomfort and the nausea of pregnancy, then you had the agony of childbirth to bring the baby into the world, and then you suffered every time they fell over when they were learning to walk. Later you felt their pain whenever they were ill or unhappy. It is a terrible responsibility, having children. A life sentence really.

It's worse for a woman, of course. Everything is worse for a woman. And the children never realise just how much you love them until they have children of their own and learn what it is to love with such fervour. But I could see that Pask was suffering to see his only son in terrible peril. Poor Pask, he had endured enough already, losing Elsie like that.

But Michael could never suffer enough. I reflected that his agony would last for all eternity, and that eternity is a very long time. Michael had never understood other people's pain. Of course, he was interested in the well-being of the union men under his care, but that was his job. He was paid to take care of them. But sympathy and empathy never came easily to Michael. He was a selfish, self-centred man.

When I was upset about Rudolph Valentino's death, for example, he had laughed. He actually said I was silly. In fact, he said that all the women all around the world who had mourned Valentino's death were silly. Millions of women were devastated, and Michael just said they were silly. Insensitive, that's what he was.

And of course there was that business of what he had done to Mary. I would never forgive him for that. How anyone could deliberately set out to harm a child was beyond my belief and my understanding.

Pask and I took turns to hold Bob. When Bob's fever rose, we put him back into the bath, and when it abated, we took him out and dried him and held him until the fever came back.

I boiled water on the stove and made more hot compresses and wrapped them around Bob's neck. The angel of death would not snatch him from us if I had anything to do with it. I had lost Molly. I would not lose Bob. I would do everything I'd learned since Molly's death to save this child.

Somehow, despite our agony, Pask and I must have dozed off. We woke to find the sun had risen and the kitchen was full of light, and magpies had begun singing in the trees outside the house. Bob was sprawled across his father's knees. I was afraid to touch the boy, fearing to find him stiff and cold.

But Pask was smiling. 'I reckon he's going to be all right, Mrs W. I think the fever's gone. His breathing seems better now too. He'll be out chasing sheep again in no time. Might even be able to go to school soon. I'll take him tomorrow if he wants to go. I'll make the time for him. I've been selfish keeping him away from his mates.'

'He's not going anywhere for weeks, Pask. He's going to stay in bed indoors, wrapped up in a red blanket in a well ventilated room and he's going to drink lots of nourishing broth and he's going to convalesce. And maybe have more kero on sugar if he seems up to it. There won't be any sheep chasing until I say so.'

'Whatever you say, Mrs W. You're the boss. I don't know what I would have done if you hadn't been here. Bob would have died for sure. You've saved his life, Mrs W. Just like you saved those lambs and that rosebush out by the back door. You're a lifesaver, a miracle worker.'

34

'Auntie Rose, Auntie Rose!' Bob croaked.

If he hadn't been tugging at my apron I mightn't have heard him. I was so surprised to see him that I slopped some of the milk from the pail I was carrying from the dairy to the house.

'You're supposed to be in bed, Bob,' I scolded. 'You know you've been really sick. You shouldn't be out here barefoot. Just look at the frost on that grass. How does your throat feel?'

While I was milking the cow I had decided on another Friar's Balsam inhalation for Bob. It was a week now since the crisis, and although the boy seemed recovered, I was still worried. I didn't want any relapses. He shouldn't be running around the farmyard just yet. Visions of my little sister Molly's death kept coming back to me. And memories of that dreadful night when we thought we'd lose Bob.

'I'm not too bad now, Auntie Rose,' Bob gasped. 'But Annie's crook. She's real crook. You've got to come quick.'

The bucket clanged as I dropped it. The milk spilled over the stiff grass. I had to get back to the house. Had to help Annie. I'm fifty years old. I'm old and I'm fat. I can't run fast any more. But I must run fast. As fast as I'd run for Molly. Faster.

'Where's your dad?' I gasped.

'Gone up to the three-mile paddock to shoot that fox that's killing the new lambs,' Bob whispered. 'Is Annie going to die, Auntie Rose? She can't talk and she breathes funny and her neck's red. Her face looks blue. Like Mum's did when she died.'

Bloody Pask has gone to save the lambs, I swore under my breath. What about my lamb? What about my Annie? She'll die just like Molly died. Bloody diphtheria. My little Annie. She'd been all right when I left to milk the cow. It was Bob I was worried about. Annie just had a bit of a cough. She had no fever last night or this morning. Now she'd die like Molly.

I reached the house. Annie was lying on the floor in front of the wood stove. It was not a good place for her, the wood was damp today and the stove smoked badly. The smoke would make her worse. She was as limp as the rag doll that lay beside her.

I lifted the child and put her on the kitchen table. She weighed nothing. Had her life, her soul, her substance, already drained away? I laid her on her back and put my face close to hers. I tried to hear if she was breathing. I brushed the long pale hair away from her face. Bob was right. Annie's little face was blue.

I moaned, remembering how Bob had found Elsie dead in front of that wood stove. And now he had found Annie there. I glanced at him as he stood by the door, afraid to enter, afraid to leave. He leaned against the door frame, his body shaking. I couldn't help him. I must help Annie.

I grabbed the rag doll and pushed it under her neck so that the child's head fell backwards. I opened her mouth to make the air enter her throat. There was no breath. Her chest was as still as the doll's. I banged on her chest. Was her heart still beating?

'Breathe, Annie, breathe,' I implored. 'Don't die, you mustn't die!'

My heart pounded. I was back at Molly's death. Back in that dreadful night when Molly was two years old and she'd had the diphtheria and I was six years old and my mother had sent me out in the night to find the doctor and I'd run all the way to the doctor's door – how far had it been, really? It seemed miles and I'd run and run and with every step I begged God to save Molly, and I couldn't find the right door to bang on because I couldn't see for the tears and the darkness.

Then I found the doctor's door and I hammered on it until the doctor opened his door and the white light spilled out of the room on me. He grabbed his bag and followed me and when we reached my home I crouched on the floor beside our kitchen table and I watched as the doctor opened his bag and took out a scalpel and made a hole in Molly's throat and the air whistled through the hole for a moment. Then Molly's face had collapsed and her chest caved in and blood gushed out of her mouth and she was dead.

The doctor said if he'd been there a few minutes earlier Molly would have lived. I knew then that I had killed my sister. I had failed her. I had not run fast enough. I had not prayed hard enough. It was my fault that Molly had died.

I would not let Annie die. I had beaten off the angel of death when he came for Bob, and I would save Annie too.

I grabbed the kitchen knife, the one I used to peel the potatoes. No time to sterilise it with Condy's crystals. Germs or no germs, it would have to do. I needed a tube to put in the hole that I was about to make, the hole that would allow air to enter Annie's windpipe and keep her breathing. What could I use to hold the airway open?

I saw one of Annie's school books on the floor. The cover was made of soft cardboard.

'Bob, tear the cover off that book,' I ordered.

He looked at me blankly.

'Just do it and put it on the table next to Annie's face. Roll it up tightly and put a rubber band around it. Do it now!'

Obediently, he tore the cover from the book. I knew that he thought I'd gone mad, but either he was in shock because of his fear for his sister's life or he was still too ill to argue with me. Before his illness he would never have been so compliant.

Annie had been well yesterday! How could this happen so quickly? Or had she been sickening and I hadn't noticed because I was preoccupied with Bob? It had been Bob I was afraid for yesterday, and was still afraid for this morning. Not little Annie. Now Annie was dying on the kitchen table and Bob was crouched on the floor beside the table just as I had crouched the night that Molly died.

I felt for the bands of hard gristle in Annie's throat and when I thought I had the right spot I steeled myself to plunge the knife into her. I knew I had to get the blade into the right spot. I had to puncture the windpipe. I might kill her if I didn't make the hole in the right place, but she would die unless she got air into her lungs.

I had heard people say that there would not be much blood if it was done properly. This was something we had discussed at the Women's Fellowship back home. Diphtheria was something every mother feared.

Was that the subject on the agenda the night that Michael had violated Mary?

'Jesus, Mary and Joseph save this child,' I prayed. 'Jesus, Mary and Joseph save this Annie, Jesus, Mary and Joseph save my Annie!' I shrieked.

I pushed the knife into Annie's throat and made the hole just as Pask walked into the kitchen. I saw him from the corner of my eye. The rifle and the dead fox he was carrying by the tail both fell to the floor. The clatter of the rifle (thank God Pask always checked his guns were unloaded when he carried them) and the thud of the dead fox almost covered the sound of the air whistling into Annie's windpipe.

I heard the whistle more than the clatter because I was listening for it with my face close to her throat. I blew into the hole. Her chest rose and she opened her eyes and I saw her eyes roll up and I shouted at Pask. 'Stick that tube into the hole. Quick!'

To his credit, he did as he was told. He said afterwards that he didn't know what the hell was going on, but he wasn't going to argue with me. He said I looked like Abraham sacrificing Isaac and for a moment he wished he'd brought a sheep with him instead of the fox.

'Not that I ever would argue with you, Mrs W. Tell you what, though, those Roman prayers you were yelling were pretty good, too. Don't reckon God himself would have argued with you, to tell the truth.'

We were all pretty shaken, and although Annie was obviously alive from the way she clung to me, I insisted that we put her in the cart and go off to see the doctor. I wasn't sure that the doctor would do anything much more, but I wasn't about to take any chances. I held the tube in her throat in place all the way there and Annie kept breathing although her eyes were wild and terrified.

When we got to the hospital, Pask and Bob had to sit on hard chairs out in the long corridor, but I went in to the surgical area with Annie because she refused to let go of me. I had to hold her while the doctor and two nurses did horrible things to her throat. I looked the other way. It's one thing to take a vegetable knife to a kiddie in the heat of the moment, but another to see strangers hurt her even if it is for her own good.

The doctor said what I'd done was called a tracheotomy and I'd done a good job and Annie would have died otherwise. He also said kerosene on sugar wasn't an acceptable treatment, but Bob had pulled through pretty well on that kero, and doctors aren't always right, just because they've been to school to learn a bit about medicine and they have a brass plate with their name on it hanging by their front door.

I'd known what to do, although I didn't tell the doctor, because I'd vowed that I would never let what had happened to Molly happen to my own children. If anyone was talking about diphtheria I would always listen carefully, and if I saw something written in the paper about the disease I would read it and cut it out to keep.

The angel of death had never come for my own children, but thank God, I had known what to do when he came for Bob and Annie.

Pask and Bob went home to look after the cow and the chooks and the sheep, but I stayed in Orroroo to be with Annie. The nurses found a bed for me so I could sleep at the hospital because every time I tried to leave Annie was distraught.

It took a few weeks, but Annie and Bob were soon both as right as rain again. Annie was left with a little scar on her neck, but that was a small price to pay for deliverance from the angel of death.

The good thing that came out of it was that Bob was a changed boy. He couldn't do enough for me. I almost missed the old Bob; at least you knew where you stood with him. The new Bob kept opening doors before I got the chance to put my hand on the knob, and clearing off the table before we had finished eating, and washing dishes. Sometimes he washed clean dishes before they were dirty. It was a bit unnerving, really. He smiled and laughed at my jokes, even ones I didn't think were funny, and he didn't seem jealous the way he used to be when he saw Pask and me talking together. Bob was particularly nice to Annie and seemed to have a new respect and even love for his father that I had never observed in the boy before.

After a while, Pask and I decided that the children could go off to school. We all went along for the first day and the kids took me by the hand and showed me around their schoolroom. It wasn't like St Joseph's school back in Norwood. There was only one schoolroom and one teacher for quite a lot of children and there were at least three grades being taught in the same room.

There were some sad little empty desks and the teacher whispered to us that five children from the school had died during the diphtheria epidemic. We had been fortunate to have our children survive, Pask and I.

35

Then another letter came from home. Mavis had had her baby. It was a boy, but a sickly boy. It had been a long labour and a difficult birth. They had named the baby Michael. I groaned when I read that. Michael was not a name I would have given to any child, although Harry had been christened Harold Michael, back in the days when I felt differently. But Harry and Mavis were not to know why I no longer liked the name.

I stuck the letter into the book I had been reading when Pask brought in the mail. I sighed. I should have been there to support Mavis when she needed me. If I had been there, I would have suggested some other name. Rudolph, perhaps, or even Cedric. It was too late now; the baptism had taken place. Of course, they didn't know about the incest, and I wasn't going to enlighten them on that subject. That was between Mary and me now. Little Michael had had to be baptised quickly because he had not been expected to survive. Father Flaherty had insisted on it. Harry and Mavis apologised to me for doing it while I was away in the country.

Harry wrote that Mavis was depressed and unhappy and finding it hard to cope with little Michael. She had no family in Adelaide; they were all in Sydney and could not come to South Australia. They were too busy reading Sydney newspapers and buying expensive fashionable clothes to visit Mavis, I supposed. I had never been to Sydney, and I really didn't understand why anyone would want to live there, but then I hadn't understood why anyone would want to live at Orroroo until I tried it.

Harry and Mavis needed my help with the baby. Little Michael couldn't keep his milk down, he had reflux, croup and cradle cap and a terrible rash on his bottom. Mavis was distraught. Amy tried to help her, but she didn't know what to do. Mavis had written to Mary for advice and she had written back with advice, but she couldn't come to Adelaide because she was pregnant again.

I was a bit annoyed when I read that Mavis was asking Mary's opinion. I was the baby's grandmother. Why hadn't Mavis written to me for advice? Did she think I'd forgotten how to raise children? Charlie sounded surprised when he wrote that Mary had announced that she was pregnant. I did smile when I read that bit. At least Mary had told me about her pregnancy before she told anyone else. Charlie was desperate. I was needed in Adelaide. Could I get the next train from Orroroo?

'I will have to go back,' I told Pask. 'But what will happen to you and the kiddies?'

'I could get my sister over for a bit,' he said doubtfully. 'She's not much use, but she'd be better than nothing. I don't know how long she'll stay, though. She came when Elsie died, but you saw what the place was like when she left. She's not the most reliable of people and the kids don't like her much. She pinched all of Elsie's good stuff too. She said she'd look after it for us. And her cooking is pretty terrible. Especially compared with yours.'

I really smiled at that. They say the way to a man's heart is through his stomach. But I wondered if it was my cooking or my lovemaking that was my main attraction.

'We could put up with her for a couple of months if we really have to, I suppose. I reckon the kids will be unhappy, though. They'll miss their Auntie Rose something awful.'

'And you, Pask, will you miss me?'

'Too right I will, Mrs W. You'd better not be gone too long, or me and the kids will have to come looking for you. It would embarrass you something awful, I reckon, if the kids and me and a mob of sheep turned up on your doorstep in Adelaide.'

I had a sudden thought. It was November now. Christmas was not far. I had to go back to help with the baby at once, of course, and I had wanted to spend Christmas with my own family, but how could I be away from Pask and Annie and Bob, who had become my other family, at a time like that? Christmas is such a special time. You need all your loved ones around you then. And now I had loved ones at home in Norwood and at Orroroo too. In fact, now I really had two homes.

What was I going to do? I felt as if I was being torn apart So much for being an independent widow woman! I had managed to saddle myself with two burdens instead of one. There must be a way out of it, though.

'Could you and the children come down to Adelaide for Christmas, Pask? I would prefer you didn't bring the sheep, though. My backyard at Norwood isn't really big enough for them and I have a feeling that Mrs Williams would complain about the noise and the smell. But could you come? Would it be possible?'

I had a sudden vision of Pask's sheep running around in suburban Norwood, bleating and farting, smelling as only sheep could do. That would upset Mrs Williams. The stink of a lot of animals in a confined area would probably be worse than that old coat I had doused in kerosene and burned in the incinerator. Especially if it rained. Nothing smells worse than a wet sheep. It wouldn't only be her curtains that would smell, it would be her whole house. And the noise would be even worse than Charlie's trumpet.

But if Pask and the children and a few sheep came for Christmas, no one could turn them away. You couldn't tell a shepherd and his sheep that there was no room at the inn at Christmas time.

It would be amusing to take Pask and the sheep over to the church, though. I could suggest to Father Flaherty that they could run a sort of nativity scene. Mavis could bring the baby and perhaps Charlie and Joe and Brian could be the three wise men. Not that Joe was all that wise.

Charlie would definitely qualify as a wise man, though. His letters had helped me so much during my exile. I suddenly realised that now I'd have a new problem. If Pask came to visit, we could hardly spend the night together in my family home. It could be months before I'd share a bed with Pask again.

I closed the collected works of Shakespeare. I'd tired of Lord Alfred Tennyson and wanted something meatier. I was reading *Romeo and Juliet* and I'd stuck Charlie's letter in the pages where Romeo was explaining how they could deceive their families by apparent suicide.

It occurred to me that Pask and I might be star-crossed lovers too. Elderly ones, perhaps, but my family wouldn't be too thrilled to learn what their mum had been up to at Orroroo. I certainly wasn't about to drink poison and pretend to be dead.

I tapped Pask on the shoulder. 'Come on, we're wasting good time here. Let's go to bed and see how loud we can make the springs creak. It's your turn on top tonight.'

'You haven't given me a chance to make up my mind yet about whether I'm coming to Adelaide yet, Mrs W. But I don't think I can go too long without a bit of bed acrobatics, so I suppose I will have to come down. It's a long time since I got on the Adelaide train. Are those Scotch thistles still out there along the track?'

'You mean the blue roses?' I said. 'They were there when I came up here.'

He rose to follow me to the bedroom, but paused at the doorway. 'I was wondering about something, Mrs W. I know it isn't quite a year yet since your husband died, and it may not be what you want to hear right now, but I wonder if you might consider, when you feel that the time is right and things are decent,' he paused to take a deep breath, 'I was wondering if you might think about marrying a one-eyed sheep-chasing farmer? Would you consider making an honest man of me?'

I was flabbergasted. I had never considered that he might want to marry me. I was so much older than he was, to start with. And I was quite happy with things as they were. I was not at all sure that I wanted to alter the present arrangements.

This must be how the lady in that film, *The Sheik*, felt. She didn't want to marry Rudolph Valentino because she didn't want to lose her independence. I didn't want to lose my independence either. I was fond of Pask, and the fact that he had one eye certainly didn't worry me, but I did feel a certain reluctance to tie myself irrevocably to him. Marriage was such a permanent step to take.

It was nice being an independent widow woman. I'm becoming a suffragette, I thought. This is how Emily Pankhurst and her followers felt. Muriel Matters, that was the Adelaide woman who went over to London and got herself arrested by yelling 'Votes for women' in the House of Lords and chaining herself to the grille in Parliament House.

I'll be chaining myself to a railing next. At least we already have the female franchise in South Australia so I won't be out campaigning for the vote here. We had it before the Pommie women, too.

If I didn't marry Pask, I could come and go as I wanted between Adelaide and Orroroo. But if I did marry him, I'd be tied to one life, a life as a farmer's wife. I didn't want one life. I wanted two lives. I wanted the freedom to choose where I lived and how long I stayed here or there. I had tasted liberty and I had enjoyed it.

I'd been confined to my home at Norwood all my married life with Michael, and then the cage door had opened and I'd flown out. I had spread my wings like the magpies that lived in the trees around this house. You couldn't keep one of those magpies in a cage, and I didn't want to live in a cage like Pask's cocky, either. I was a free spirit now and, despite the magnetism of Orroroo, I wasn't about to surrender my freedom.

But I didn't want to upset Pask either. He was a lovely man. But a man nevertheless. Sometimes men changed after you marry them, that was another point. Michael had certainly changed, although the Great War may have played a part in that. And men don't take kindly to women who say they want independence. However, men don't enjoy rejection either. I decided to stall for time.

I might think of a way out later. Or he might see a younger more attractive prospect and decide that a younger chicken would suit his hen house better. That would hurt, but I could probably learn to accept it. Or, hopefully, he'd learn to accept that he had to live in sin if he wanted my company. He did seem to be enjoying his nightly sin.

What I needed to do was to stop him reading the Bible and find another book with fewer moral lessons in it for him. Perhaps I could find Michael's copy of *Ulysses* when I got back to Norwood. Michael said it was unsuitable for me to read, so it must be pretty good.

'It's much too soon after my husband's death to be thinking of marriage, Pask,' I said demurely. 'My family would be very unhappy. Let's keep marriage in the back of our minds for the future. In the meantime, I'll race you to the bed. The last one to get their clothes off is a fuddy-duddy.'

In the morning we told the children that I'd be leaving for Adelaide soon.

Annie burst into tears and rushed into my arms. 'No, Auntie Rose, you can't go. Mummy died and went away and we were all alone and then you came and made us happy and you have to stay with us. We love you, we need you.'

The old stony look returned to Bob's eyes. I thought for a moment that he was going to say something like 'Good riddance to bad rubbish', but then he, too ran to embrace me.

'Is it something I did, Auntie Rose?' he sobbed. 'Have I upset you? It's my fault that you are going, isn't it? If it is because of me, I'm really sorry and it isn't fair to go and leave Dad and Annie because of me. I'll go away if you like, but you have to stay to look after Annie. I don't want Annie to get sick again.'

'It isn't anything that you've done, Bob. It's because my family back in Adelaide need me for a bit. I have to go and help a sick baby and sort out a few things and then I will come back. I promise. And you kids and your dad might be coming down to spend Christmas with me and my family in Adelaide, if Dad can find someone to look after the sheep and the property while we're all away. What do you think about that?'

The children's eyes grew larger as they thought about the prospect of a trip on the train and a holiday in Adelaide.

'Billy at school's going to be so jealous when I say we're all going to Adelaide,' said Bob. 'You are wonderful, Auntie Rose. I never thought I'd go to Adelaide. Or have a ride on a train, either!'

'Will we see Amy and your other children?' asked Annie. 'Where will we sleep? Can I share a room with Amy?'

The sleeping arrangements were preoccupying me, too. Brian was still using Amy's room, and Amy was at Mavis's house, although she'd want to come home when I returned. Charlie and Joe shared the sleep-out. That left my bed vacant, but I wanted to use that myself. That left Pask and Bob and Annie to find beds for.

It would be nice if Pask and I could sleep together, but I didn't think the family would take kindly if I walked in and said, 'This is my lover and he's going to share my bed.' My family were just not that modern, not that forward-thinking, not that Bohemian.

I had a feeling that Pask was going to end up on a mattress in the front room, probably in about the same spot as that previously occupied by Michael's coffin. And Amy, Annie and I would share my bed. Any accompanying sheep would have to lodge in the chook run.

36

Wearing my black coat and my hat trimmed with blue roses, I sat on the train bound for Adelaide. The parting from Pask, Annie and Bob had been very difficult, almost as difficult as when I'd left Norwood. The children had clung to me as though they'd never see me again, and even Pask looked a bit emotional, although he was loath to let anyone see it in public.

But I would come back. And they were definitely coming to Adelaide for Christmas. It was settled. Tim and Anastasia would take the cow over to Pekina for a month, and the neighbours would make sure there was water enough for the sheep. It was only a month away, I had reassured Amy and Bob. And it wasn't all that far from Orroroo to Adelaide, I told them.

Was I mad not to jump at the chance to marry Pask? It would be so easy. It would solve a lot of problems. But it would create more different ones, I reminded myself. Perhaps one day I might feel differently about marriage, but for now I wanted my freedom.

And now, thanks to Michael's resurrected bankbook, I had the money to come and go as I pleased. I could spend half my time in Adelaide, and half my time at Orroroo. And I could go to Mount Gambier to visit Mary and her family any time I wanted to, as well. I could take Amy, and even Annie, with me, too.

I might bring Amy up to Orroroo when I came back. She would get along well with Annie and Bob. She could even go to school at Orroroo and see what a state school was like, for a change. I could teach her to milk the cow, and the children could show her all their secret places on the farm. They could show her how to catch yabbies in the dam. She would learn to love Orroroo as much as I did. It would broaden her horizons. It would do her good to see the real Australia.

It was early November. The pastures we were travelling through were still green with the flush of spring. The land was full of life and of promise. Perhaps the drought was over for a couple of years. I knew it would come back, though. Droughts always come back. The secret of living out here was in knowing how to live with the drought years. Perhaps that's the secret to living anywhere, I mused. You have to know which are the drought years and which are the years of plenty. It isn't always obvious.

The little black girl's people would have known how to live out here, though. How long had they been here before we whites came? How many places with rocks bearing secret, sacred messages from the past on them, like that rock I had seen by the side of the creek at Orroroo, were out there, hidden from eyes that wouldn't understand the message they carried?

Young lambs frolicked and played beside their watchful mothers. Those were late lambs, I thought. Pask's ewes had already lambed. There were a few older, more staid young sheep lying quietly in the grass, creatures at the Amy and Annie stage of life, too young to leave their mother's side, but beginning to learn the ways of the flock.

Children had to learn some independence. You couldn't keep them tied to your apron strings forever. I knew I'd done the right thing for everyone by going to Orroroo. I had given my children the chance to grow up. Perhaps I had grown up too, in my own way. Only what sort of welcome awaited me in Adelaide? Did they really want me back?

There was a man sitting opposite me. He had his face buried in a newspaper. Just like Michael, I thought. What was he? A commercial traveller, an insurance man? Did the union send men up here? Shearers had unions, I knew. They'd had a big strike recently. We were lucky to get the shearers in when we did. I was almost sure that this fellow was a union man. He didn't look like a shearer. Shearers enjoy life.

'Statesman wins Melbourne Cup' the headlines read. I leaned forward and tapped the man on the knee. He lowered his newspaper and looked over it at me with distaste. I noticed that he'd been studying the financial pages. Had Michael been right about impending disaster? Perhaps that was why this man wore such a sour expression. Or perhaps he doesn't like talking to strangers on trains, I thought. He's not even bothering to look out the window at this beautiful country that we're passing through. No soul, no feelings. No appreciation of Australia. He'll miss the lot. What a waste not to enjoy the wonders of the countryside.

'Excuse me, sir, I'm sorry to disturb you,' I said, 'but if you look out of the window right now you'll see the blue roses of Orroroo.'

He glanced out of the window. 'Those are Scotch thistles, lady,' he said. His eyes went briefly to my hat and then he buried his face in *The Advertiser* again.

37

When the train reached the Adelaide station, my Adelaide family was there waiting. Harry and Mavis had brought the baby. Young Michael looked quite bonny. He had the Walsh trademark red hair and I couldn't see any of the crust of cradle cap in it. He was quite a chubby little fellow, so I had my doubts about the reflux story too. Either someone had been fibbing or the kiddie had improved markedly. And they had named him Michael. I sighed, hoping he'd turn out better than his grandfather. I decided I'd call him Mickey after that new cartoon mouse Walt Disney is drawing in America.

Charlie was holding Amy's hand to stop her from jumping under the train wheels. Now who's mollycoddling her, I thought. Amy was holding a bunch of Michael's roses wrapped in damp newspaper. The first roses of spring are always the best ones, Michael always said. That must have been one of the few occasions when he was telling the truth, when he said that.

These weren't quite the first roses of the season, they would have begun blooming in September, but November roses are still lovely, even if a bit past their prime. A bit like me, I suppose. A terrible thought occurred to me. Had Michael been referring to young girls when he spoke of gathering the first rosebuds of the spring?

'They all said I should wait to give you these when you got home, Mum,' Amy said. 'But I wanted to give you to them here. The same as I did for Mary when she went back to Mount Gambier. Mary wrote and said she wishes she could be here. She sends love and kisses. She said I should bring roses to the railway station when you came back.'

'You did the right thing, love,' I said. 'But haven't you grown! Mavis must have been looking after you well.' And now it's my turn, I thought. I held her close and wished that I could hold Mary to me as well.

I was a little dismayed when I got home. The boys had swapped Jesus for Michael. They had brought the portrait of my dead husband back from the shed and hung it in its old place. Jesus had been hung over my bed. Charlie said that they thought I might be in need of religious solace after my stay at Orroroo. How much did Charlie suspect?

My boys were a sardonic crowd. Michael had been a bad influence on them, I decided. I was a bit uncomfortable to see Michael hanging over the mantelpiece again. He was wearing such a smug expression, as if he was saying, 'I'm back and there's nothing you can do about it.'

But the problem was, I had intended to put the mattress for Pask on the floor just in front of the fireplace. And I fully intended to sneak out of my bed, when I was sure that all the family were asleep, to join Pask on that mattress. We would be in full view of Michael when we performed our nightly acrobatics.

I grinned. That would be the ultimate revenge. Talk about an eye for an eye and a tooth for a tooth. I'd heard of widows swearing that they would dance on their dead husband's graves. This was even better. Our lovemaking would take place in the exact spot where Michael's coffin had stood that night when I had taken an axe to it. I giggled.

'That will show you, Michael Walsh. That's what comes of raping your daughter and committing incest and destroying your family, of being a hypocrite and breaking people's hearts, and betraying your wife. You've driven me to fornication and independence and I'm loving every minute of it.'

I checked that no one could hear me. They were all out in the kitchen, fussing over little Mickey. I even looked out of the window to make sure that Mrs Williams wasn't in her garden and eavesdropping.

I raised my voice and told the photo, 'Your wife has turned into a shameless hussy, Michael. Pask is a much better lover that you ever were. And when I leap on top of him on the mattress on the floor in the place vacated by your coffin it's going to be in full view of your photo, and you are going to wish that you had an axe in your hand. And there won't be a thing that you'll be able to do about it. You're dead, Michael Walsh, and I am alive! And I won't marry Pask because I'm going to keep your name and bring shame on it every time I fornicate.'

I was an evil woman and I knew it. I was almost as evil as Michael. No, I wasn't that evil. No one was as vile as Michael. Let the evil be buried with Michael. I had been reborn. I was a new woman with a new life, and I was revelling in it.

I counted off the days until Pask and the kiddies arrived. It wouldn't be long before they came. I must get a start on making the Christmas puddings and cake. But there were more pressing matters to attend to first.

There was a knock at the door. I hoped Mrs Williams hadn't heard me talking to Michael's photo.

'I didn't think I would ever see or hear from you again, Mrs Walsh,' said Mrs. Williams. 'You must come over to my house and tell me everything that's happened up there at Wallaroo. I insist on hearing all the details. I've just made a pot of tea and some scones.'

'It's Orroroo, not Wallaroo,' I said. 'It would take quite a while to tell you everything. I'll just come over for a few minutes, because my family and I have a lot of things to discuss too.' I had no intention of telling Mrs Williams all the details of my stay at Orroroo, no matter how hard she insisted.

'Come over tomorrow then, Mrs Walsh,' said Mrs Williams.

'I have to go and see my bank manager tomorrow,' I said. 'I have financial matters to settle.'

'It must be hard being a widow,' said Mrs. Williams.

'There is a certain pride in being independent and able to cope on your own,' I said.

With Michael's deposit book and his death certificate in my handbag, I took the tram into town the next day and went to see the bank manager. I intended to withdraw all the cash. There was no sense in leaving the money to sit in the account. I wanted the feel of the banknotes in my hand.

'No problem, Mrs Walsh,' said the manager. 'No problem at all. It is a most fortunate time to have this much money on hand. There are rumours that there could be financial problems overseas soon. New York is a bit shaky. It would be worrisome if one believed such rumours. Personally I don't. I can recommend some very sound investments to you. Extremely safe ones.'

'Thank you very much, but I've already decided where I'm going to invest this money,' I said. I checked the notes that the teller counted out. I wasn't about to be cheated by anyone ever again.

Charlie and I dug a hole in the garden. We put the money, carefully wrapped in oilcloth and then protected by a tin, into the hole. We didn't want the worms eating it. There are lots of fat worms in our garden soil. It was due to all that horse manure we'd enriched the garden with over the years. Then Charlie and I dragged the heavy chopping block back over the top of the hole.

'This is a bit like a funeral,' said Charlie. 'Do you want me to fetch my trumpet and play the Last Post? Maybe one of us ought to say a few words over the grave.'

'No trumpets, please, Charlie. We don't need Mrs Williams looking over the fence. Let's keep this as quiet as possible. If there is a financial crash coming, I think this hole will be a lot safer place than any investment that the bank recommends,' I told him. 'And what's more, this money can be resurrected any time we want it. We will survive. Those are the only words I feel like saying.'

'Did you take the money out to pay the stonemason first?' Charlie asked.

'Yes, I paid him yesterday and we haven't got any other bills outstanding. We're financially independent,' I said.

I didn't add that I was independent now in a number of ways that no one suspected. And that I intended to stay that way. I also didn't tell Charlie that after I'd paid the stonemason, I took a hammer and a chisel out of the shed. I put the tools in my purse along with some horse-manure wrapped in a copy of *The Advertiser*, and I went off on the tram to have a look at Michael's headstone.

The stone read, 'Michael Edward Walsh, born 17.3.1876, died 16.2.28. Beloved husband of Rose, father of six, grandfather of one.'

I left most of the lies intact, but I chiselled out the word 'Beloved'.

I didn't take any roses with me, but I wore the hat.

Acknowledgements

My thanks to my long-suffering husband Frank, who cooked and encouraged; to Sister Patricia of OLSH who predicted long ago that I would write the Great Australian Novel (still working on that one, Sister Pat); to all at the Salisbury Writing Festival which conducted the Three Day Novel Writing Competition for which this novel was originally written; to Anne Bartlett for her magnificent mentorship; to the Orroroo Historical Society and especially Mr Gerald Kuerschner who helped with my research into Orroroo in the 1920s; to my IT team, Denise Visciglio, Margaret Travers and Alexander Worrall, without whom I could not function; and to Stephen Matthews and Brenda Eldridge who brought this book into existence.

www.ingramcontent.com/pod-product-compliance
Lightning Source LLC
Chambersburg PA
CBHW061612100726
47898CB00002B/633